SQUIDDING AROUND

Fish Feud!

KEVIN SHERRY

WITH COLOR BY WES DZIOBA

graphix

AN IMPRINT OF
SCHOLASTIC

To my niece Amelia
with love from your Cod-father

Library of Congress Cataloging-in-Publication Data Available

ISBN 978-1-338-63668-0 (hardcover)
ISBN 978-1-338-63667-3 (paperback)

10 9 8 7 6 5 4 3 2 1   20 21 22 23 24

Printed in China   62

First edition, September 2020
Edited by Jenne Abramowitz
Book design by Steve Ponzo
Creative Director: Phil Falco
Publisher: David Saylor

CHAPTER 1

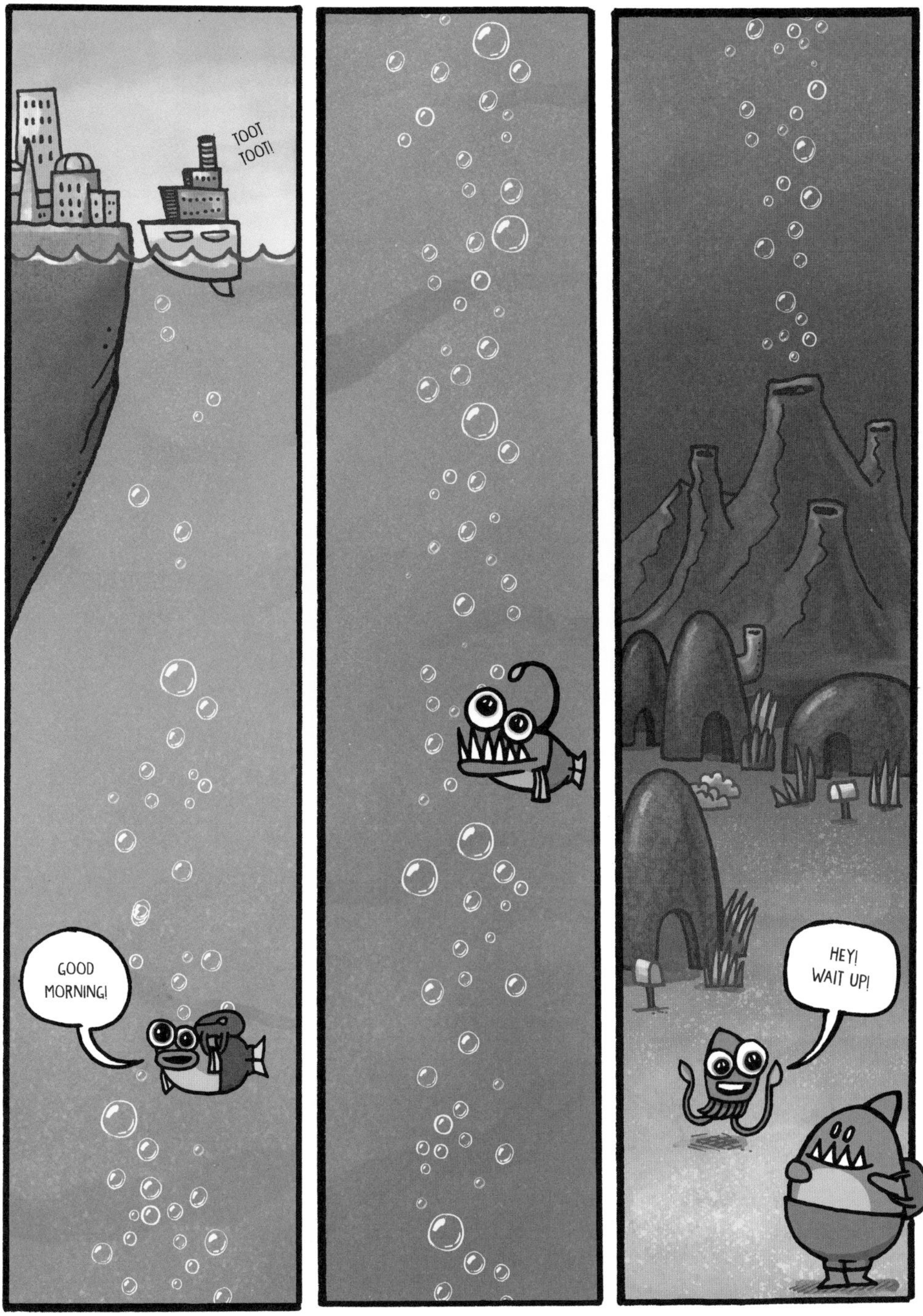
TOOT
TOOT!
GOOD
MORNING!
HEY!
WAIT UP!

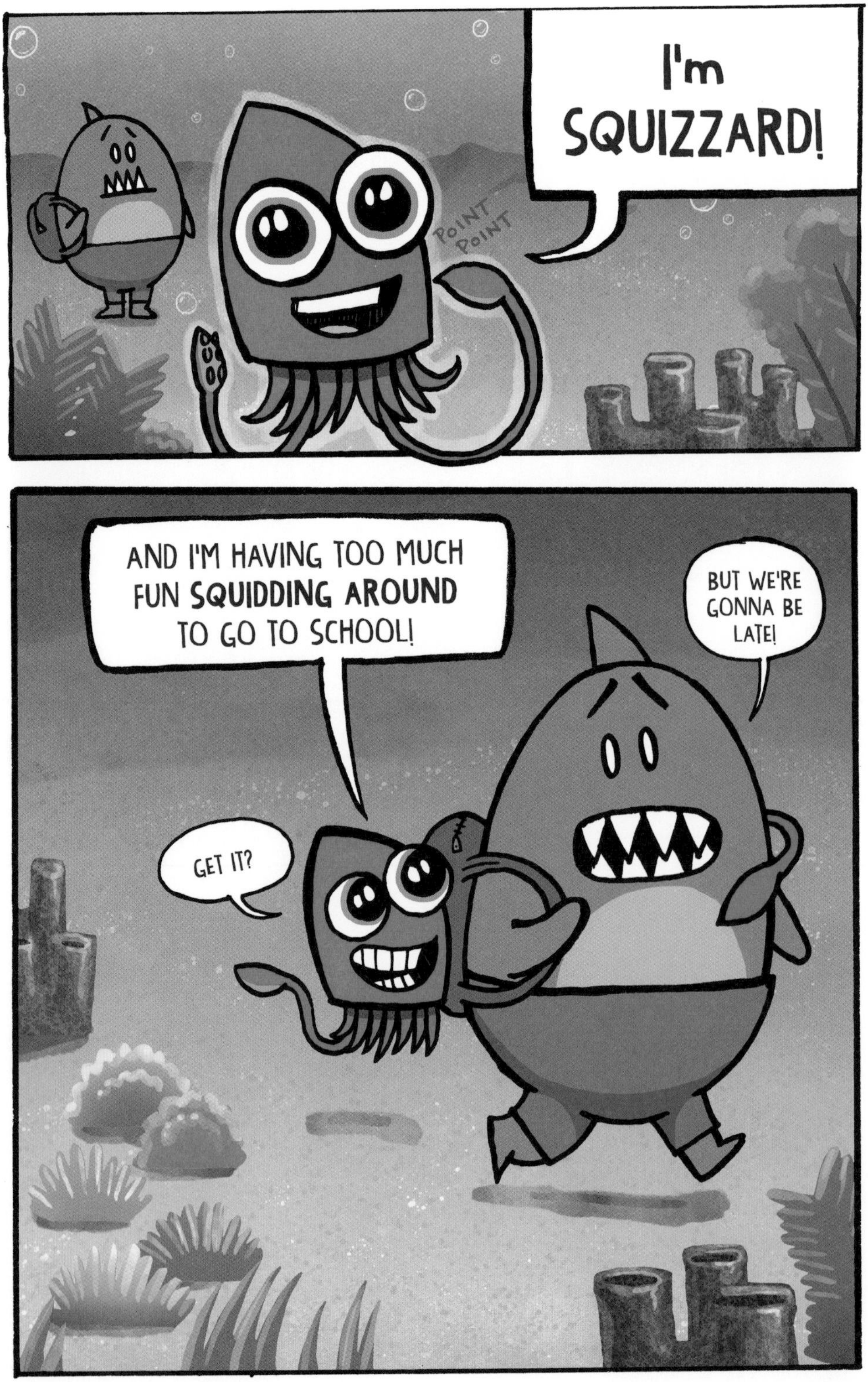
I'm SQUIZZARD!
POINT POINT
AND I'M HAVING TOO MUCH FUN **SQUIDDING AROUND** TO GO TO SCHOOL!
BUT WE'RE GONNA BE LATE!
GET IT?

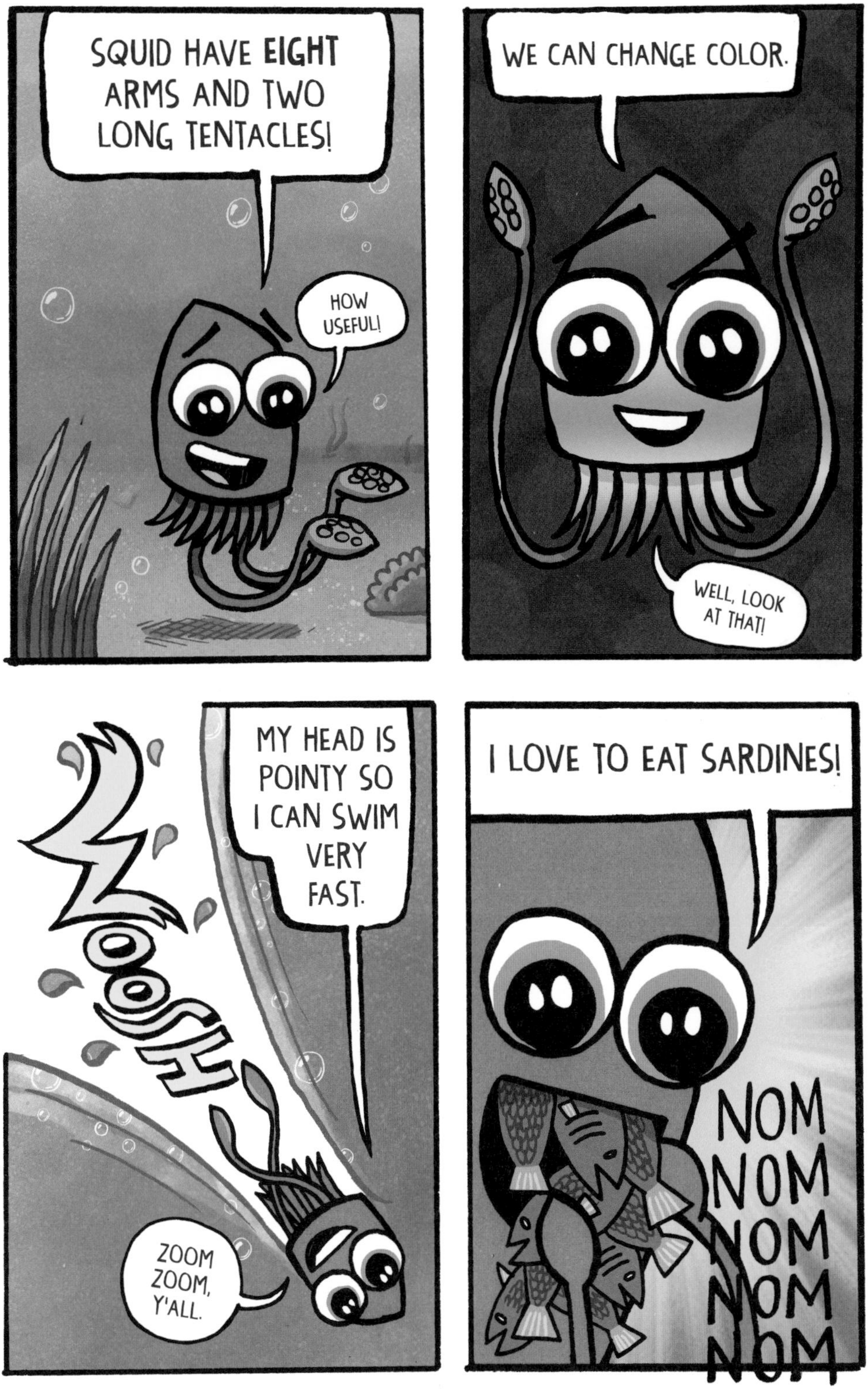
SQUID HAVE **EIGHT** ARMS AND TWO LONG TENTACLES!
HOW USEFUL!
WE CAN CHANGE COLOR.
WELL, LOOK AT THAT!
MY HEAD IS POINTY SO I CAN SWIM VERY FAST.
WOOSH
ZOOM ZOOM, Y'ALL.
I LOVE TO EAT SARDINES!
NOM NOM NOM NOM NOM

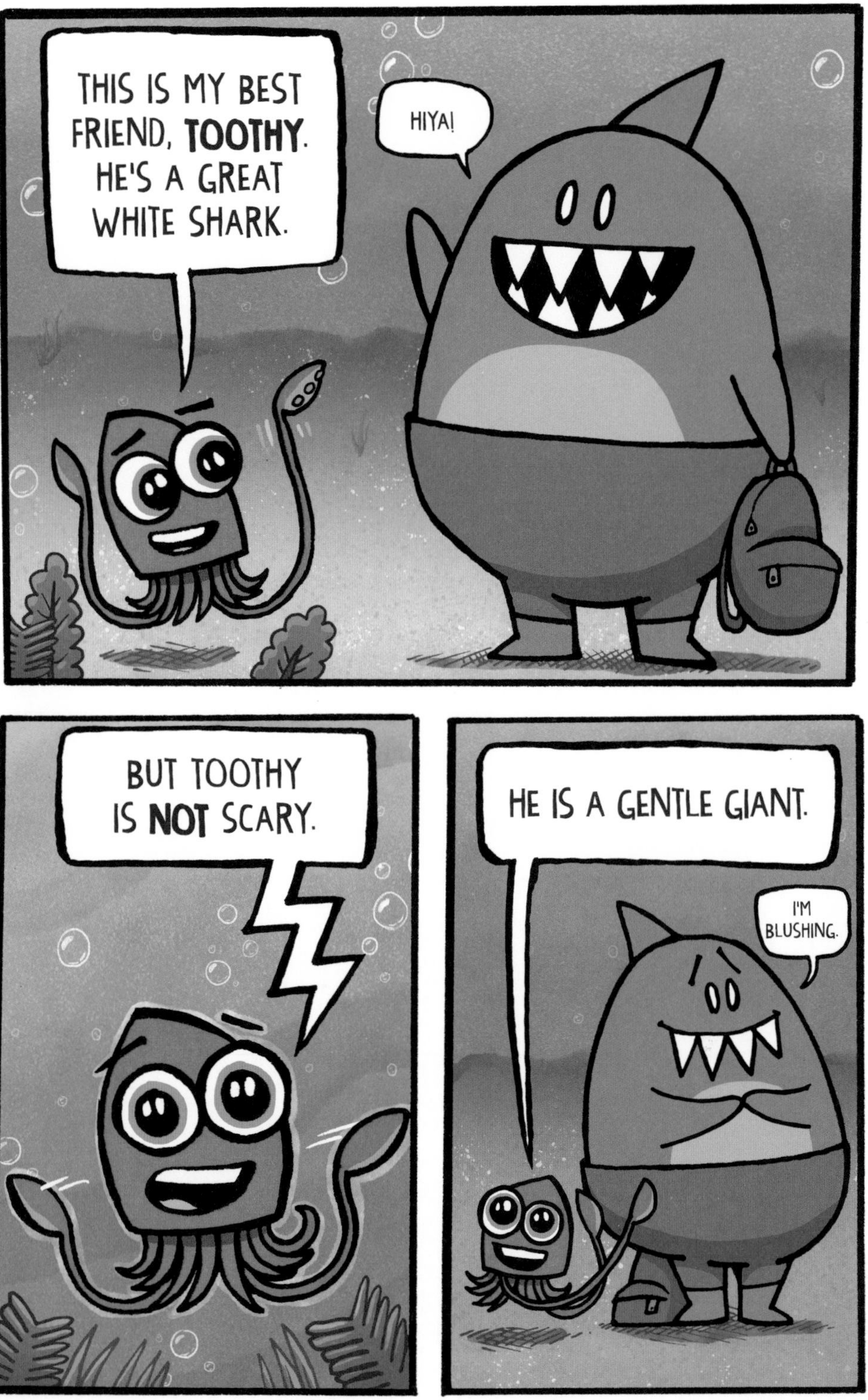
THIS IS MY BEST FRIEND, **TOOTHY**. HE'S A GREAT WHITE SHARK.
HIYA!
BUT TOOTHY IS **NOT** SCARY.
HE IS A GENTLE GIANT.
I'M BLUSHING.

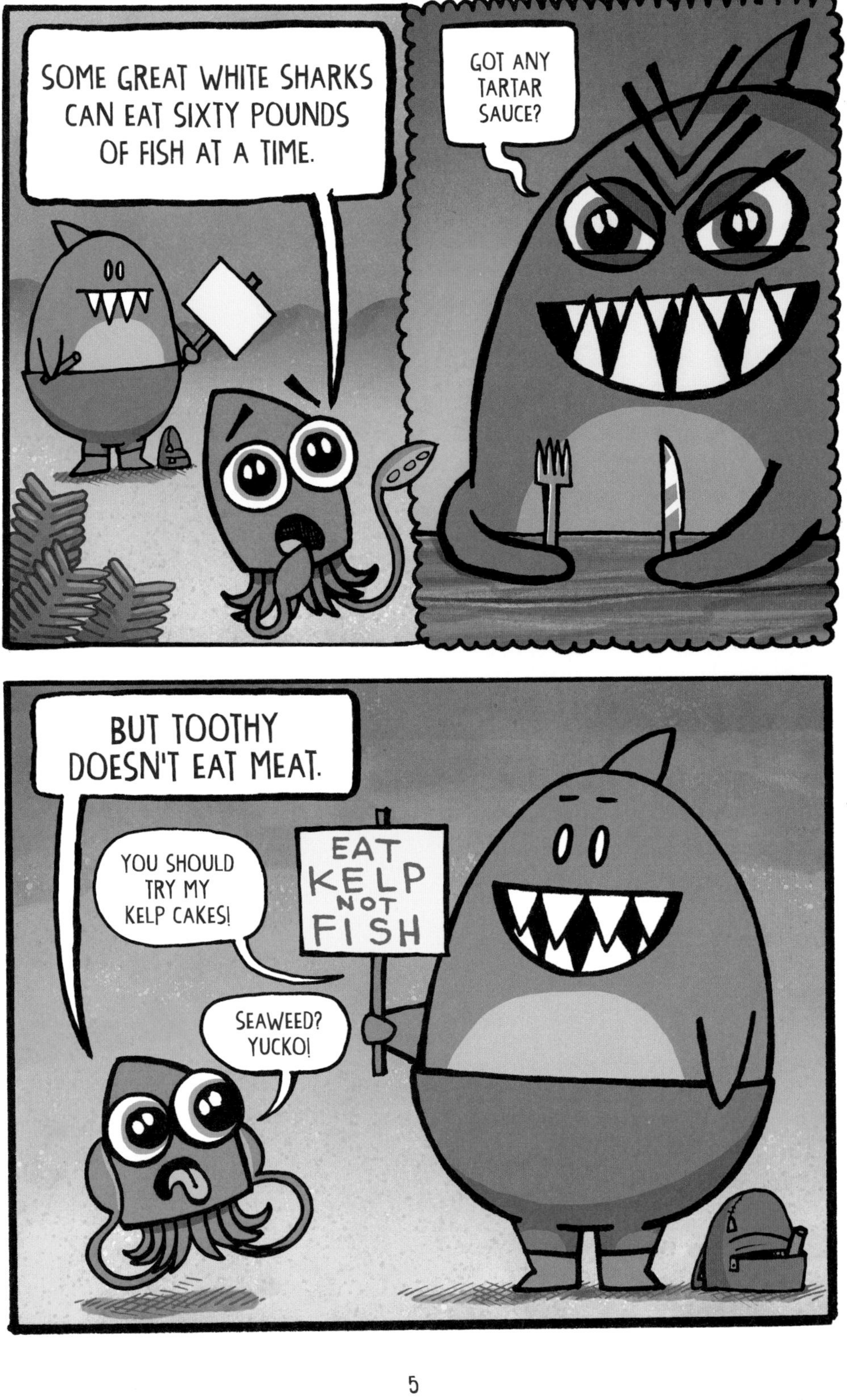
SOME GREAT WHITE SHARKS CAN EAT SIXTY POUNDS OF FISH AT A TIME.
GOT ANY TARTAR SAUCE?
BUT TOOTHY DOESN'T EAT MEAT.
YOU SHOULD TRY MY KELP CAKES!
EAT KELP NOT FISH
SEAWEED? YUCKO!

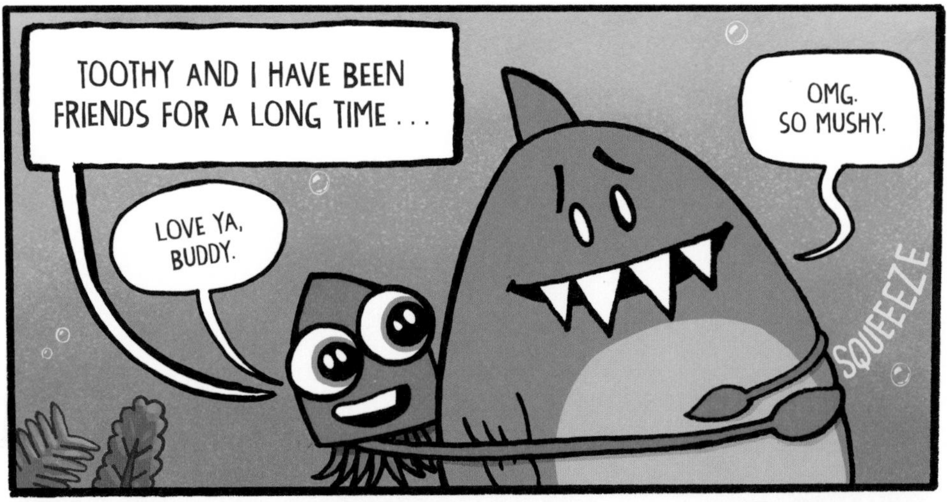
TOOTHY AND I HAVE BEEN FRIENDS FOR A LONG TIME . . .
LOVE YA, BUDDY.
OMG. SO MUSHY.
SQUEEEZE

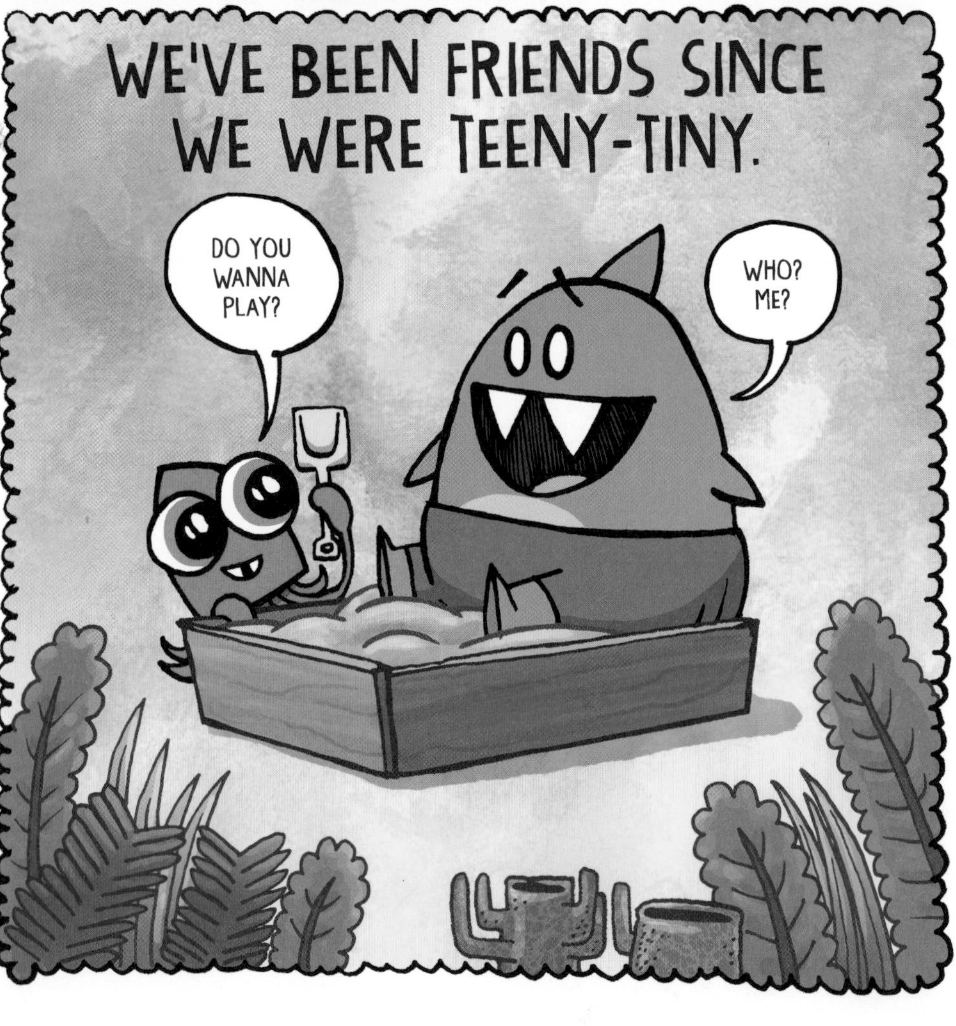
WE'VE BEEN FRIENDS SINCE WE WERE TEENY-TINY.
DO YOU WANNA PLAY?
WHO? ME?

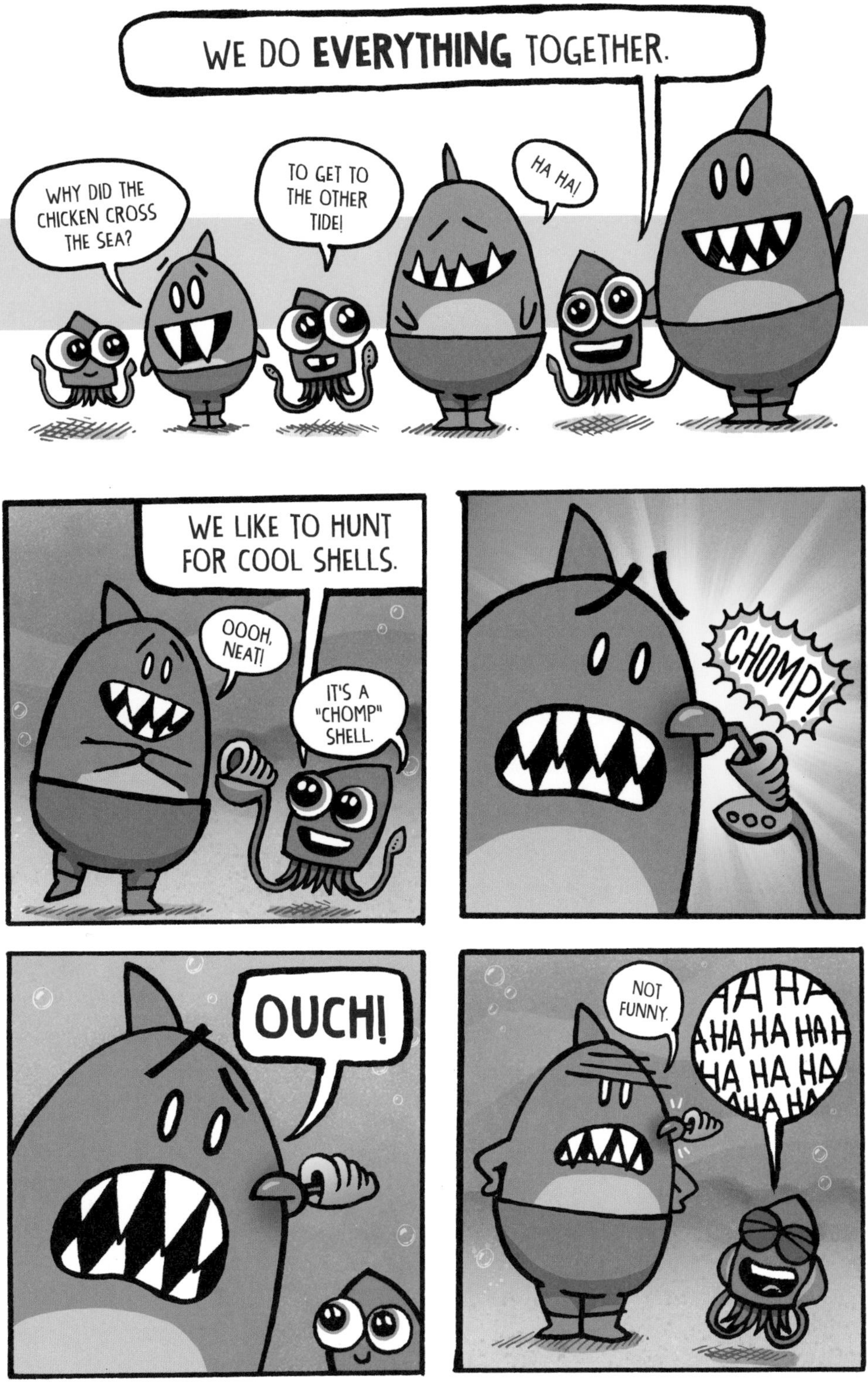
WE DO EVERYTHING TOGETHER.
WHY DID THE CHICKEN CROSS THE SEA?
TO GET TO THE OTHER TIDE!
HA HA!
WE LIKE TO HUNT FOR COOL SHELLS.
OOOH, NEAT!
IT'S A "CHOMP" SHELL.
CHOMP!
OUCH!
NOT FUNNY.
HA HA HA HA HA HA HA HA

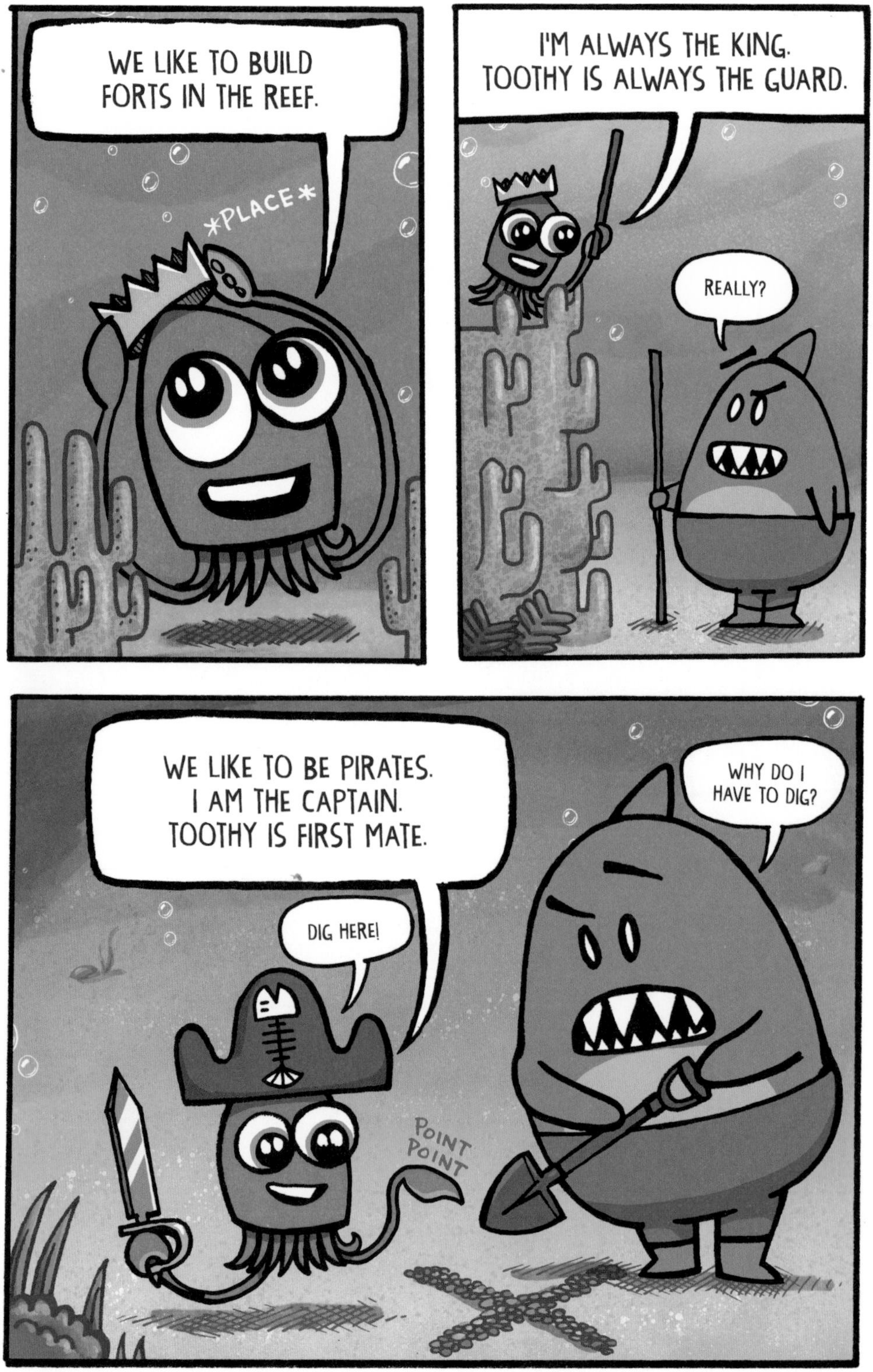

WE LIKE TO BUILD FORTS IN THE REEF.
PLACE
I'M ALWAYS THE KING. TOOTHY IS ALWAYS THE GUARD.
REALLY?
WE LIKE TO BE PIRATES. I AM THE CAPTAIN. TOOTHY IS FIRST MATE.
DIG HERE!
POINT POINT
WHY DO I HAVE TO DIG?

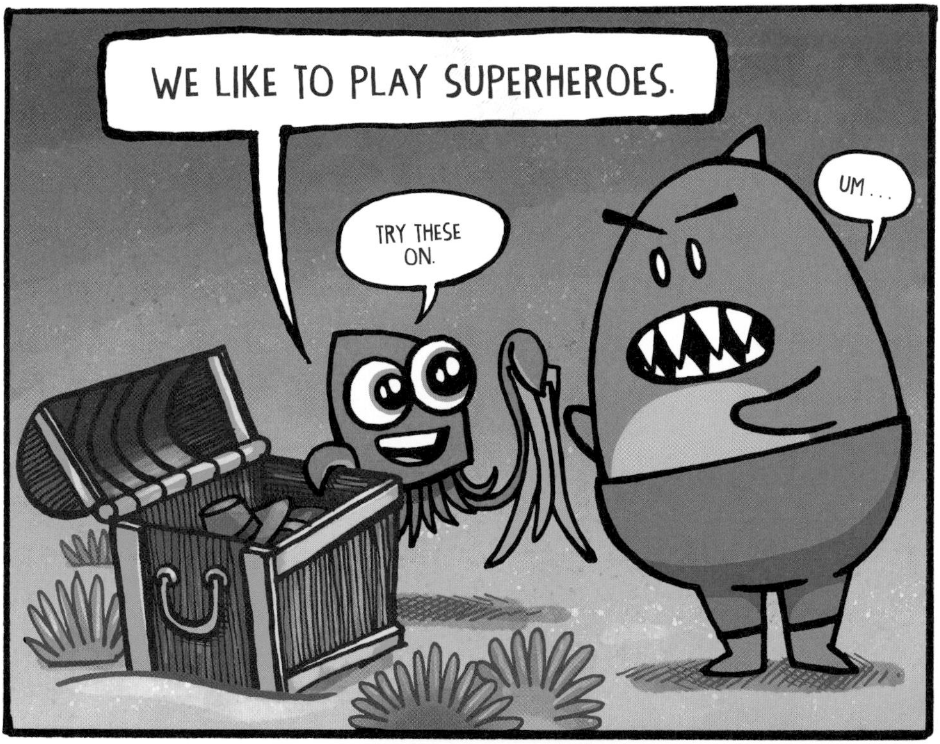
WE LIKE TO PLAY SUPERHEROES.
TRY THESE ON.
UM . . .

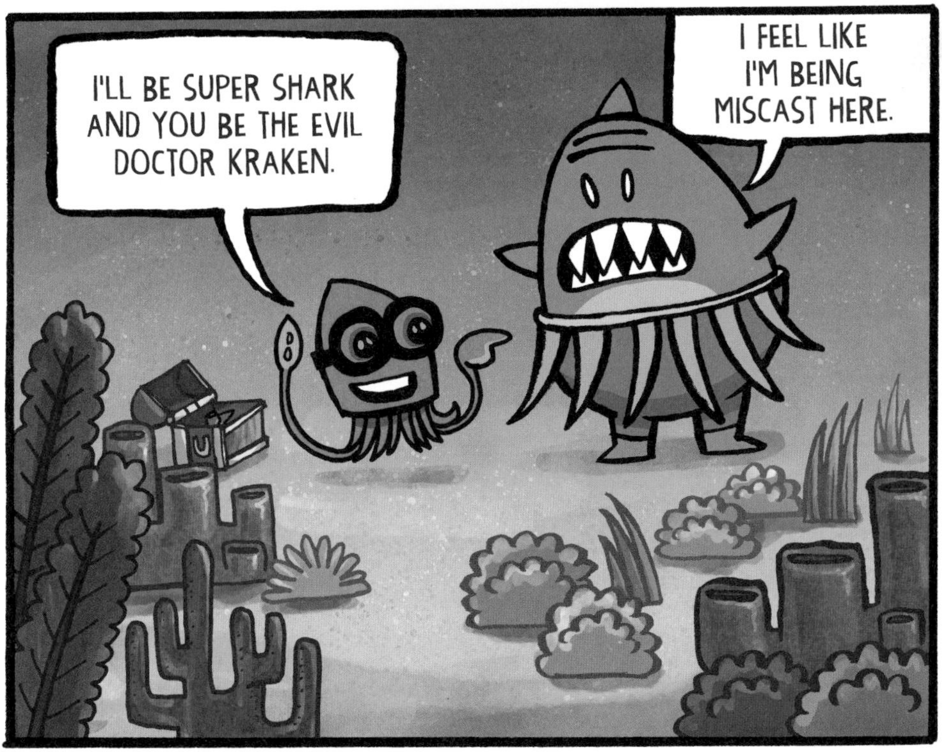
I'LL BE SUPER SHARK AND YOU BE THE EVIL DOCTOR KRAKEN.
I FEEL LIKE I'M BEING MISCAST HERE.

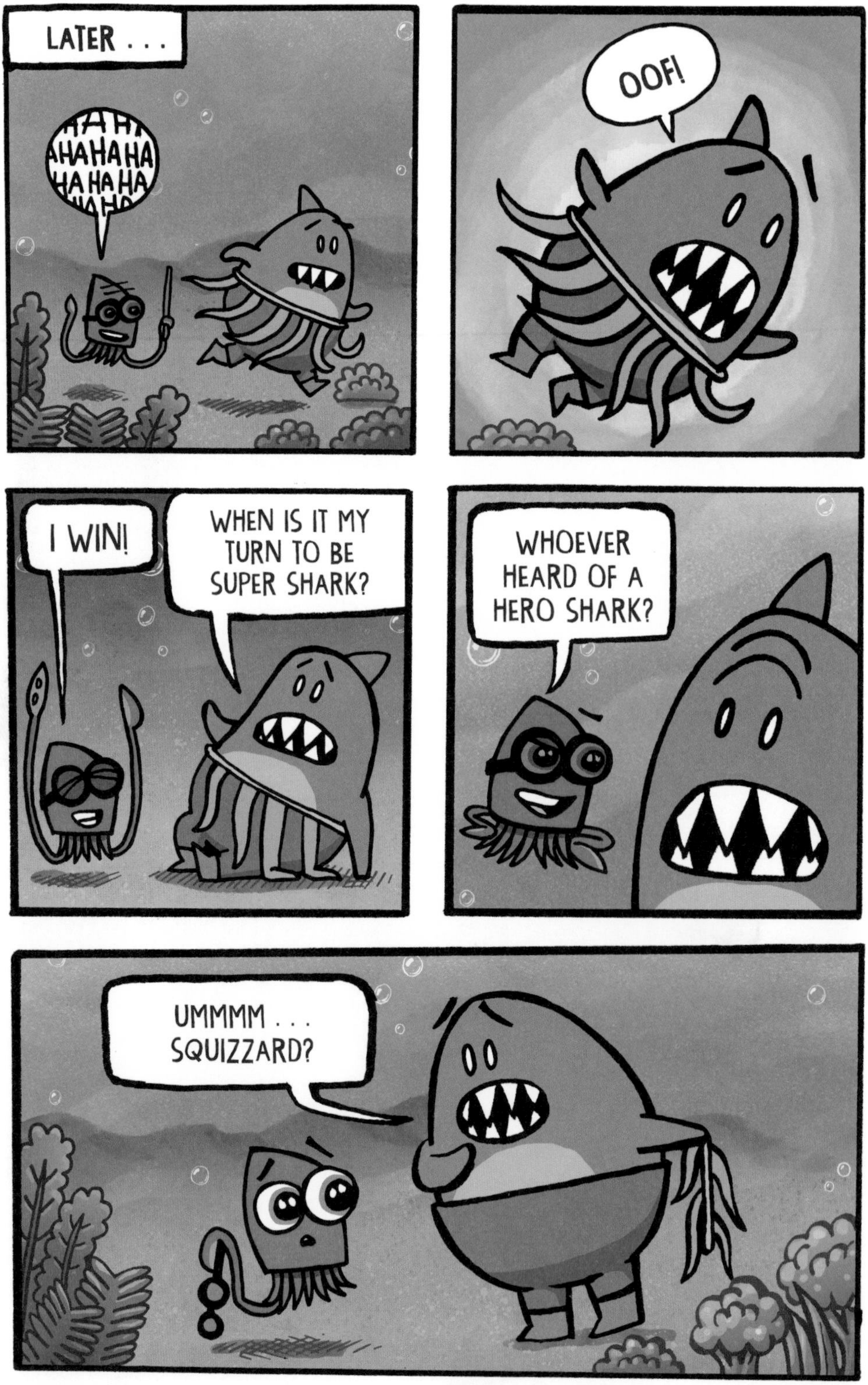
LATER . . .
HAHAHA HA HA HA
OOF!
I WIN!
WHEN IS IT MY TURN TO BE SUPER SHARK?
WHOEVER HEARD OF A HERO SHARK?
UMMMM . . . SQUIZZARD?

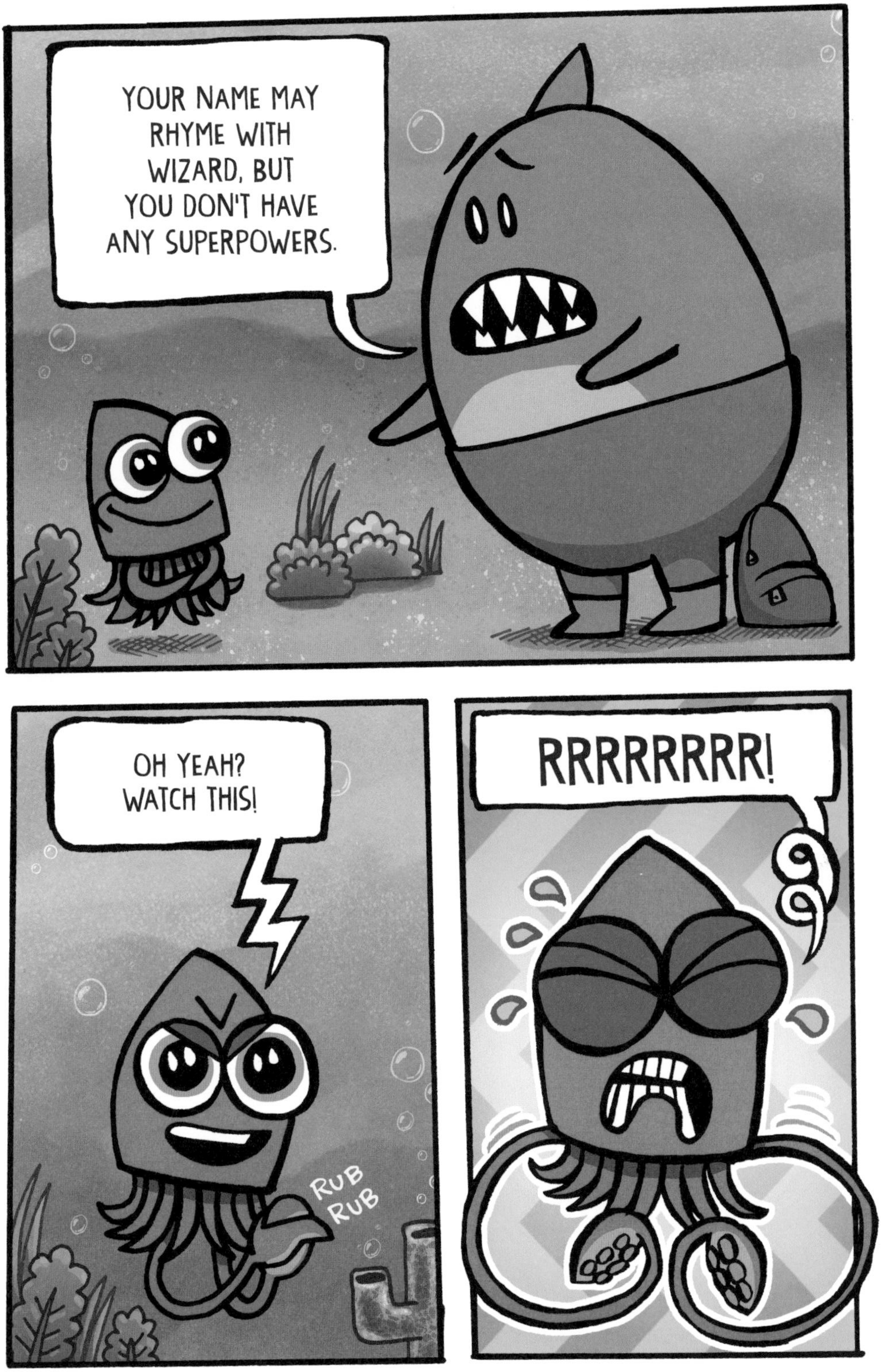
YOUR NAME MAY RHYME WITH WIZARD, BUT YOU DON'T HAVE ANY SUPERPOWERS.
OH YEAH? WATCH THIS!
RUB RUB
RRRRRRRR!

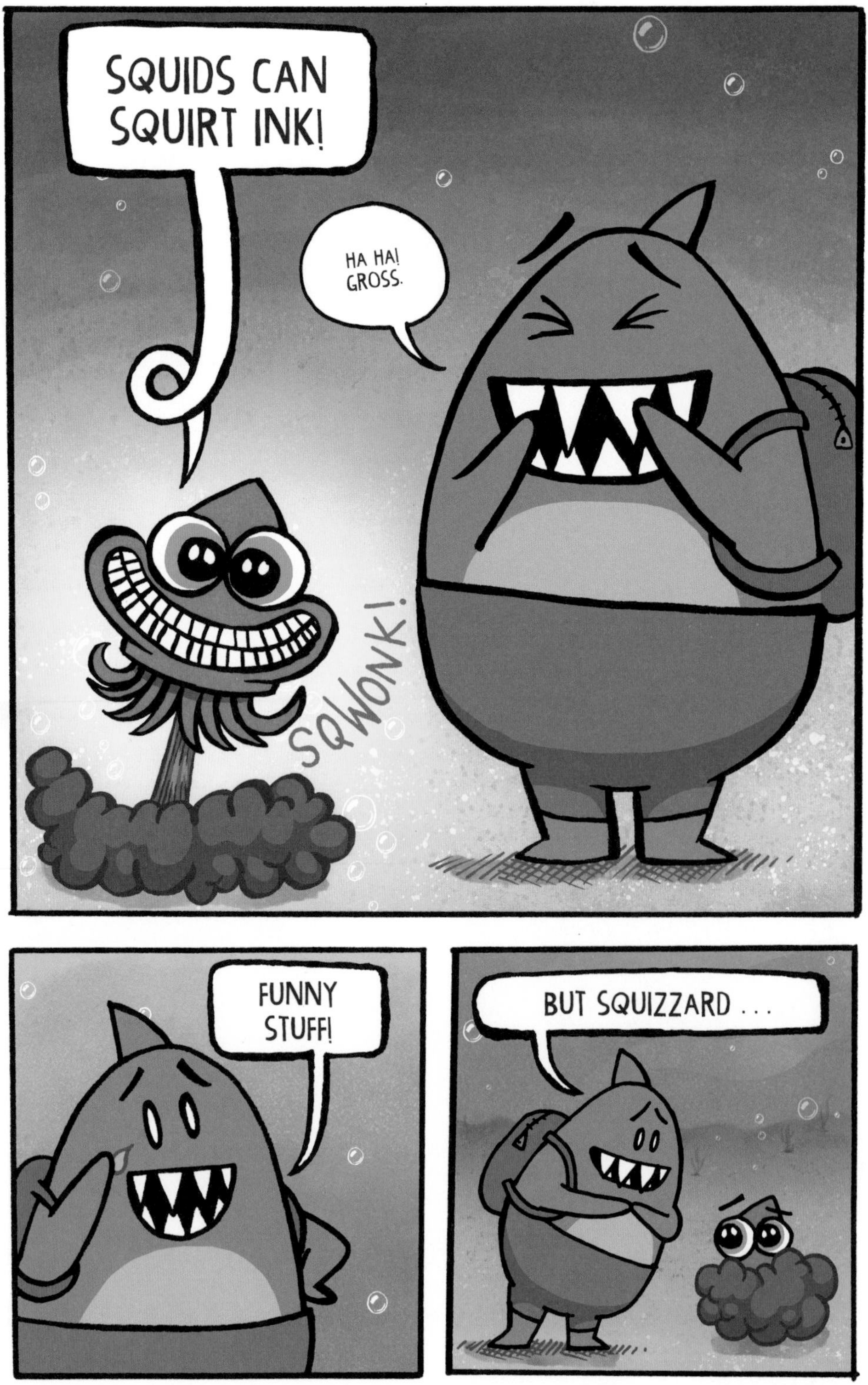
SQUIDS CAN SQUIRT INK!
HA HA! GROSS.
SQWONK!
FUNNY STUFF!
BUT SQUIZZARD . . .

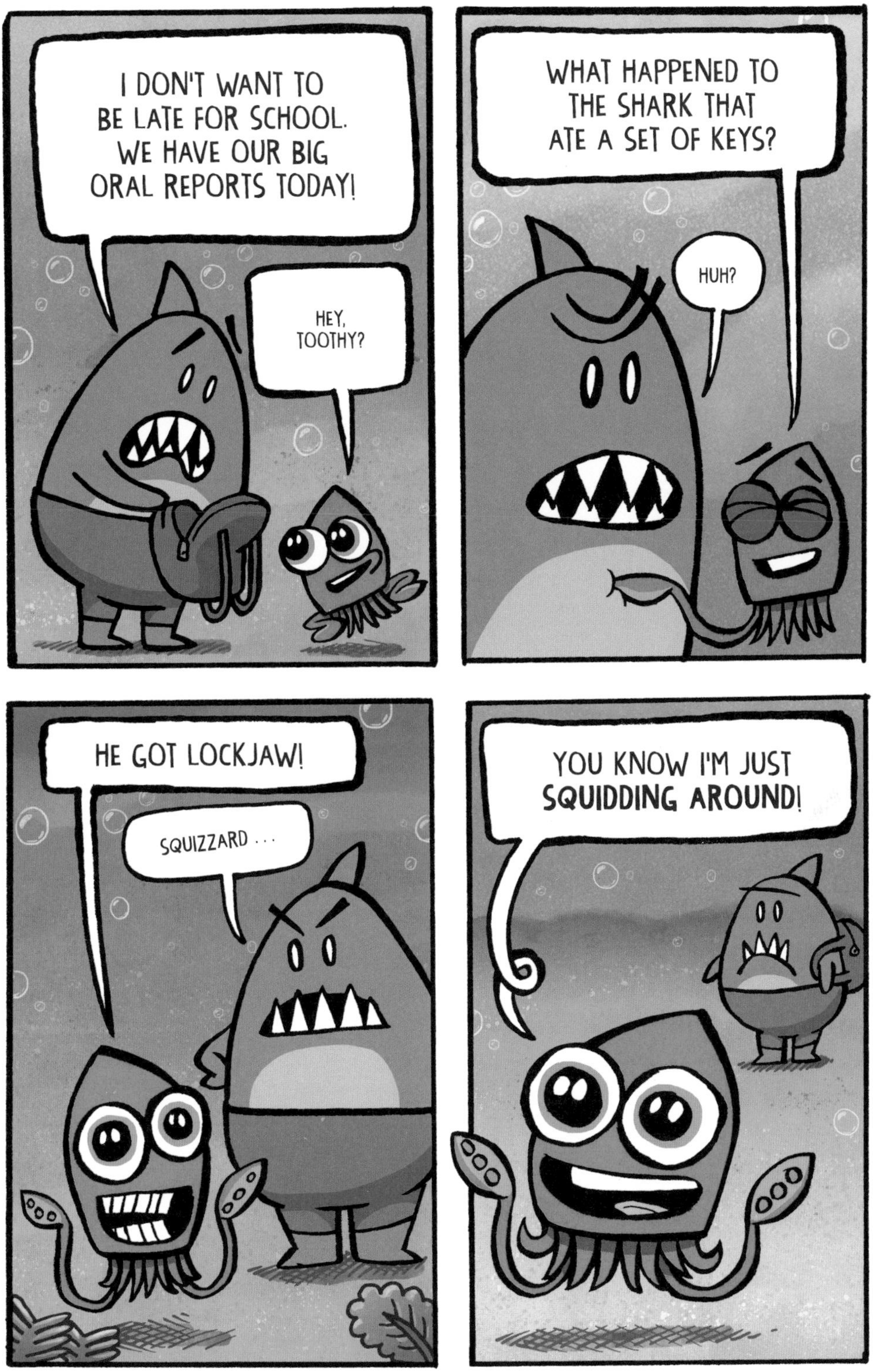
I DON'T WANT TO BE LATE FOR SCHOOL. WE HAVE OUR BIG ORAL REPORTS TODAY!
HEY, TOOTHY?
WHAT HAPPENED TO THE SHARK THAT ATE A SET OF KEYS?
HUH?
HE GOT LOCKJAW!
SQUIZZARD . . .
YOU KNOW I'M JUST **SQUIDDING AROUND**!

CHAPTER 2

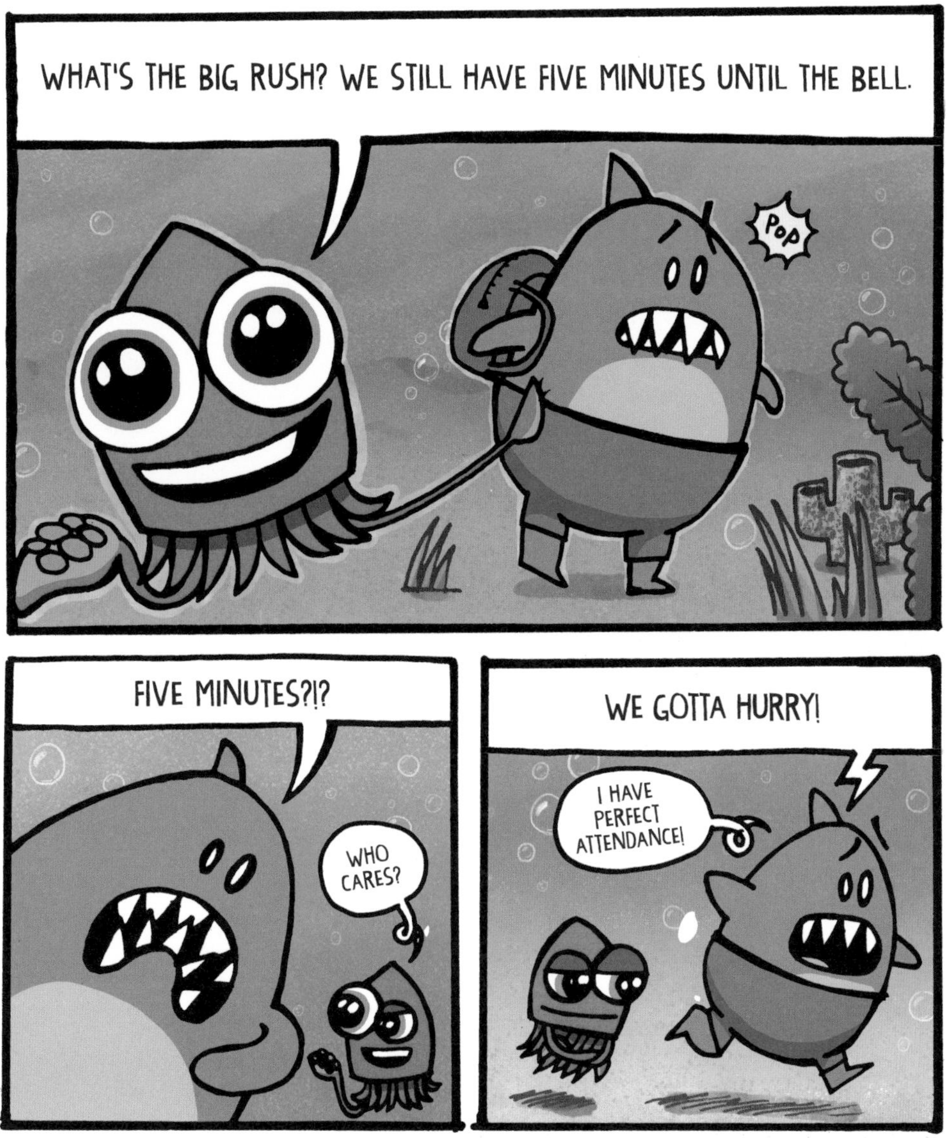

WHAT'S THE BIG RUSH? WE STILL HAVE FIVE MINUTES UNTIL THE BELL.
POP
FIVE MINUTES?!?
WHO CARES?
WE GOTTA HURRY!
I HAVE PERFECT ATTENDANCE!

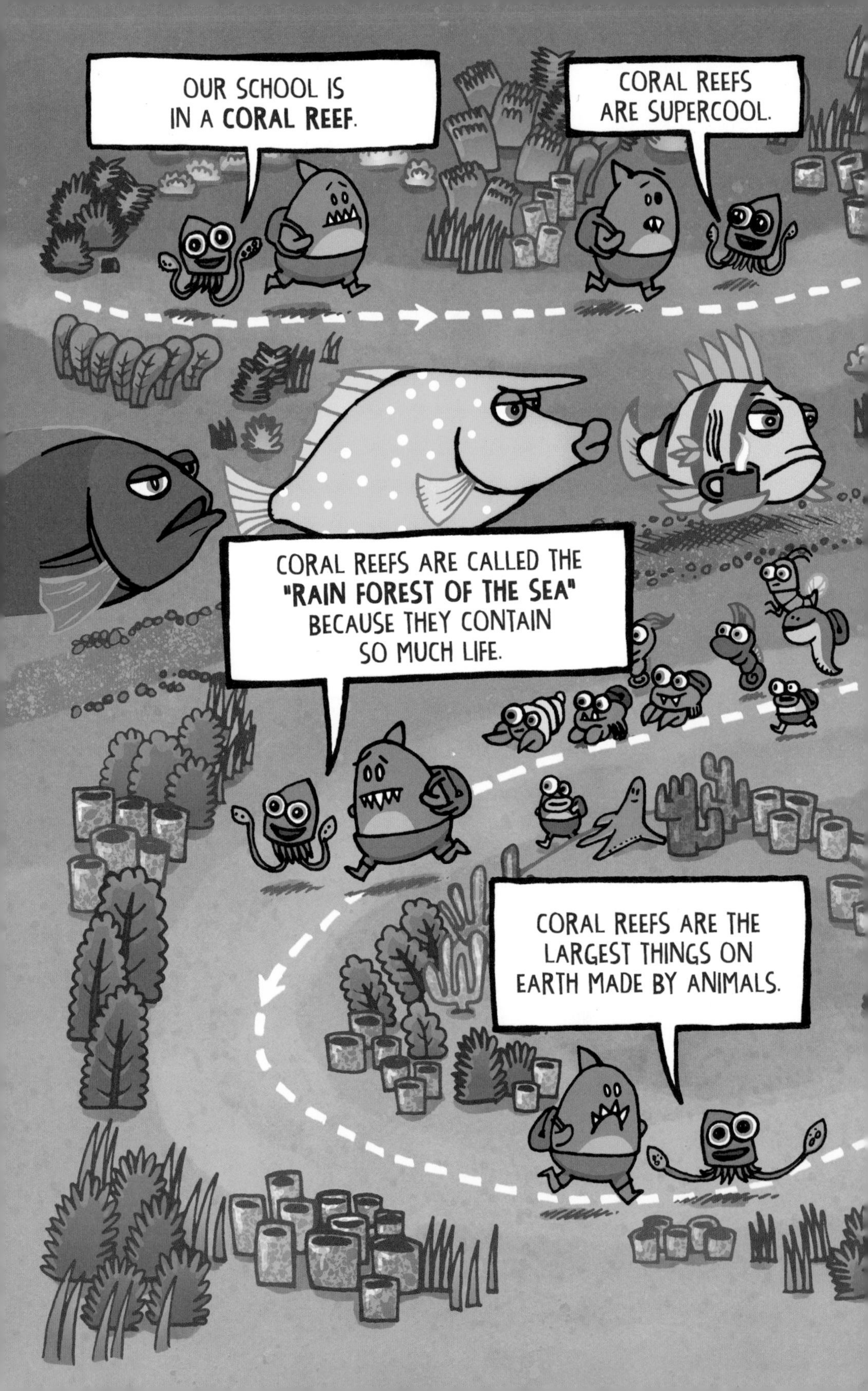
OUR SCHOOL IS IN A **CORAL REEF**.
CORAL REEFS ARE SUPERCOOL.
CORAL REEFS ARE CALLED THE **"RAIN FOREST OF THE SEA"** BECAUSE THEY CONTAIN SO MUCH LIFE.
CORAL REEFS ARE THE LARGEST THINGS ON EARTH MADE BY ANIMALS.

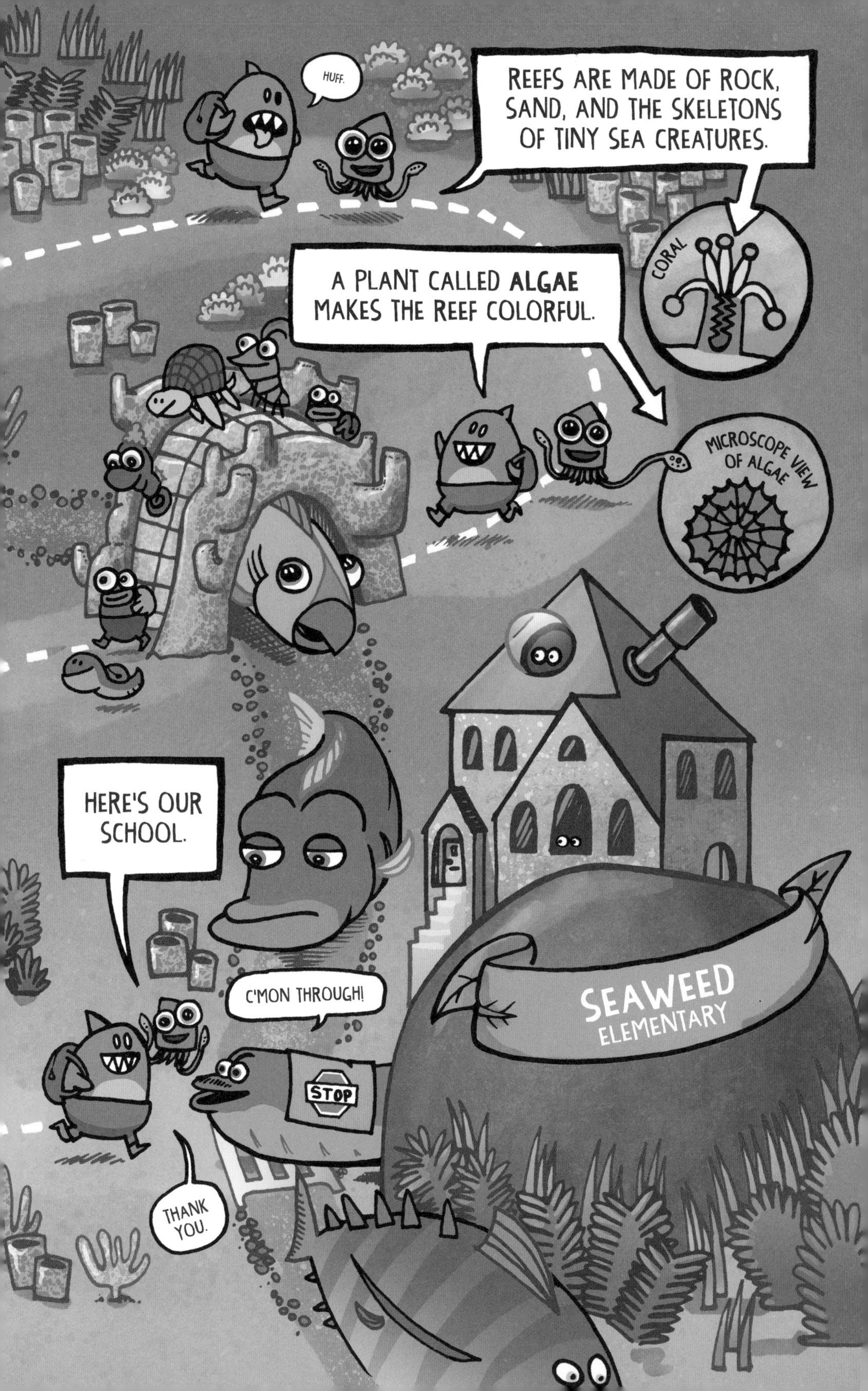
HUFF.
REEFS ARE MADE OF ROCK, SAND, AND THE SKELETONS OF TINY SEA CREATURES.
CORAL
A PLANT CALLED ALGAE MAKES THE REEF COLORFUL.
MICROSCOPE VIEW OF ALGAE
HERE'S OUR SCHOOL.
C'MON THROUGH!
STOP
SEAWEED ELEMENTARY
THANK YOU.

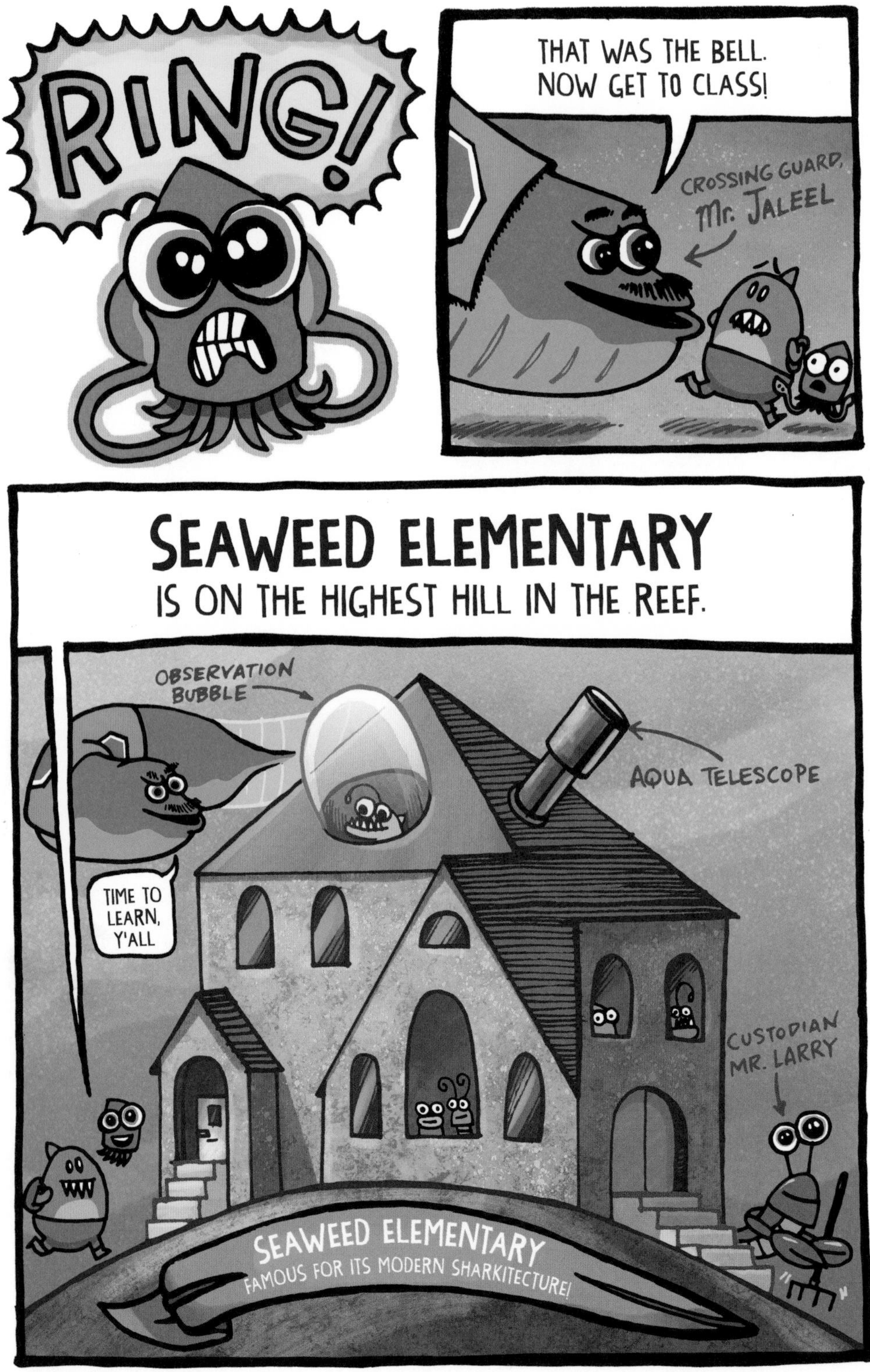
RING!
THAT WAS THE BELL. NOW GET TO CLASS!
CROSSING GUARD, Mr. JALEEL
SEAWEED ELEMENTARY
IS ON THE HIGHEST HILL IN THE REEF.
OBSERVATION BUBBLE
AQUA TELESCOPE
TIME TO LEARN, Y'ALL
CUSTODIAN MR. LARRY
SEAWEED ELEMENTARY
FAMOUS FOR ITS MODERN SHARKITECTURE!

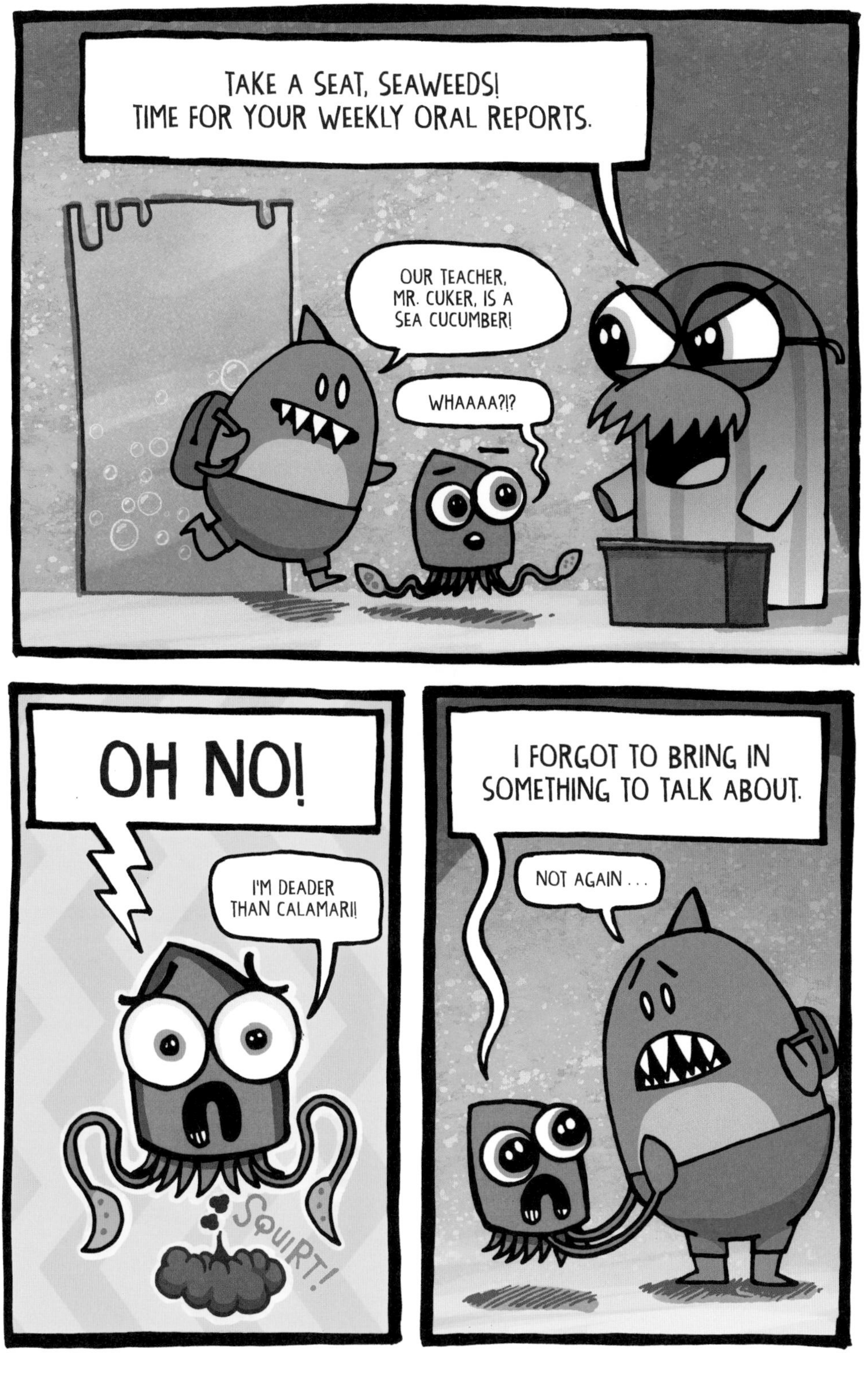
TAKE A SEAT, SEAWEEDS! TIME FOR YOUR WEEKLY ORAL REPORTS.
OUR TEACHER, MR. CUKER, IS A SEA CUCUMBER!
WHAAAA?!?
OH NO!
I'M DEADER THAN CALAMARI!
SQUIRT!
I FORGOT TO BRING IN SOMETHING TO TALK ABOUT.
NOT AGAIN . . .

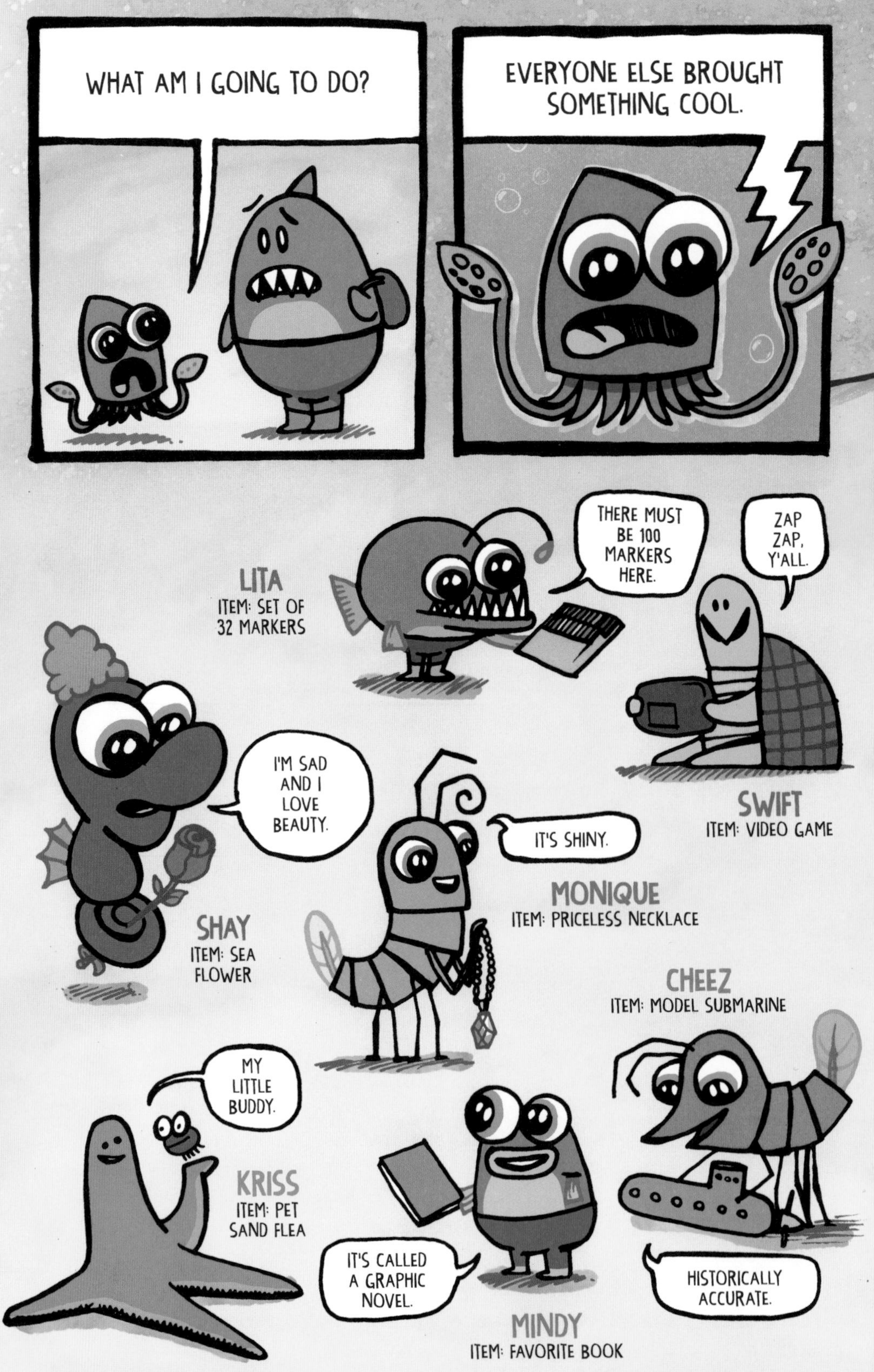
WHAT AM I GOING TO DO?
EVERYONE ELSE BROUGHT SOMETHING COOL.
THERE MUST BE 100 MARKERS HERE.
ZAP ZAP, Y'ALL.
LITA
ITEM: SET OF 32 MARKERS
I'M SAD AND I LOVE BEAUTY.
IT'S SHINY.
SWIFT
ITEM: VIDEO GAME
MONIQUE
ITEM: PRICELESS NECKLACE
SHAY
ITEM: SEA FLOWER
CHEEZ
ITEM: MODEL SUBMARINE
MY LITTLE BUDDY.
KRISS
ITEM: PET SAND FLEA
IT'S CALLED A GRAPHIC NOVEL.
HISTORICALLY ACCURATE.
MINDY
ITEM: FAVORITE BOOK

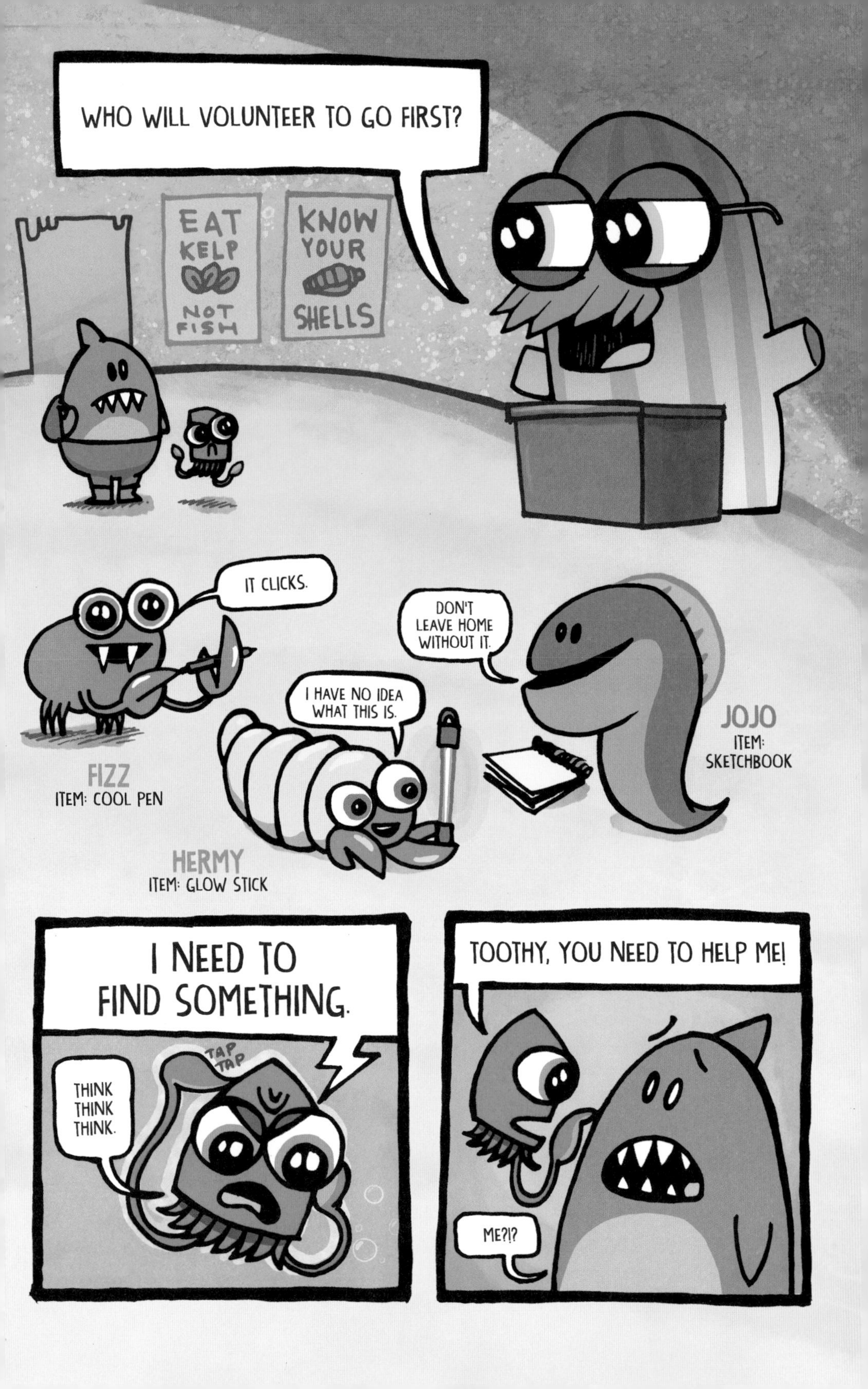

WHO WILL VOLUNTEER TO GO FIRST?
EAT KELP NOT FISH
KNOW YOUR SHELLS
IT CLICKS.
FIZZ
ITEM: COOL PEN
DON'T LEAVE HOME WITHOUT IT.
JOJO
ITEM: SKETCHBOOK
I HAVE NO IDEA WHAT THIS IS.
HERMY
ITEM: GLOW STICK
I NEED TO FIND SOMETHING.
THINK THINK THINK.
TAP TAP
TOOTHY, YOU NEED TO HELP ME!
ME?!?

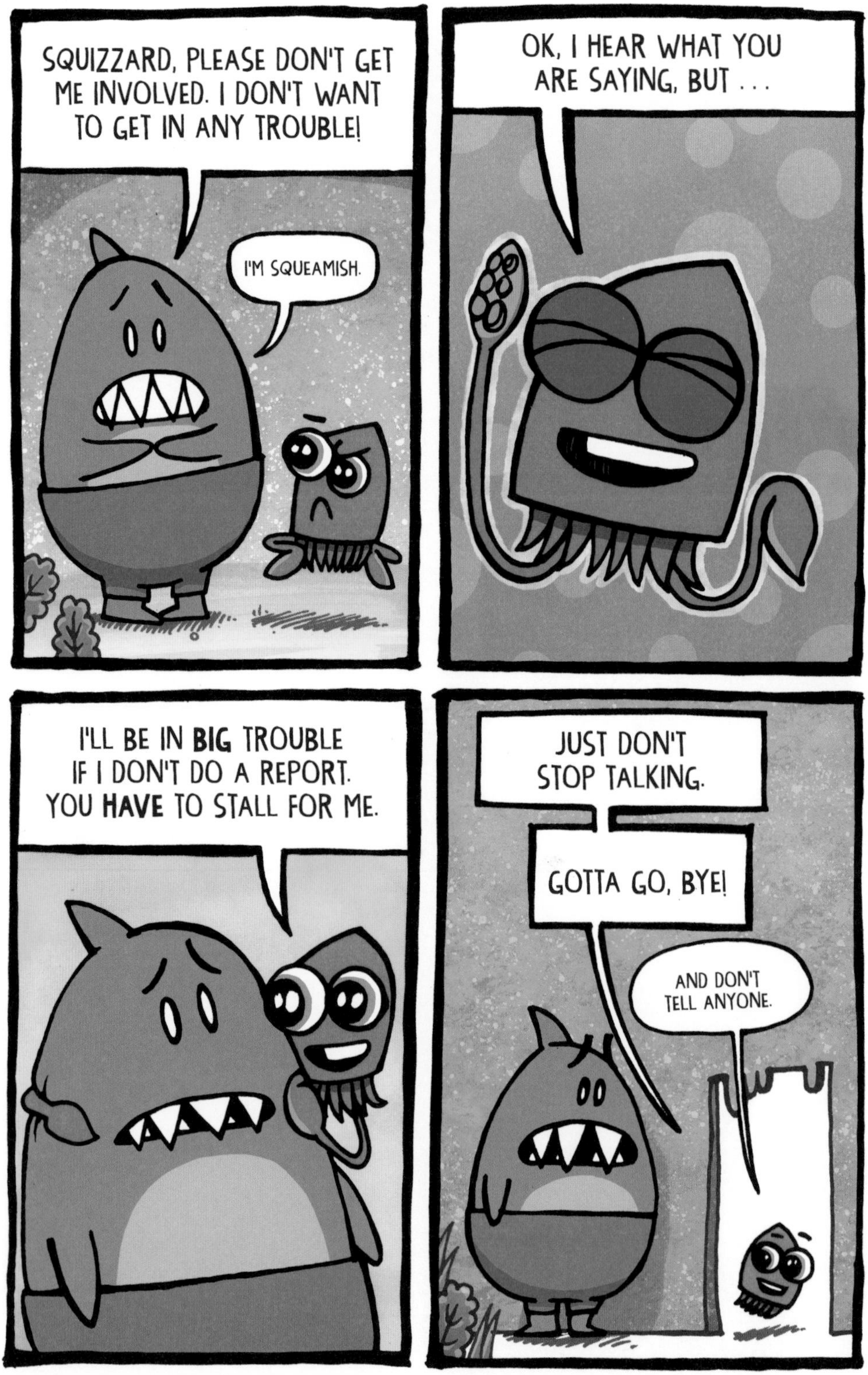
SQUIZZARD, PLEASE DON'T GET ME INVOLVED. I DON'T WANT TO GET IN ANY TROUBLE!
I'M SQUEAMISH.
OK, I HEAR WHAT YOU ARE SAYING, BUT . . .
I'LL BE IN BIG TROUBLE IF I DON'T DO A REPORT. YOU HAVE TO STALL FOR ME.
JUST DON'T STOP TALKING.
GOTTA GO, BYE!
AND DON'T TELL ANYONE.

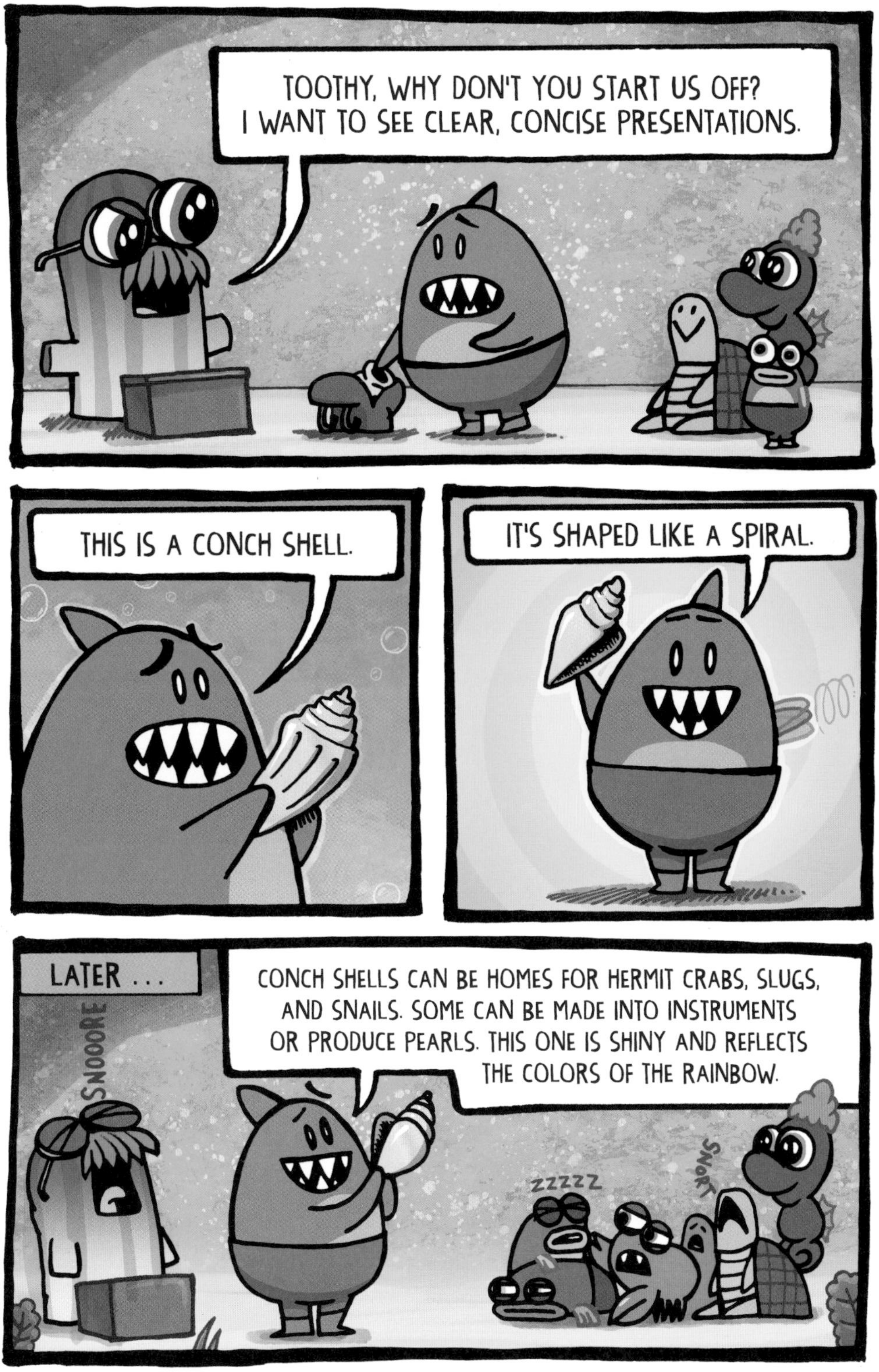
TOOTHY, WHY DON'T YOU START US OFF? I WANT TO SEE CLEAR, CONCISE PRESENTATIONS.
THIS IS A CONCH SHELL.
IT'S SHAPED LIKE A SPIRAL.
LATER . . .
CONCH SHELLS CAN BE HOMES FOR HERMIT CRABS, SLUGS, AND SNAILS. SOME CAN BE MADE INTO INSTRUMENTS OR PRODUCE PEARLS. THIS ONE IS SHINY AND REFLECTS THE COLORS OF THE RAINBOW.
SNOOORE
SNORT
ZZZZZ

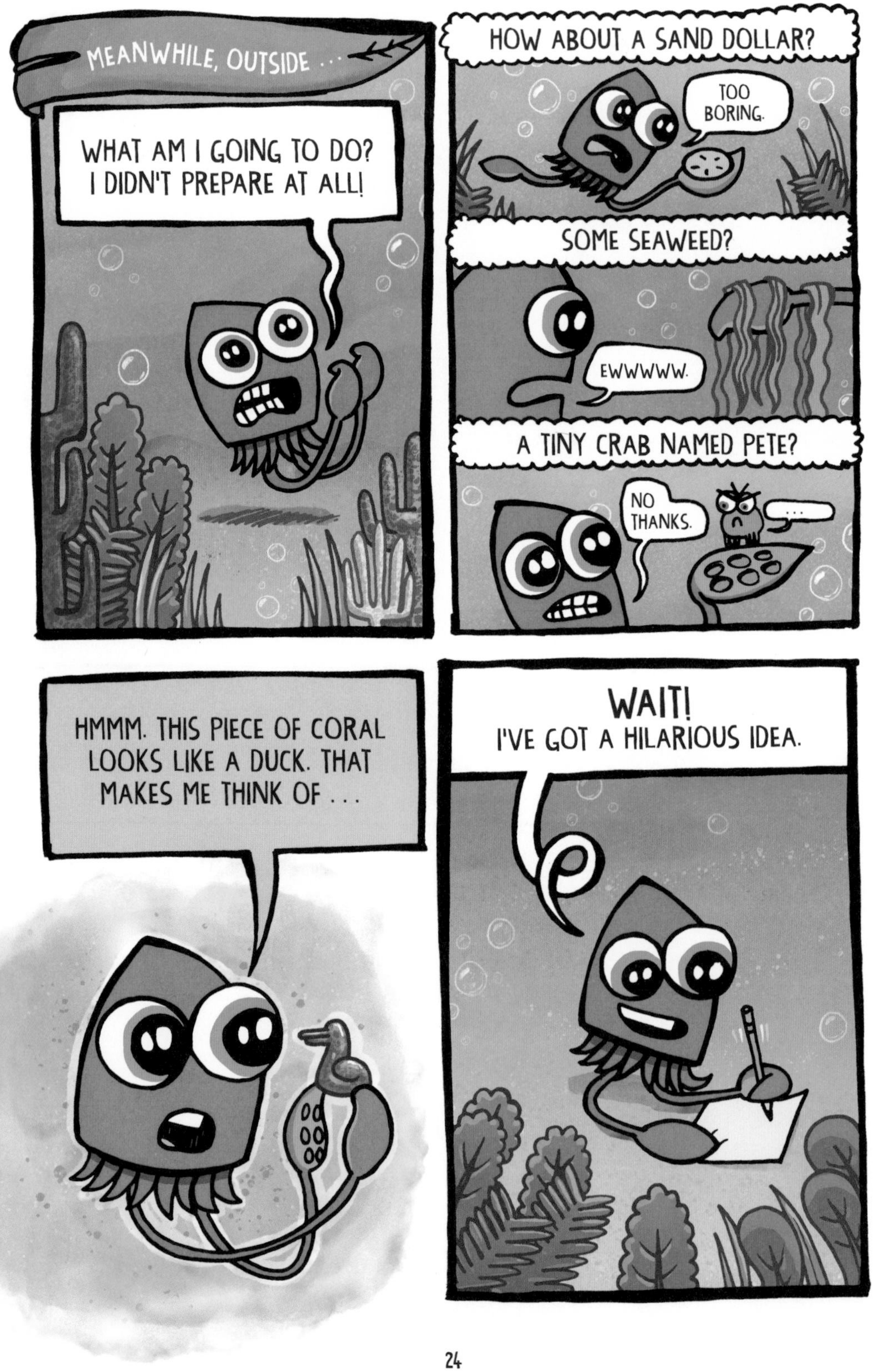
MEANWHILE, OUTSIDE . . .
WHAT AM I GOING TO DO? I DIDN'T PREPARE AT ALL!
HOW ABOUT A SAND DOLLAR?
TOO BORING.
SOME SEAWEED?
EWWWWW.
A TINY CRAB NAMED PETE?
NO THANKS.
. . .
HMMM. THIS PIECE OF CORAL LOOKS LIKE A DUCK. THAT MAKES ME THINK OF . . .
WAIT!
I'VE GOT A HILARIOUS IDEA.

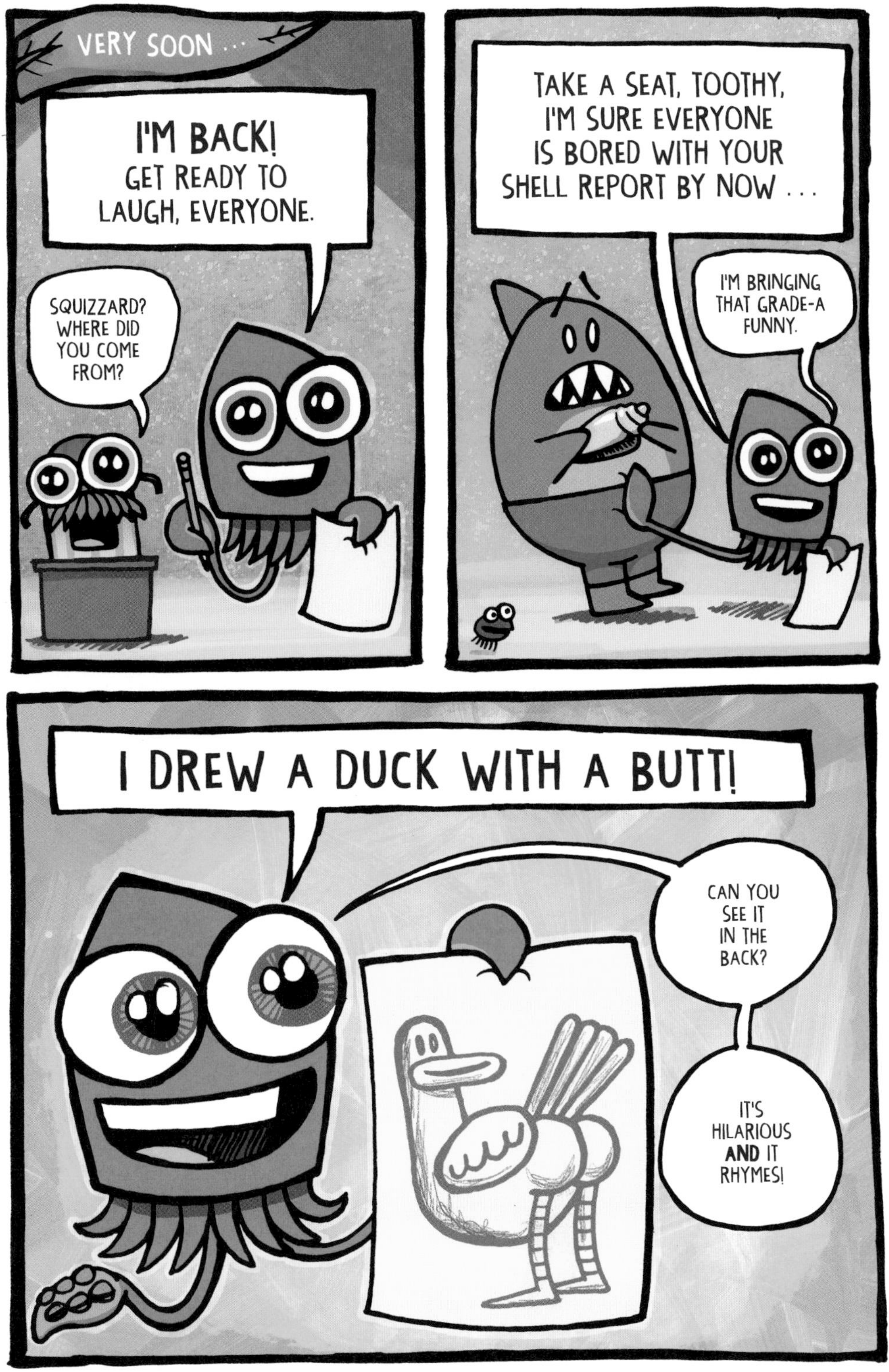
VERY SOON . . .
I'M BACK! GET READY TO LAUGH, EVERYONE.
SQUIZZARD? WHERE DID YOU COME FROM?
TAKE A SEAT, TOOTHY, I'M SURE EVERYONE IS BORED WITH YOUR SHELL REPORT BY NOW . . .
I'M BRINGING THAT GRADE-A FUNNY.
I DREW A DUCK WITH A BUTT!
CAN YOU SEE IT IN THE BACK?
IT'S HILARIOUS **AND** IT RHYMES!

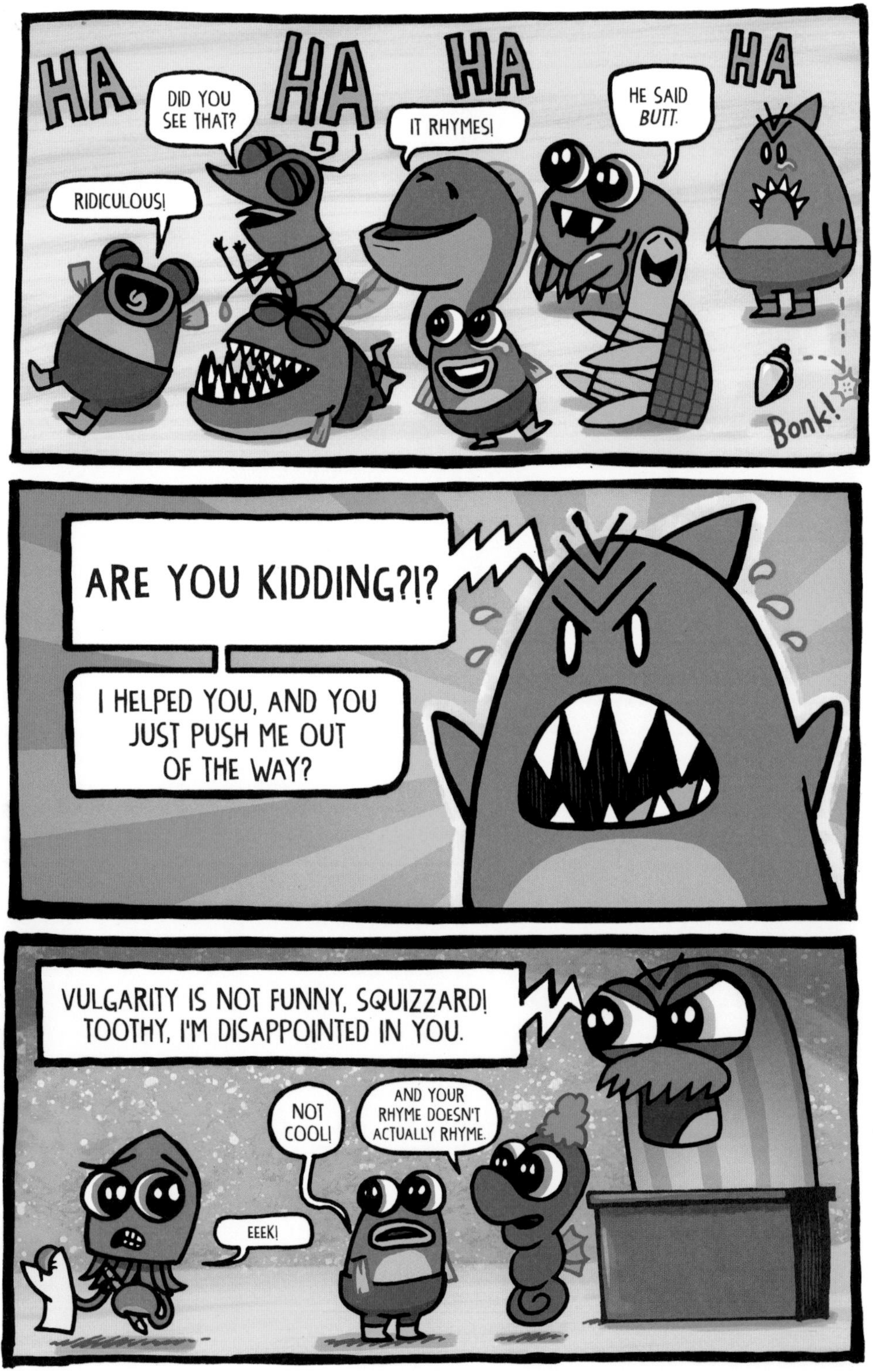
HA
RIDICULOUS!
DID YOU SEE THAT?
HA
HA
IT RHYMES!
HE SAID *BUTT*.
HA
Bonk!
ARE YOU KIDDING?!?
I HELPED YOU, AND YOU JUST PUSH ME OUT OF THE WAY?
VULGARITY IS NOT FUNNY, SQUIZZARD! TOOTHY, I'M DISAPPOINTED IN YOU.
EEEK!
NOT COOL!
AND YOUR RHYME DOESN'T ACTUALLY RHYME.

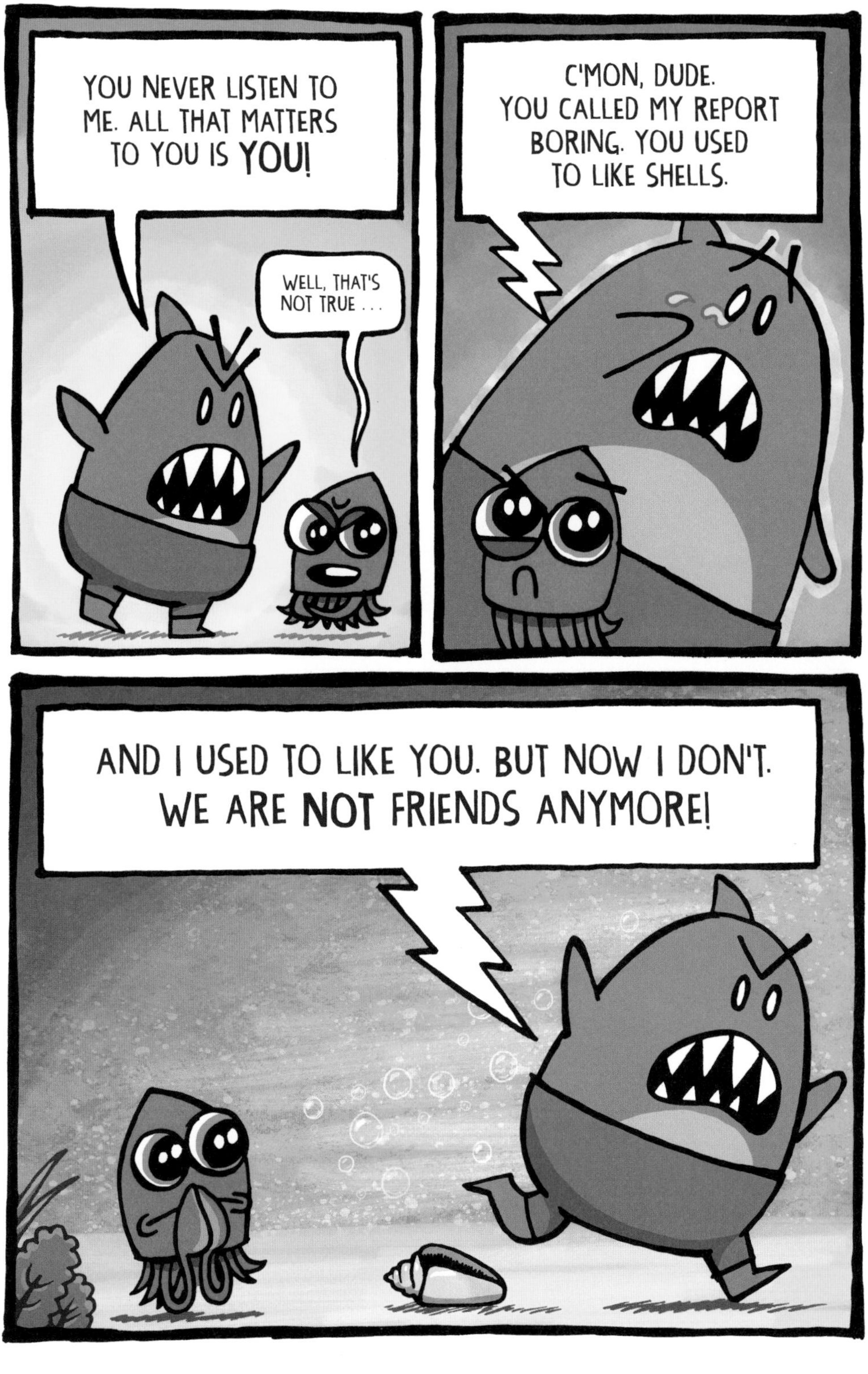
YOU NEVER LISTEN TO ME. ALL THAT MATTERS TO YOU IS YOU!
WELL, THAT'S NOT TRUE . . .
C'MON, DUDE. YOU CALLED MY REPORT BORING. YOU USED TO LIKE SHELLS.
AND I USED TO LIKE YOU. BUT NOW I DON'T. WE ARE NOT FRIENDS ANYMORE!

CHAP[redacted]

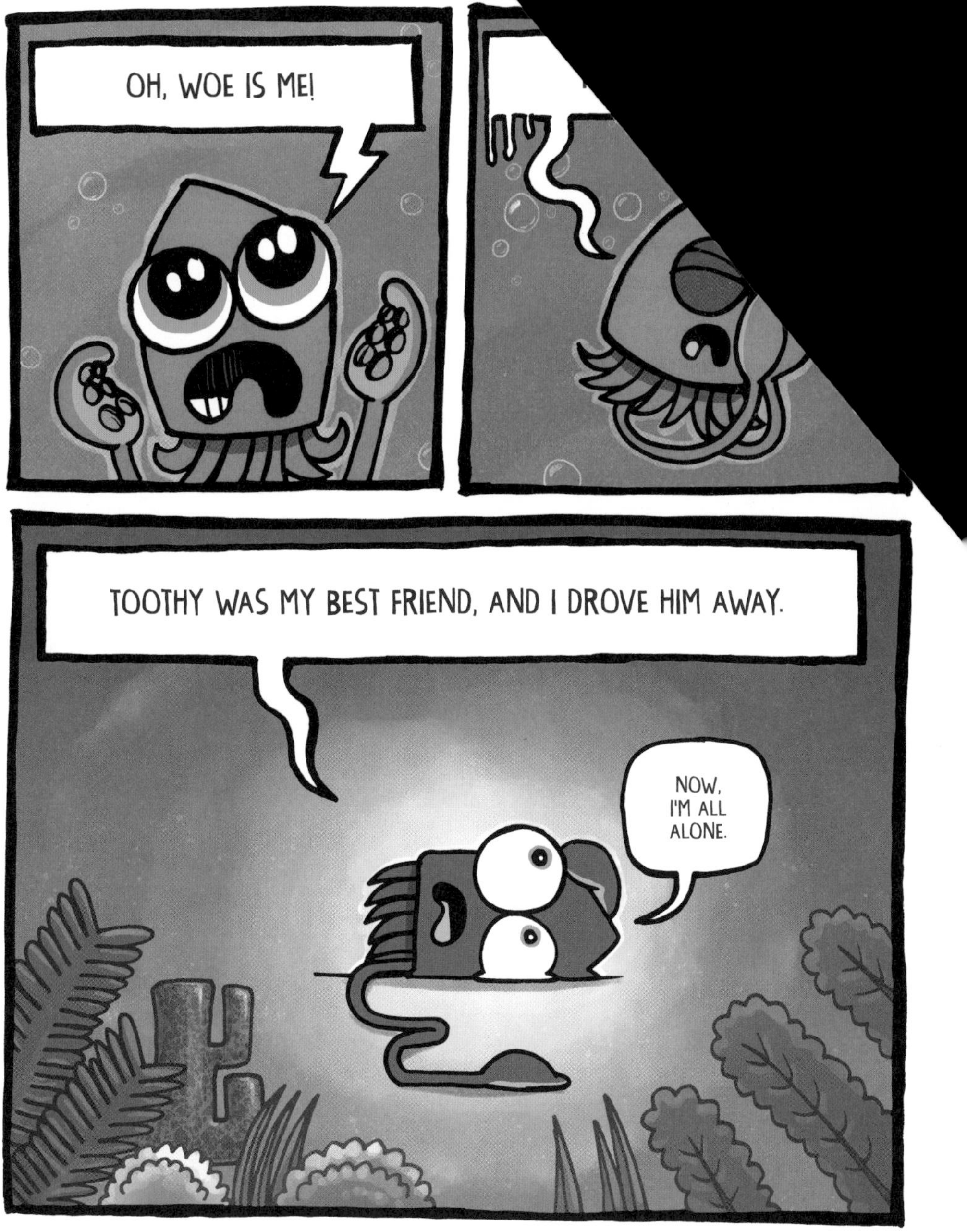
OH, WOE IS ME!
[redacted]
TOOTHY WAS MY BEST FRIEND, AND I DROVE HIM AWAY.
NOW, I'M ALL ALONE.

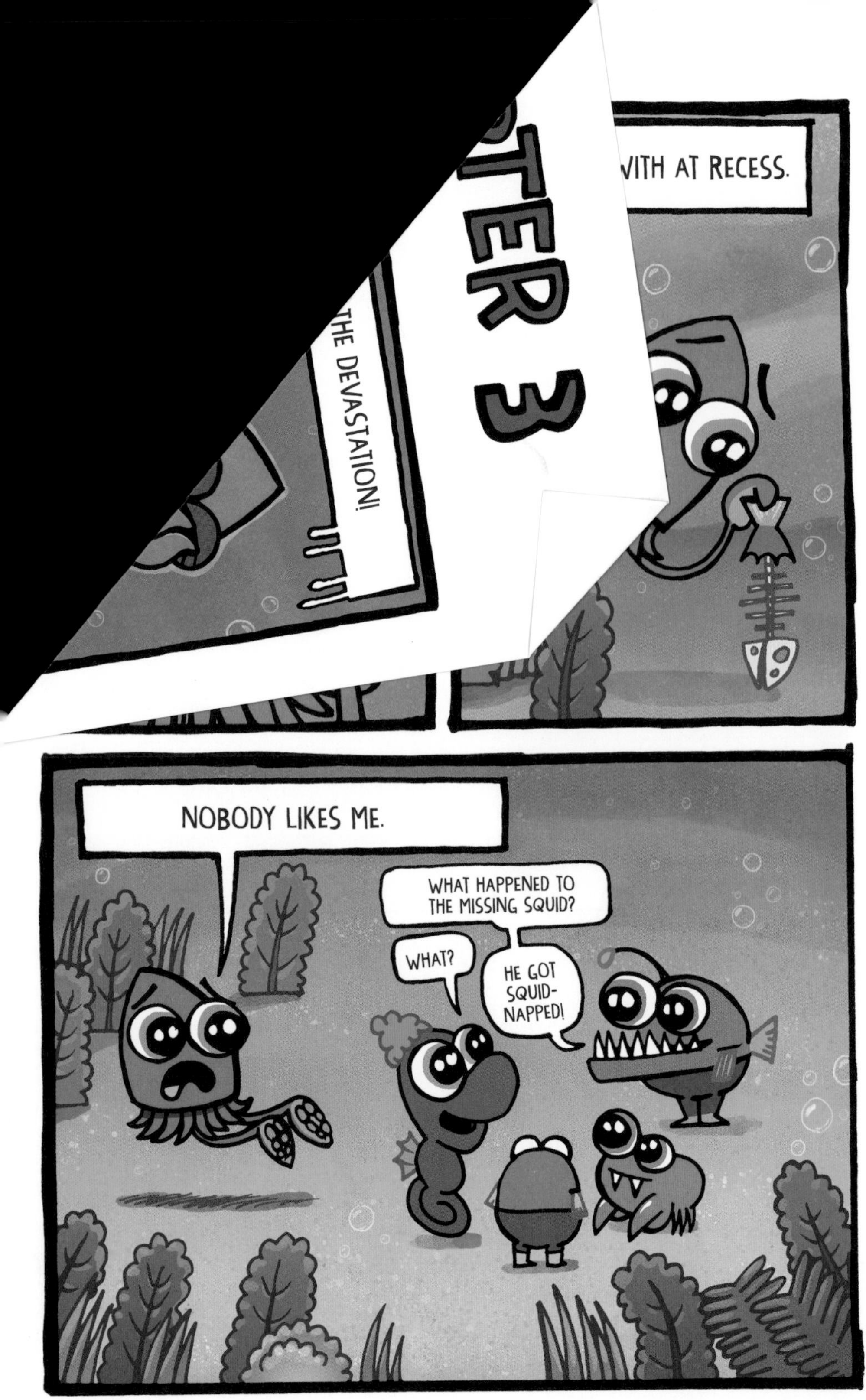

WITH AT RECESS.
THE DEVASTATION!
NOBODY LIKES ME.
WHAT HAPPENED TO THE MISSING SQUID?
WHAT?
HE GOT SQUID-NAPPED!

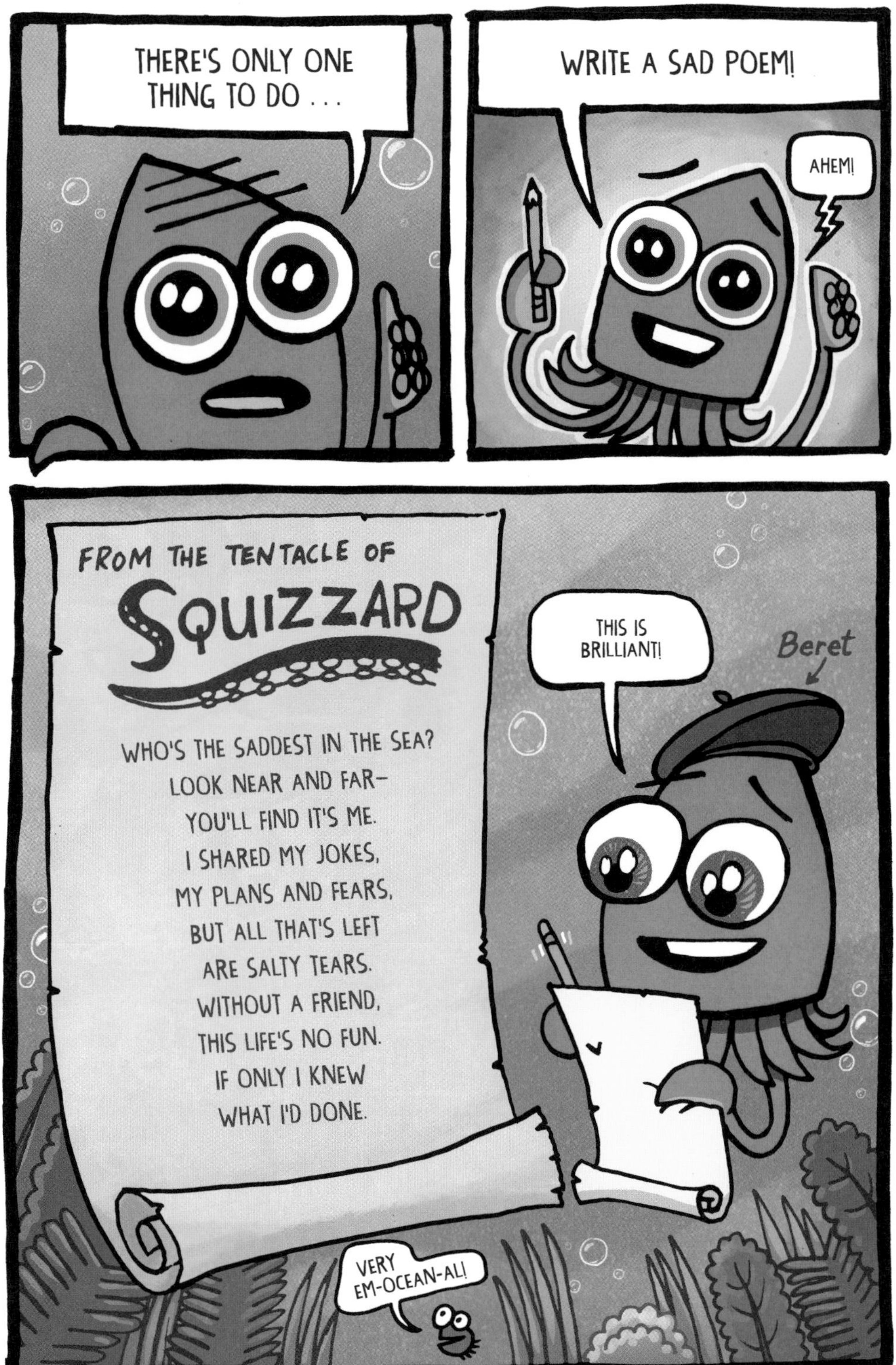
THERE'S ONLY ONE THING TO DO . . .
WRITE A SAD POEM!
AHEM!
FROM THE TENTACLE OF
SQUIZZARD
WHO'S THE SADDEST IN THE SEA?
LOOK NEAR AND FAR—
YOU'LL FIND IT'S ME.
I SHARED MY JOKES,
MY PLANS AND FEARS,
BUT ALL THAT'S LEFT
ARE SALTY TEARS.
WITHOUT A FRIEND,
THIS LIFE'S NO FUN.
IF ONLY I KNEW
WHAT I'D DONE.
THIS IS BRILLIANT!
Beret
VERY EM-OCEAN-AL!

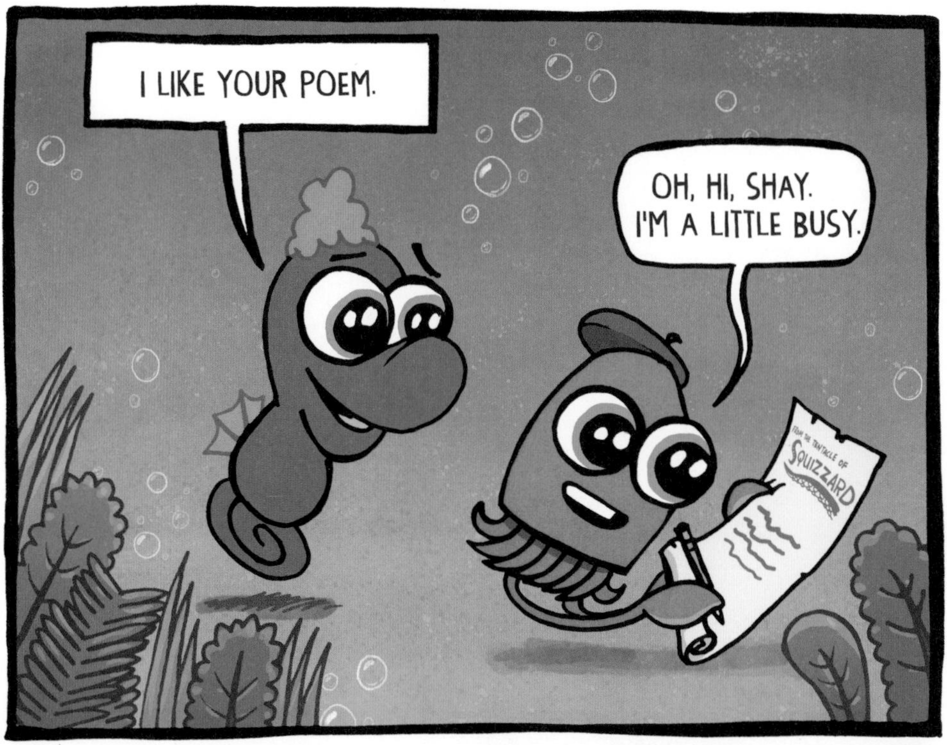
I LIKE YOUR POEM.
OH, HI, SHAY. I'M A LITTLE BUSY.
FROM THE TENTACLE OF SQUIZZARD

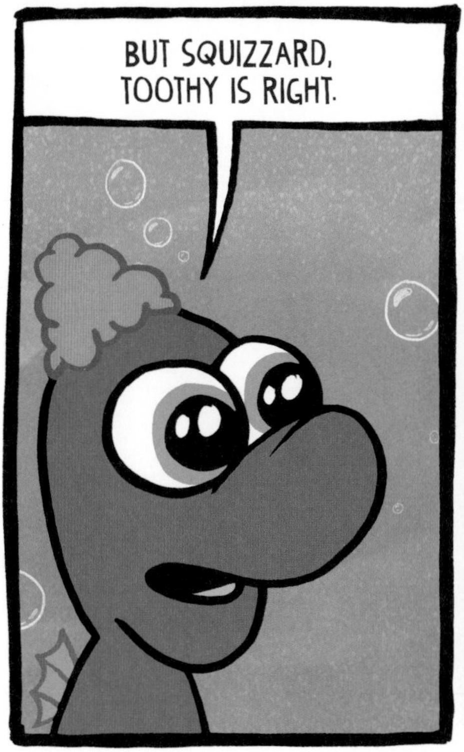
BUT SQUIZZARD, TOOTHY IS RIGHT.

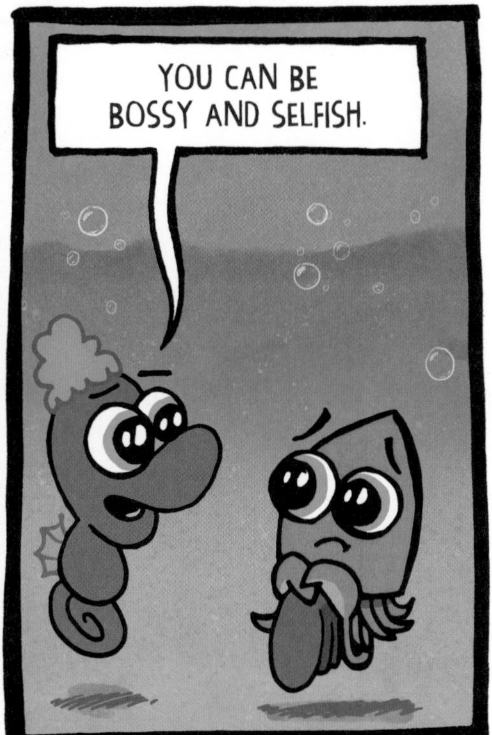
YOU CAN BE BOSSY AND SELFISH.

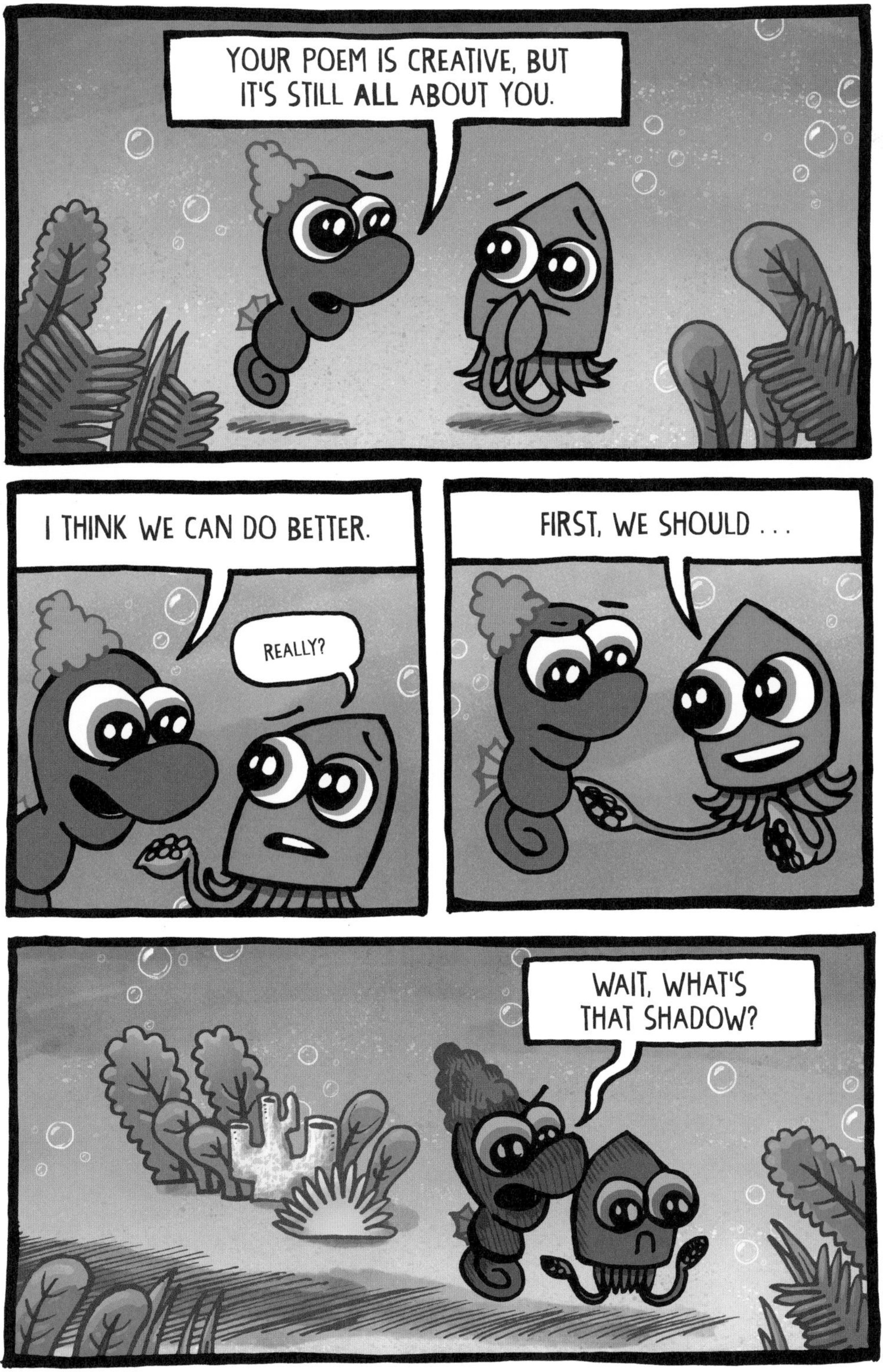
YOUR POEM IS CREATIVE, BUT IT'S STILL **ALL** ABOUT YOU.
I THINK WE CAN DO BETTER.
REALLY?
FIRST, WE SHOULD . . .
WAIT, WHAT'S THAT SHADOW?

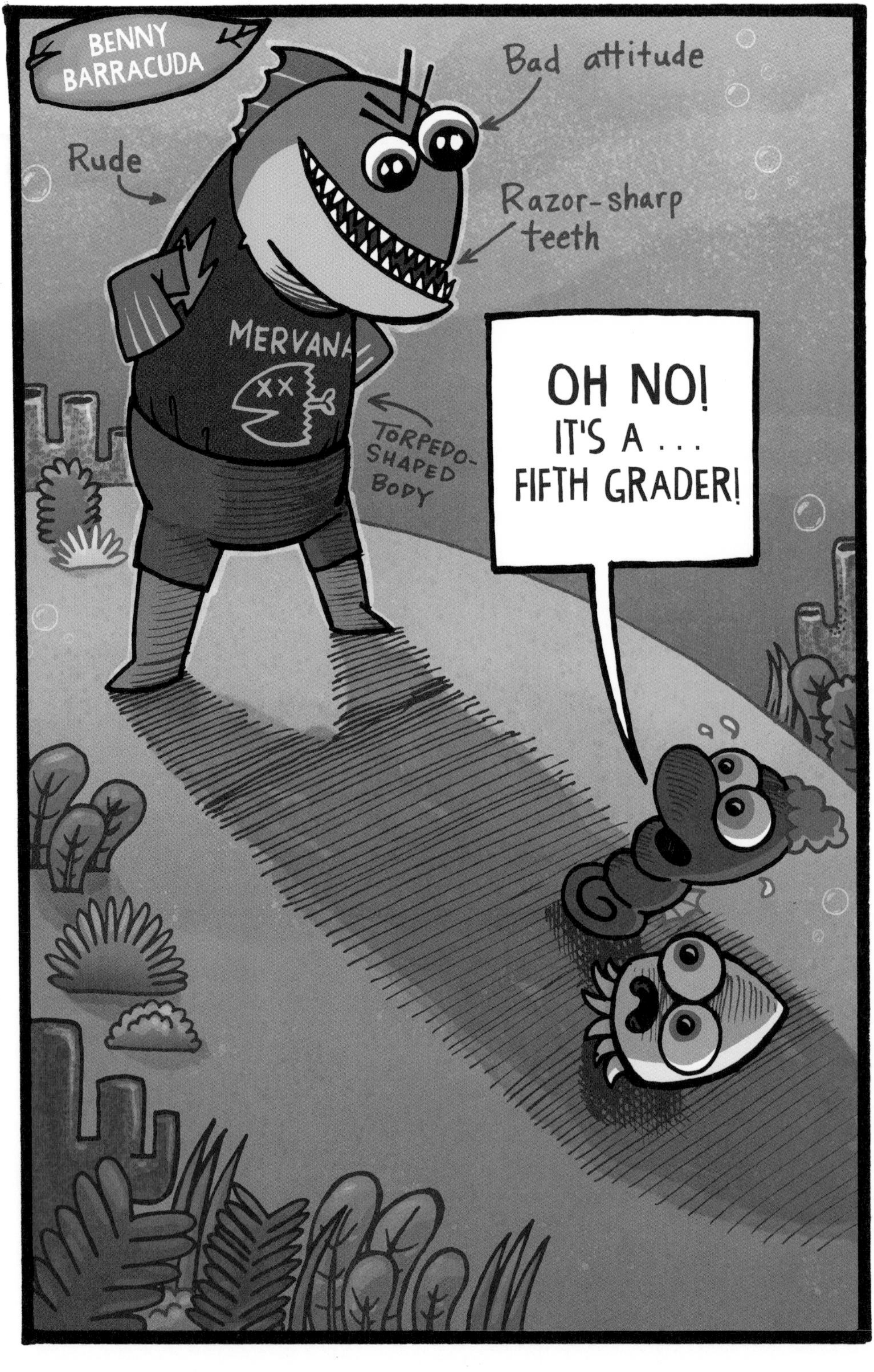
BENNY BARRACUDA
Bad attitude
Rude
Razor-sharp teeth
MERVANA
TORPEDO-SHAPED BODY
OH NO! IT'S A . . . FIFTH GRADER!

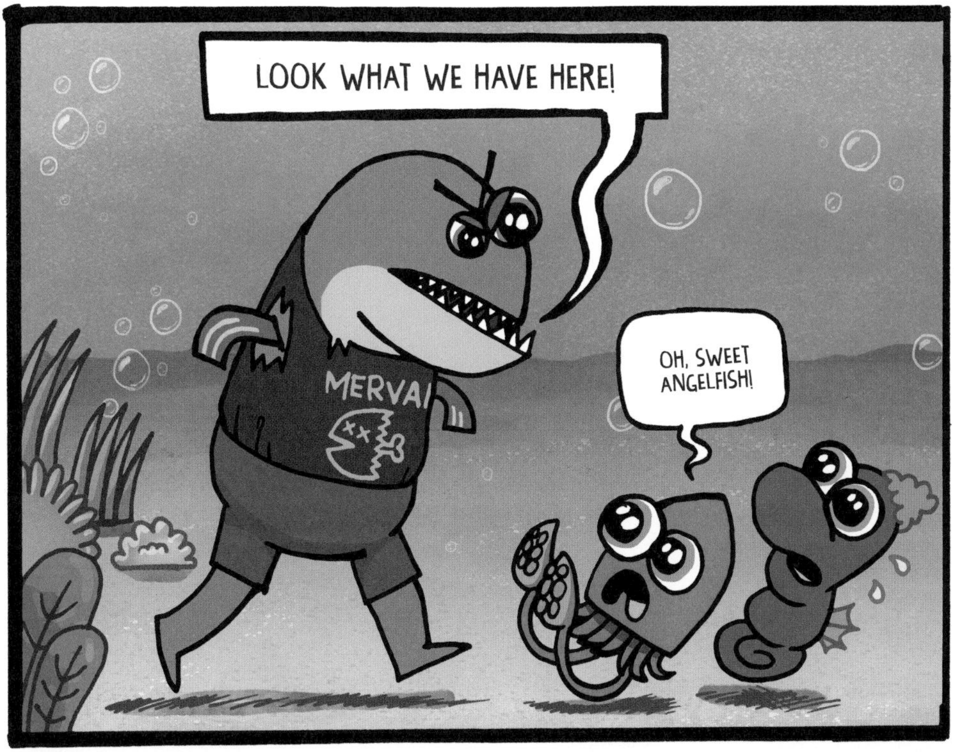
LOOK WHAT WE HAVE HERE!
OH, SWEET ANGELFISH!
MERVAL

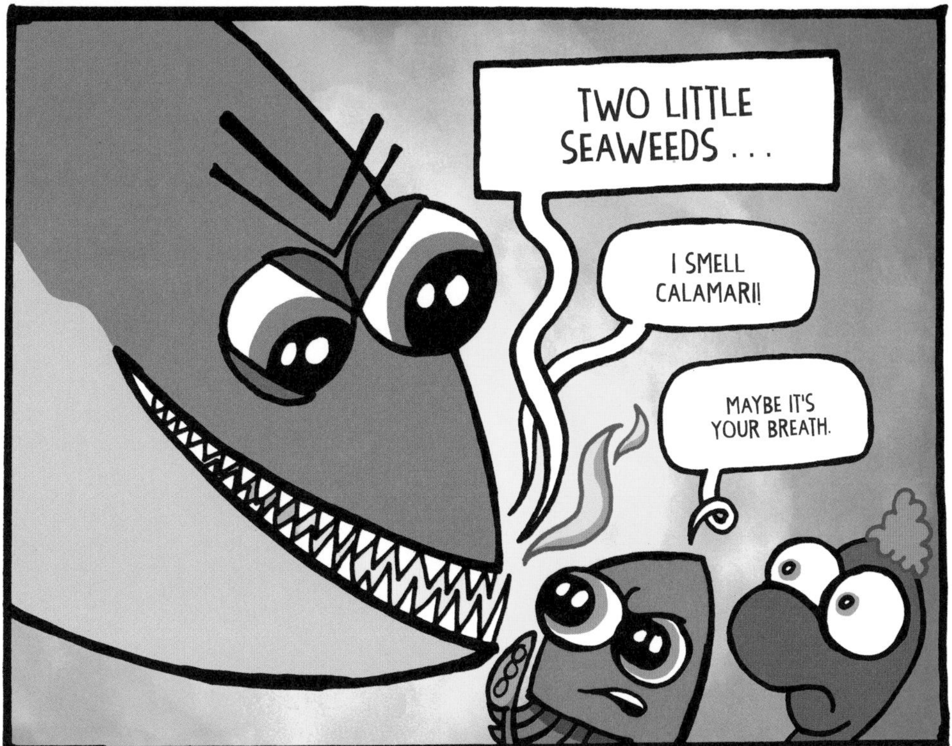
TWO LITTLE SEAWEEDS . . .
I SMELL CALAMARI!
MAYBE IT'S YOUR BREATH.

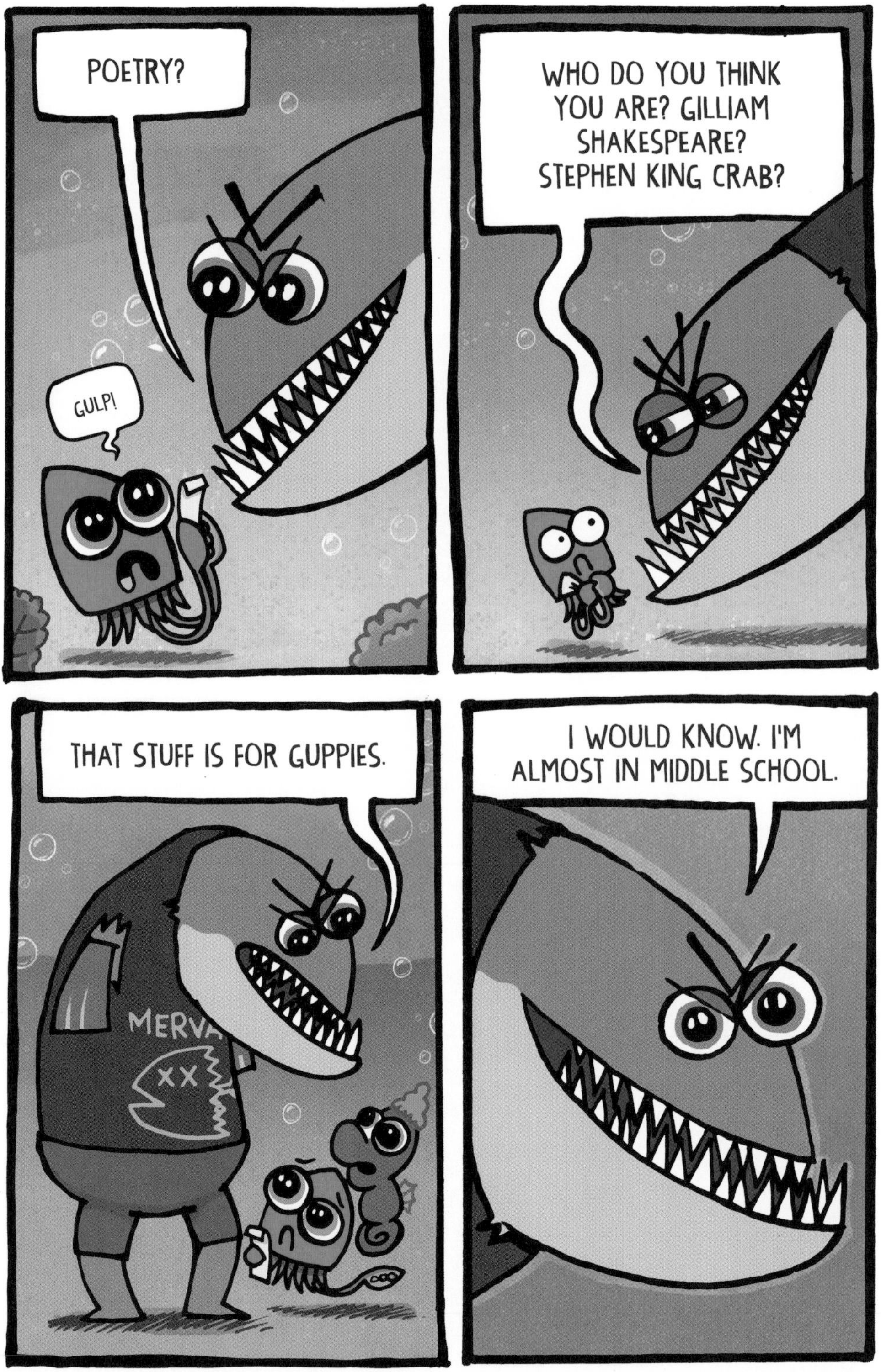
POETRY?
GULP!
WHO DO YOU THINK YOU ARE? GILLIAM SHAKESPEARE? STEPHEN KING CRAB?
THAT STUFF IS FOR GUPPIES.
MERVA
I WOULD KNOW. I'M ALMOST IN MIDDLE SCHOOL.

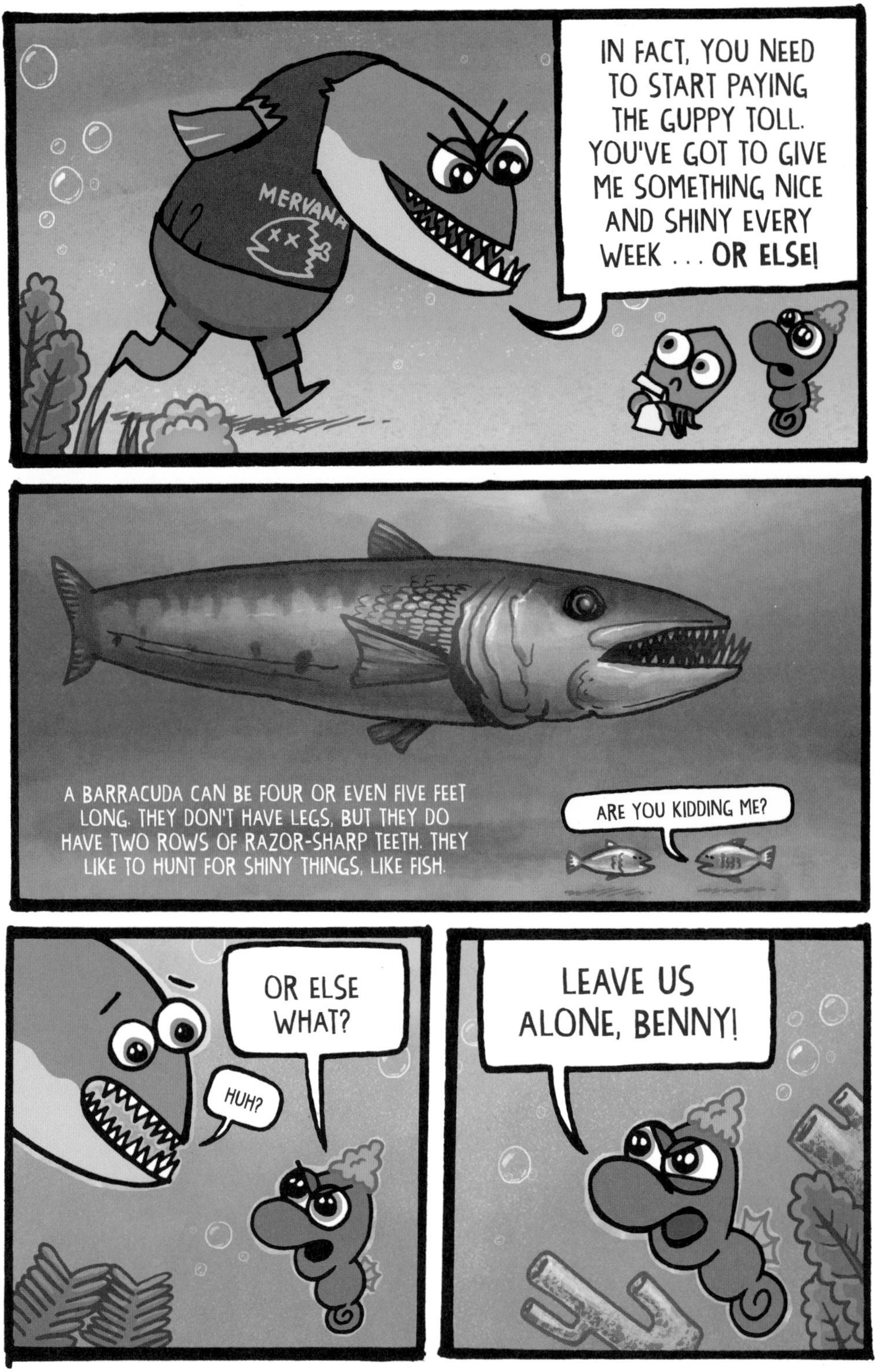
IN FACT, YOU NEED TO START PAYING THE GUPPY TOLL. YOU'VE GOT TO GIVE ME SOMETHING NICE AND SHINY EVERY WEEK . . . OR ELSE!
MERVANA
A BARRACUDA CAN BE FOUR OR EVEN FIVE FEET LONG. THEY DON'T HAVE LEGS, BUT THEY DO HAVE TWO ROWS OF RAZOR-SHARP TEETH. THEY LIKE TO HUNT FOR SHINY THINGS, LIKE FISH.
ARE YOU KIDDING ME?
OR ELSE WHAT?
HUH?
LEAVE US ALONE, BENNY!

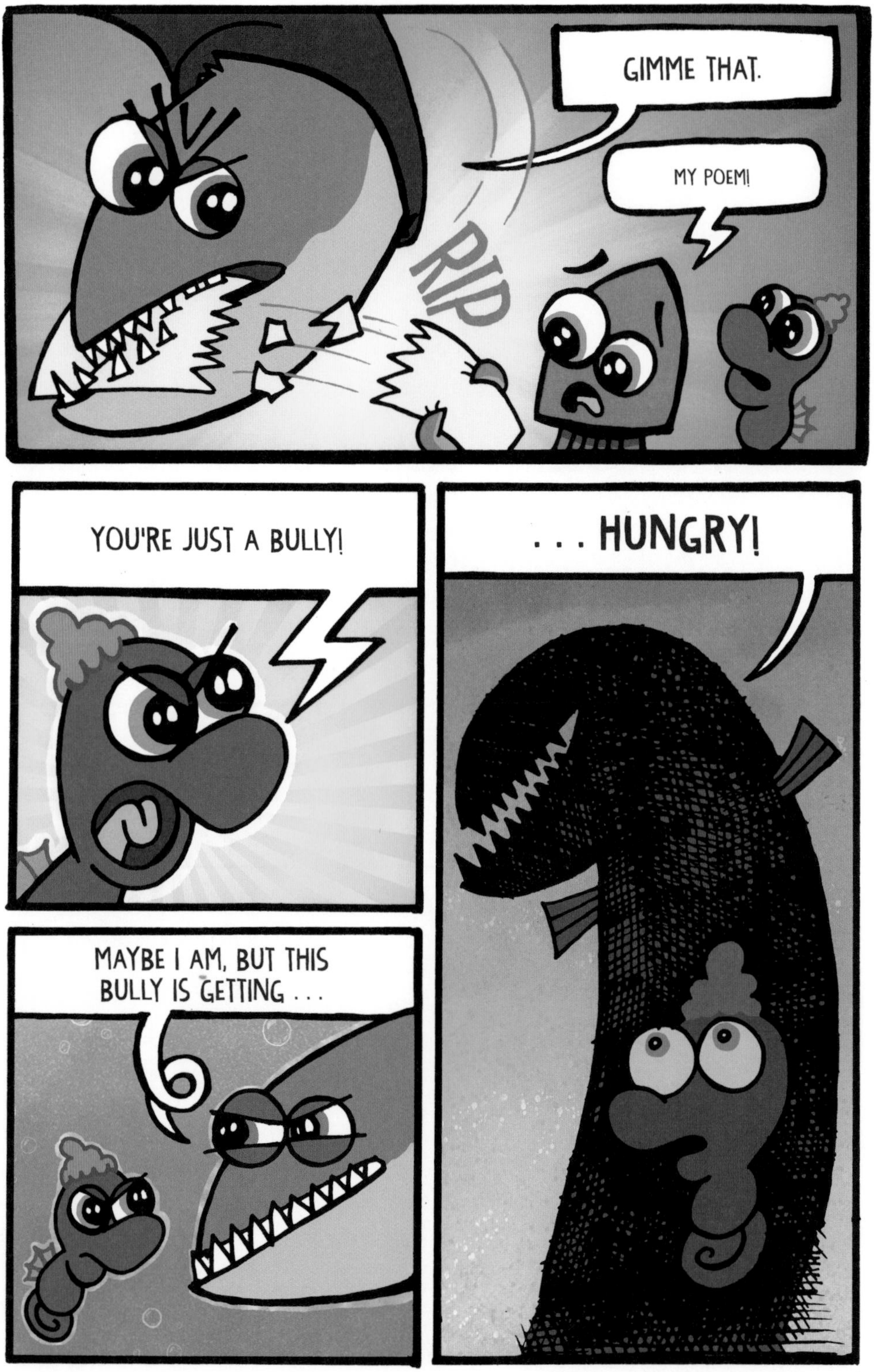
GIMME THAT.
MY POEM!
RIP
YOU'RE JUST A BULLY!
MAYBE I AM, BUT THIS BULLY IS GETTING . . .
. . . HUNGRY!

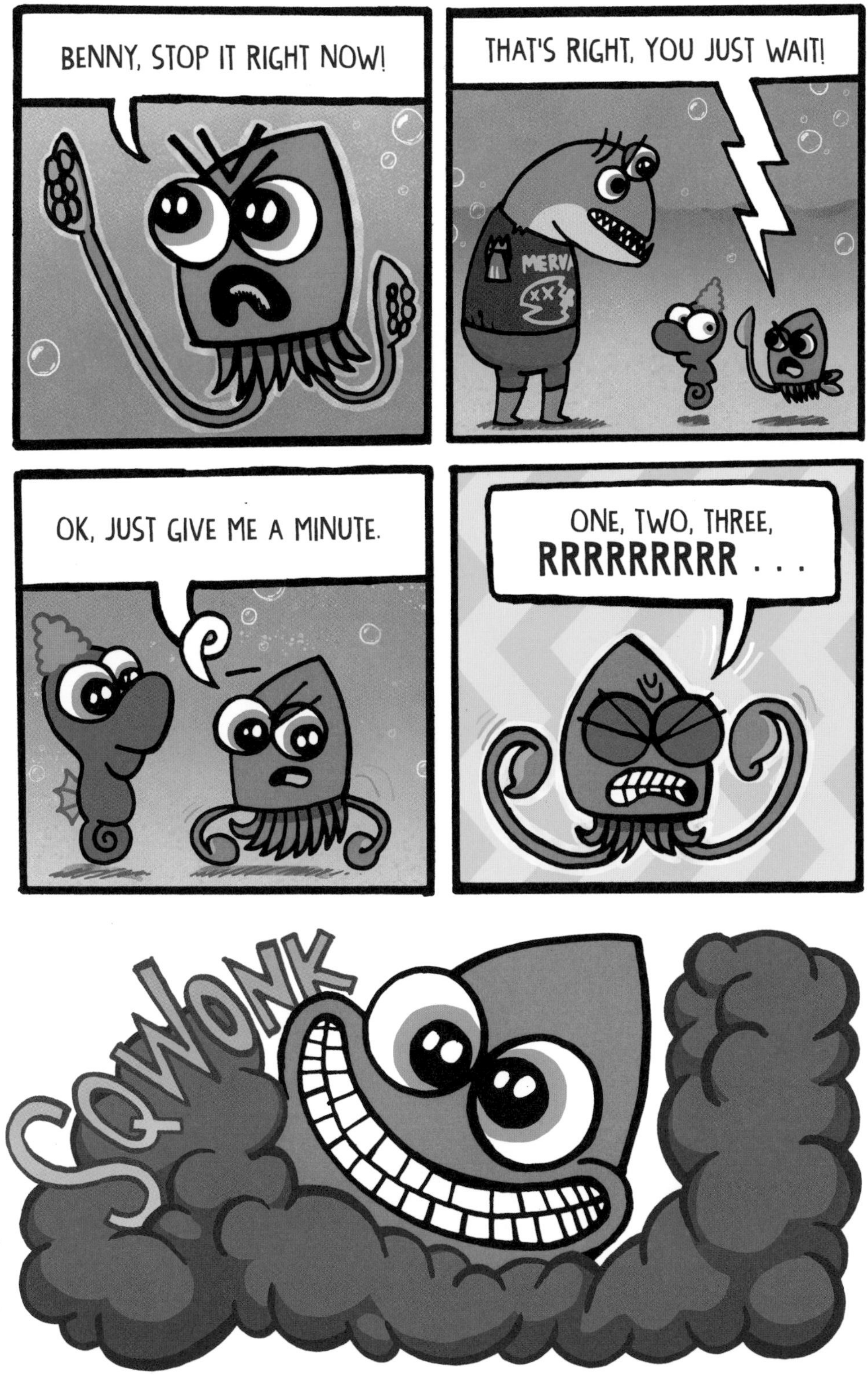
BENNY, STOP IT RIGHT NOW!
THAT'S RIGHT, YOU JUST WAIT!
MERV
OK, JUST GIVE ME A MINUTE.
ONE, TWO, THREE, RRRRRRRRR . . .
SQWONK

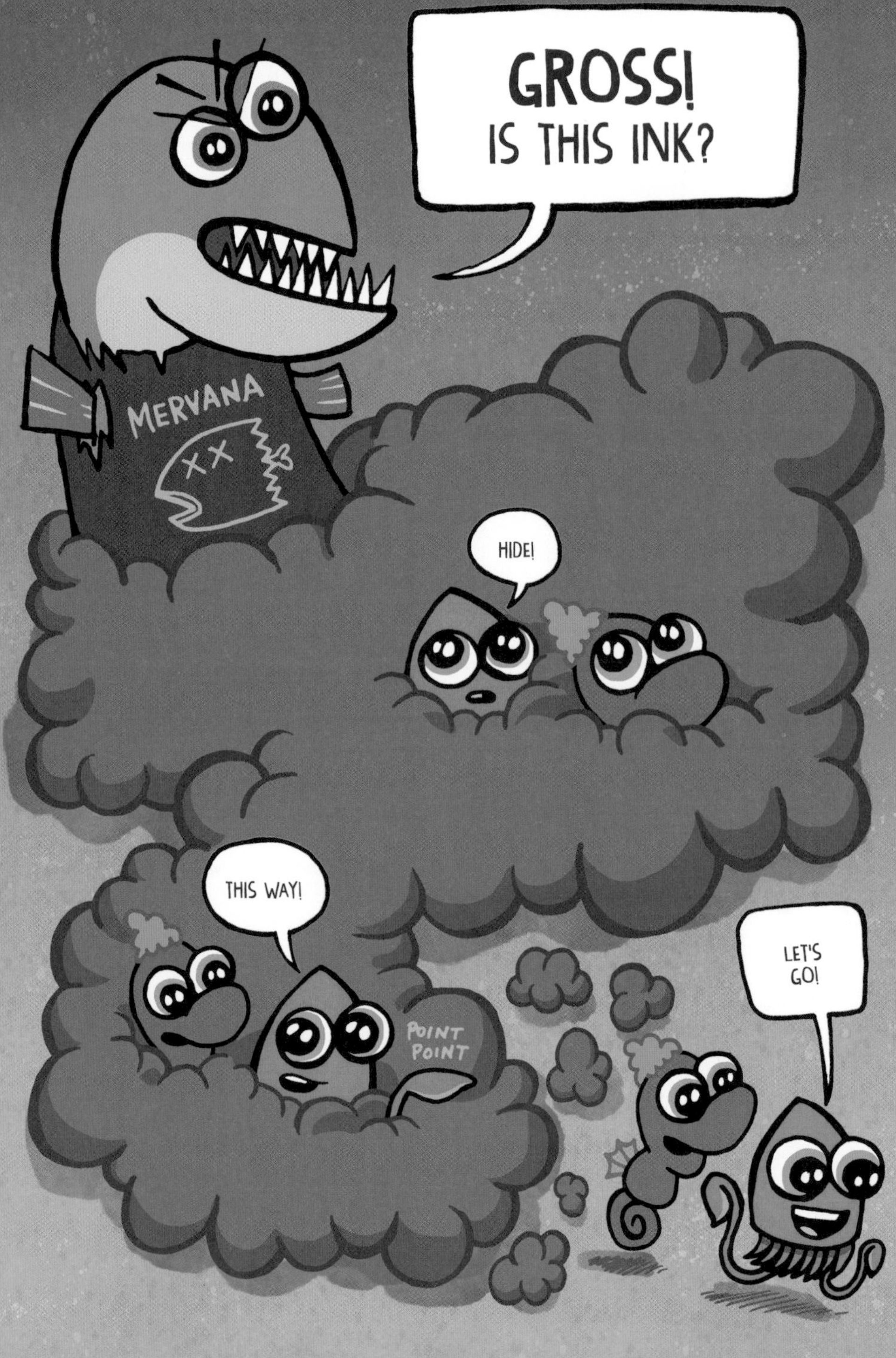
GROSS!
IS THIS INK?
MERVANA
HIDE!
THIS WAY!
POINT POINT
LET'S GO!

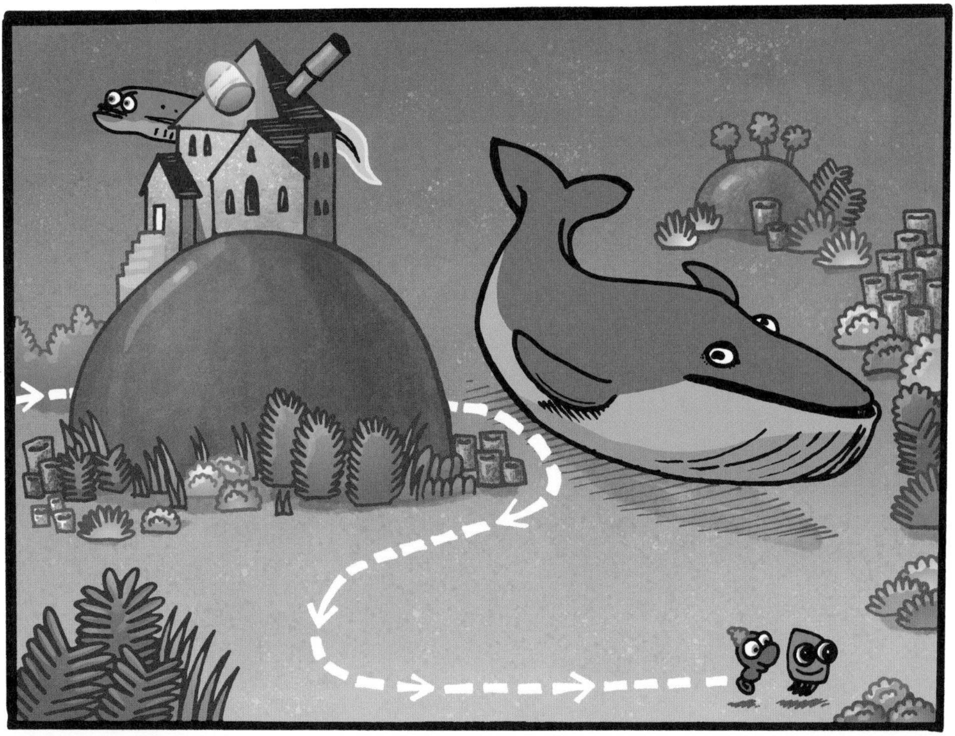

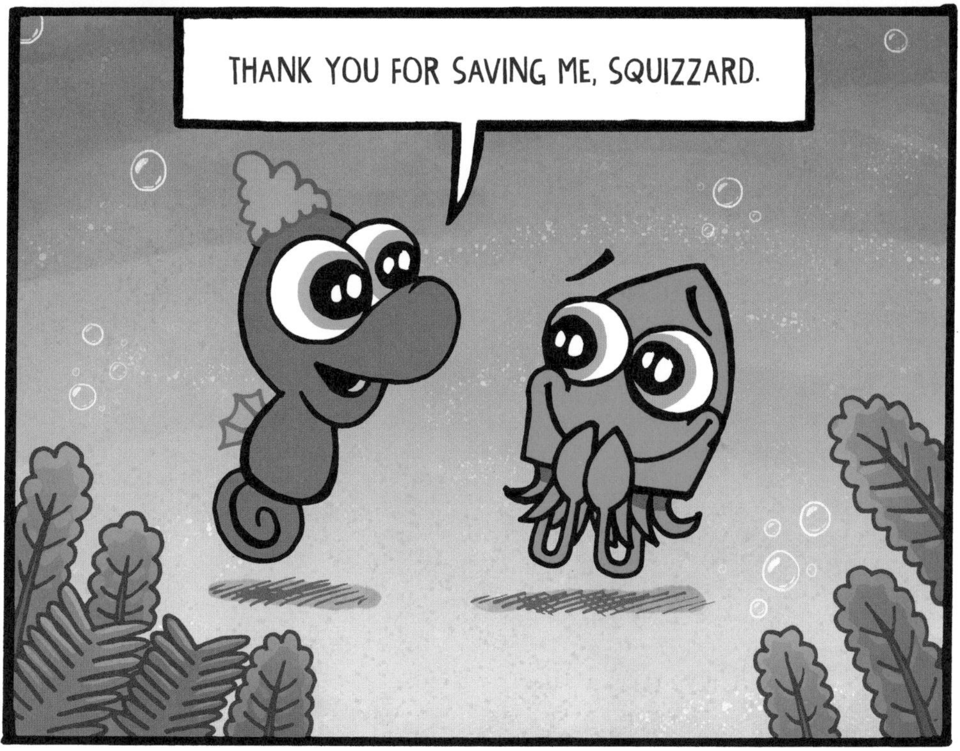
THANK YOU FOR SAVING ME, SQUIZZARD.

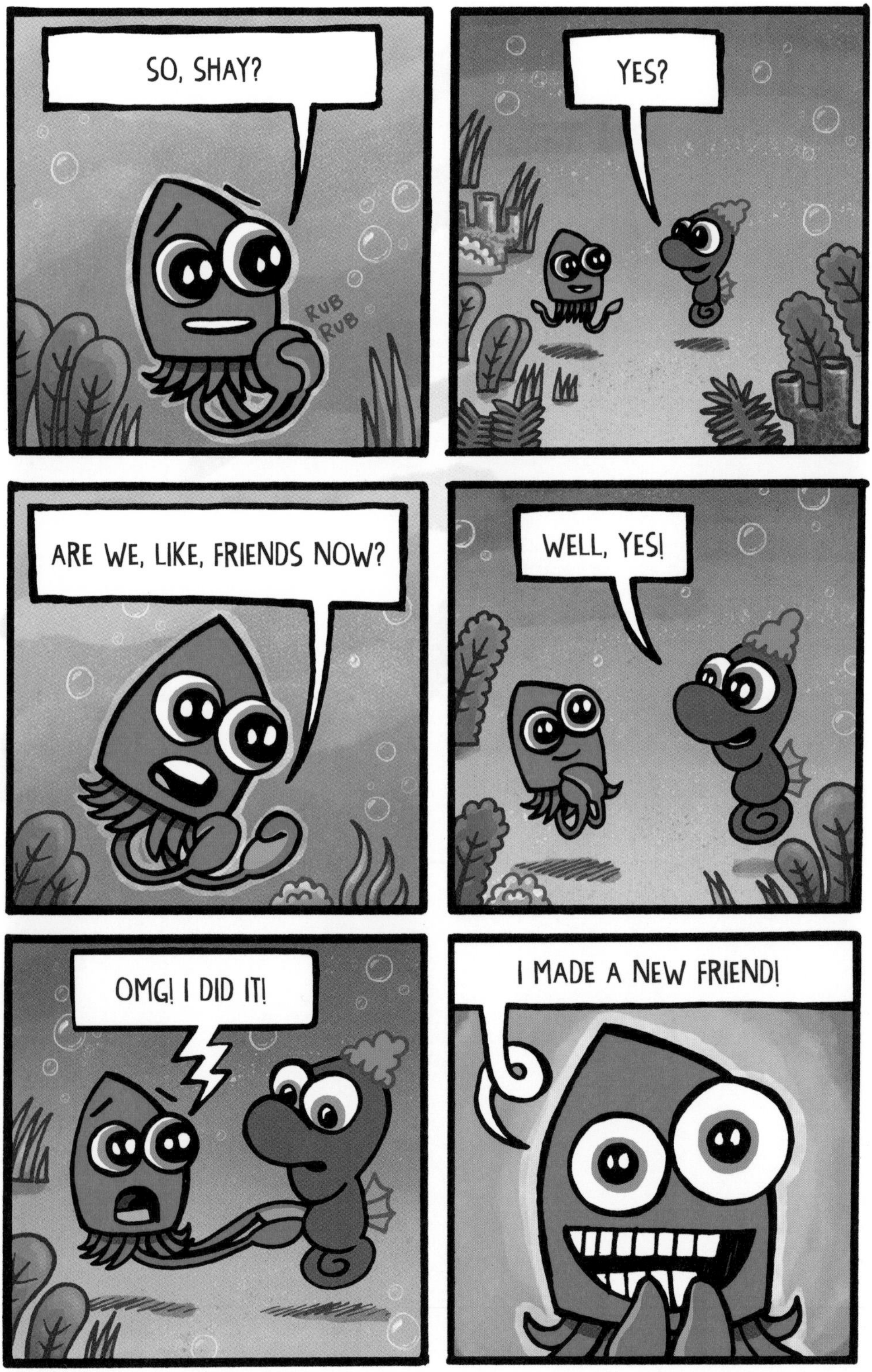
SO, SHAY?
RUB RUB
YES?
ARE WE, LIKE, FRIENDS NOW?
WELL, YES!
OMG! I DID IT!
I MADE A NEW FRIEND!

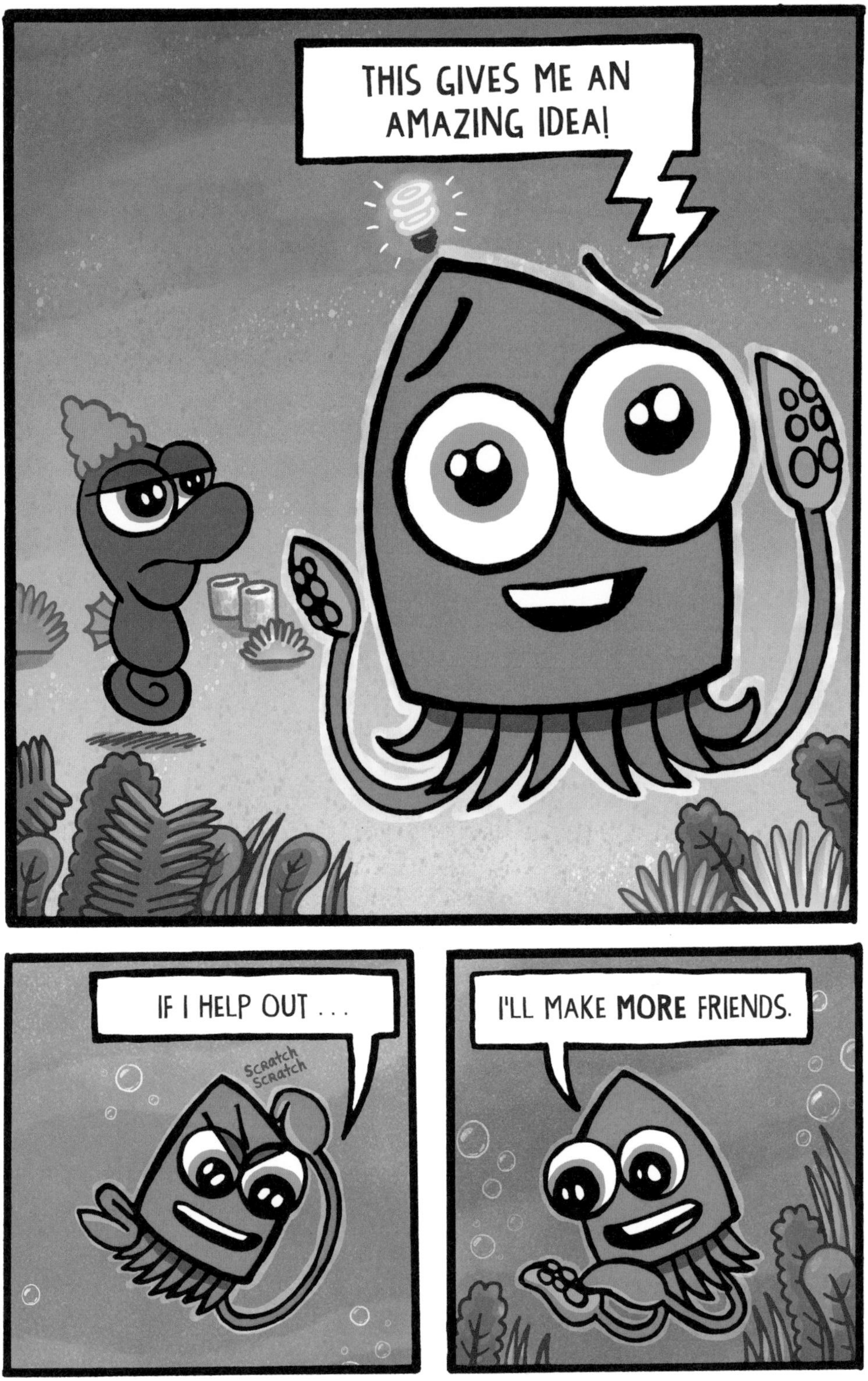
THIS GIVES ME AN AMAZING IDEA!
IF I HELP OUT . . .
Scratch Scratch
I'LL MAKE **MORE** FRIENDS.

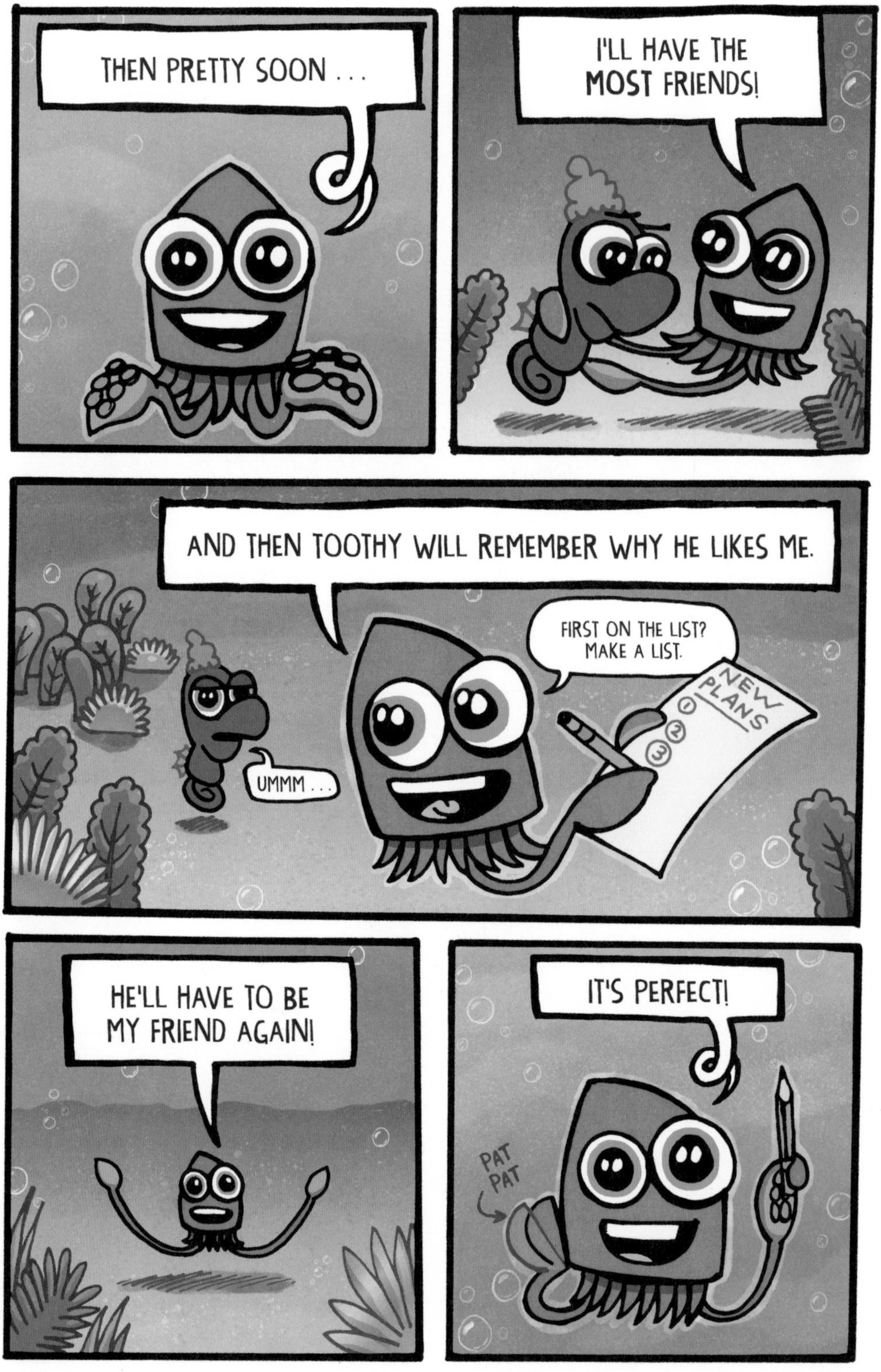
THEN PRETTY SOON . . .
I'LL HAVE THE MOST FRIENDS!
AND THEN TOOTHY WILL REMEMBER WHY HE LIKES ME.
FIRST ON THE LIST? MAKE A LIST.
NEW PLANS
1
2
3
UMMM . . .
HE'LL HAVE TO BE MY FRIEND AGAIN!
IT'S PERFECT!
PAT PAT

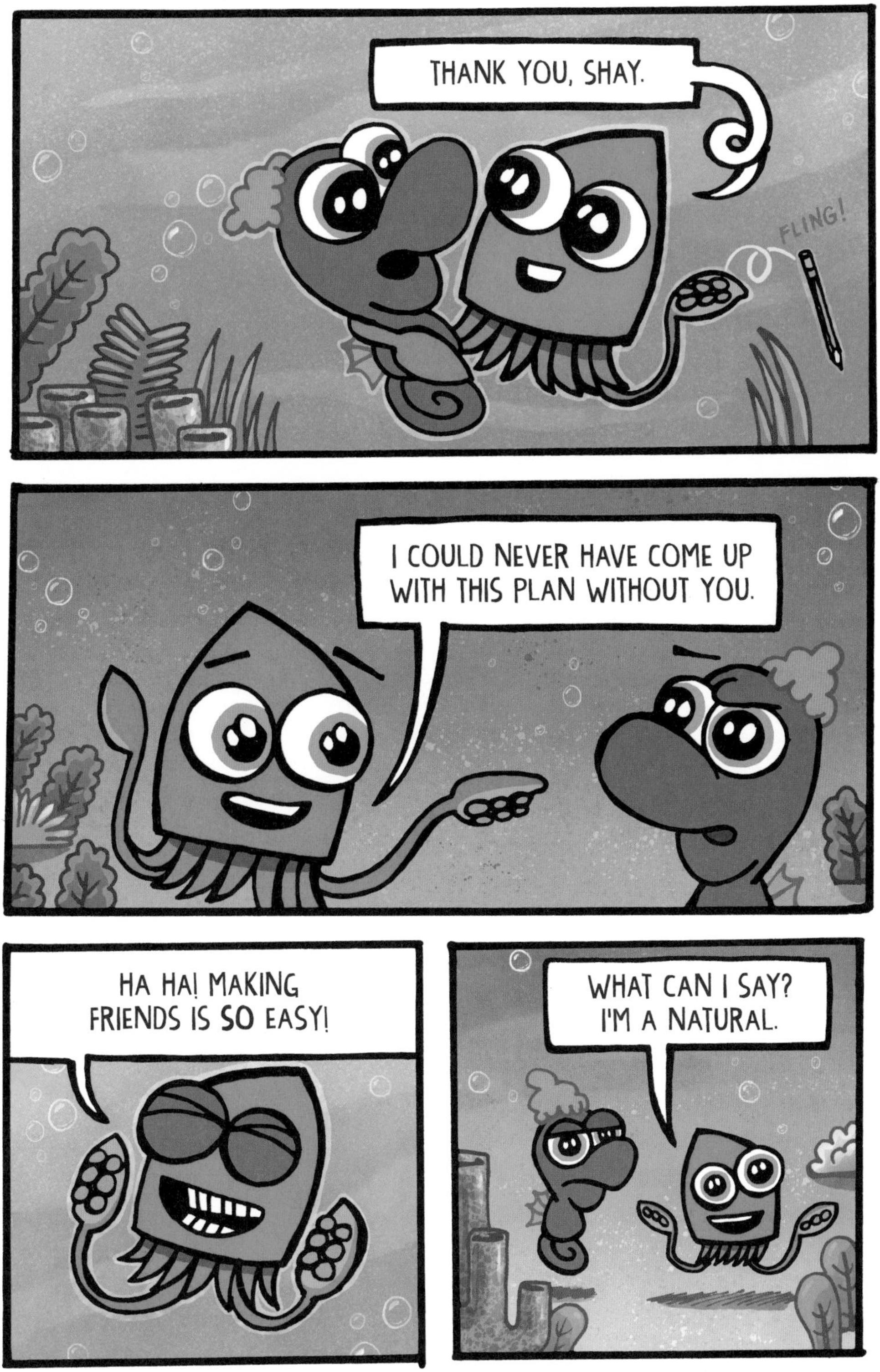
THANK YOU, SHAY.
FLING!
I COULD NEVER HAVE COME UP WITH THIS PLAN WITHOUT YOU.
HA HA! MAKING FRIENDS IS SO EASY!
WHAT CAN I SAY? I'M A NATURAL.

CHAPTER 4

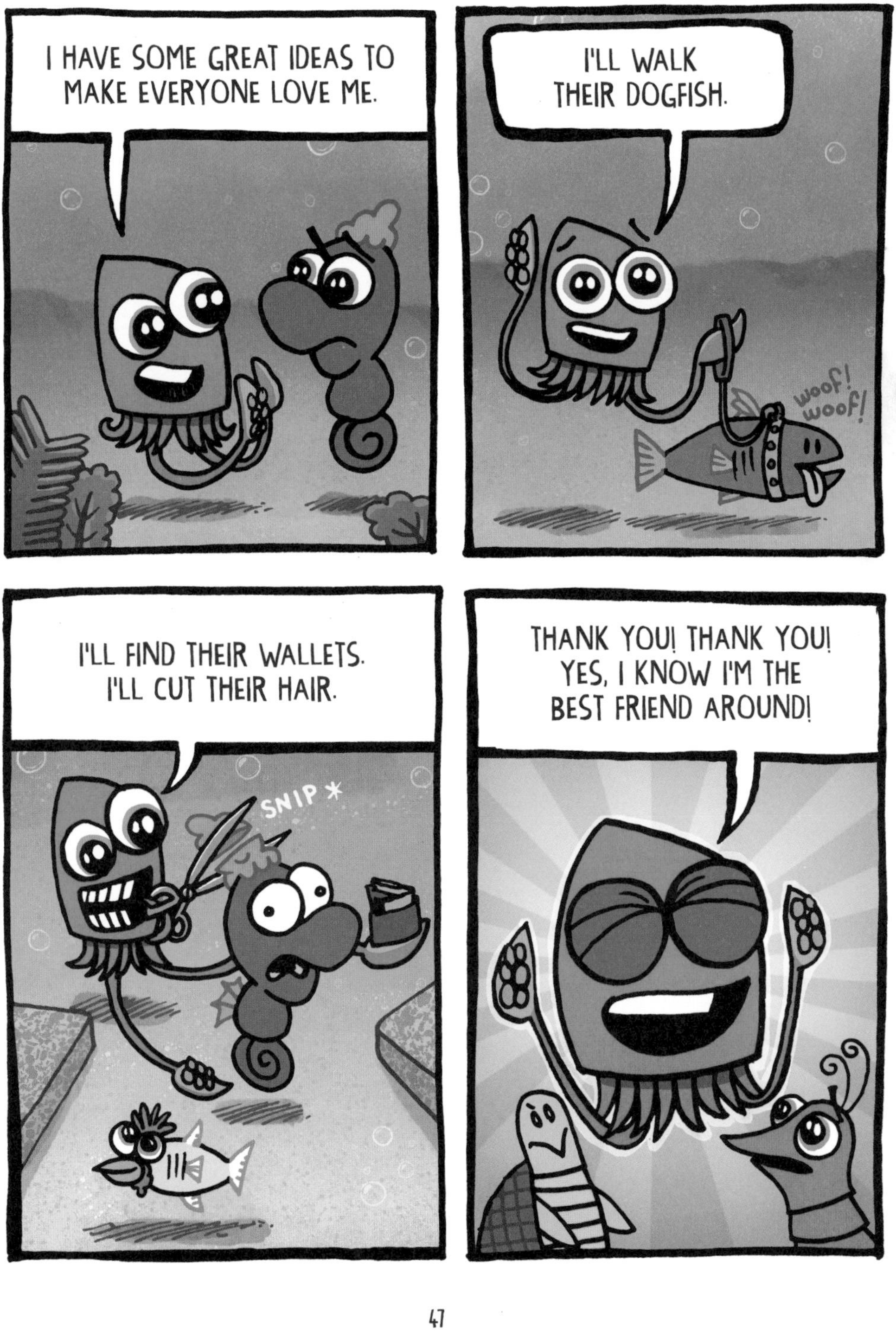
I HAVE SOME GREAT IDEAS TO MAKE EVERYONE LOVE ME.
I'LL WALK THEIR DOGFISH.
woof! woof!
I'LL FIND THEIR WALLETS. I'LL CUT THEIR HAIR.
SNIP
THANK YOU! THANK YOU! YES, I KNOW I'M THE BEST FRIEND AROUND!

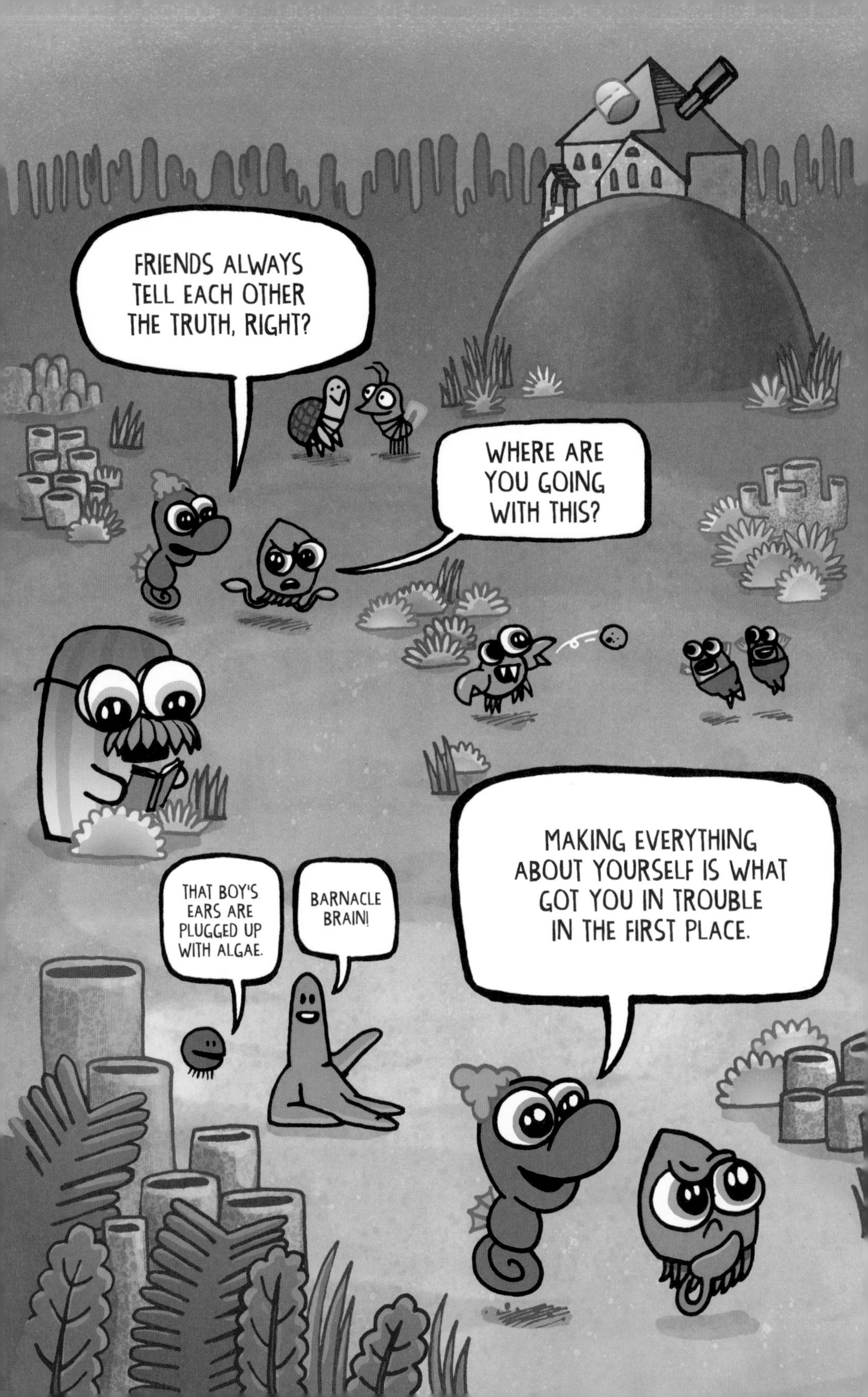

FRIENDS ALWAYS TELL EACH OTHER THE TRUTH, RIGHT?
WHERE ARE YOU GOING WITH THIS?
THAT BOY'S EARS ARE PLUGGED UP WITH ALGAE.
BARNACLE BRAIN!
MAKING EVERYTHING ABOUT YOURSELF IS WHAT GOT YOU IN TROUBLE IN THE FIRST PLACE.

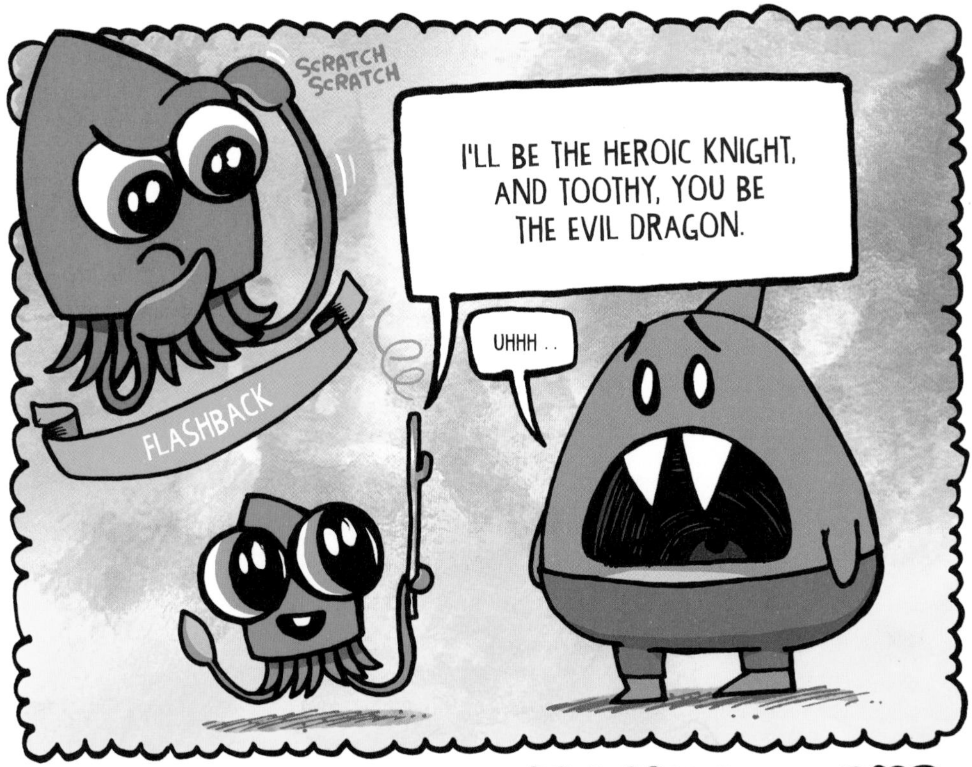
SCRATCH SCRATCH
FLASHBACK
I'LL BE THE HEROIC KNIGHT, AND TOOTHY, YOU BE THE EVIL DRAGON.
UHHH . .

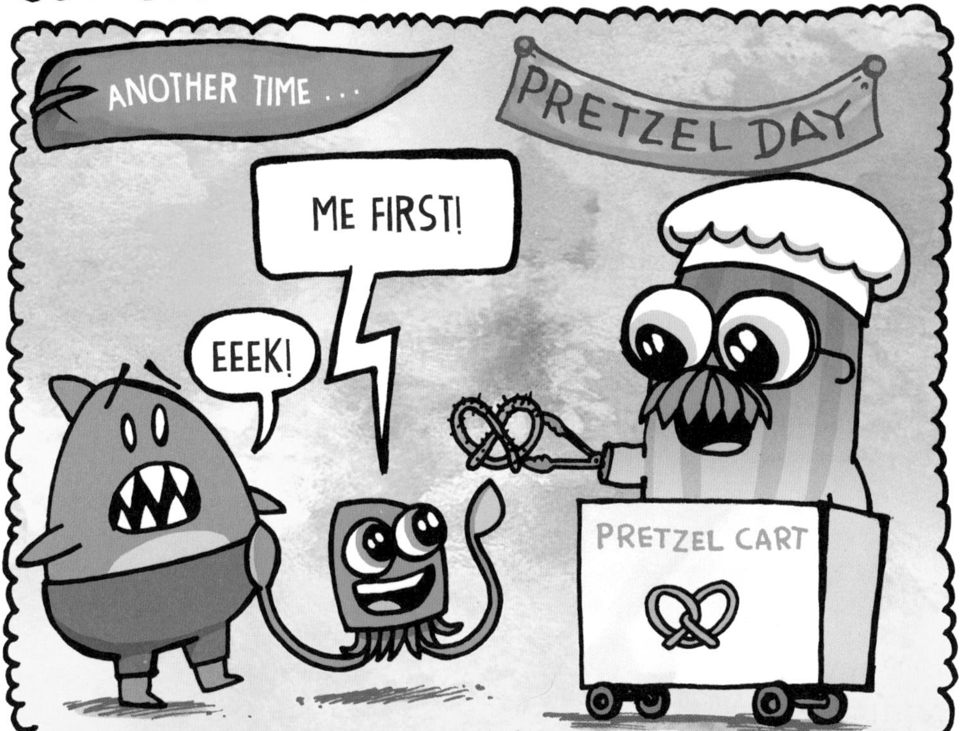
ANOTHER TIME . . .
PRETZEL DAY
ME FIRST!
EEEK!
PRETZEL CART

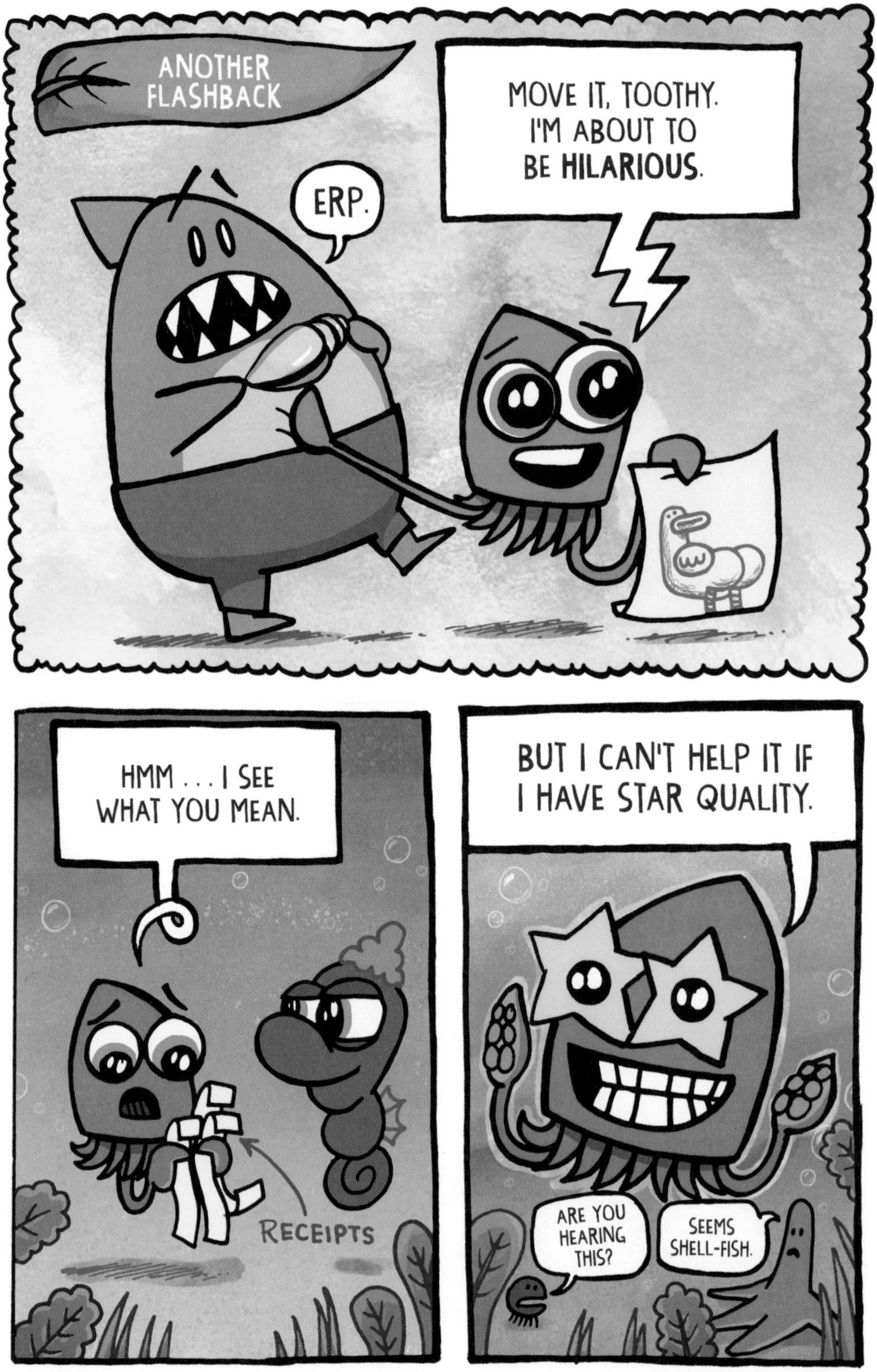
ANOTHER FLASHBACK
MOVE IT, TOOTHY. I'M ABOUT TO BE **HILARIOUS**.
ERP.
HMM . . . I SEE WHAT YOU MEAN.
RECEIPTS
BUT I CAN'T HELP IT IF I HAVE STAR QUALITY.
ARE YOU HEARING THIS?
SEEMS SHELL-FISH.

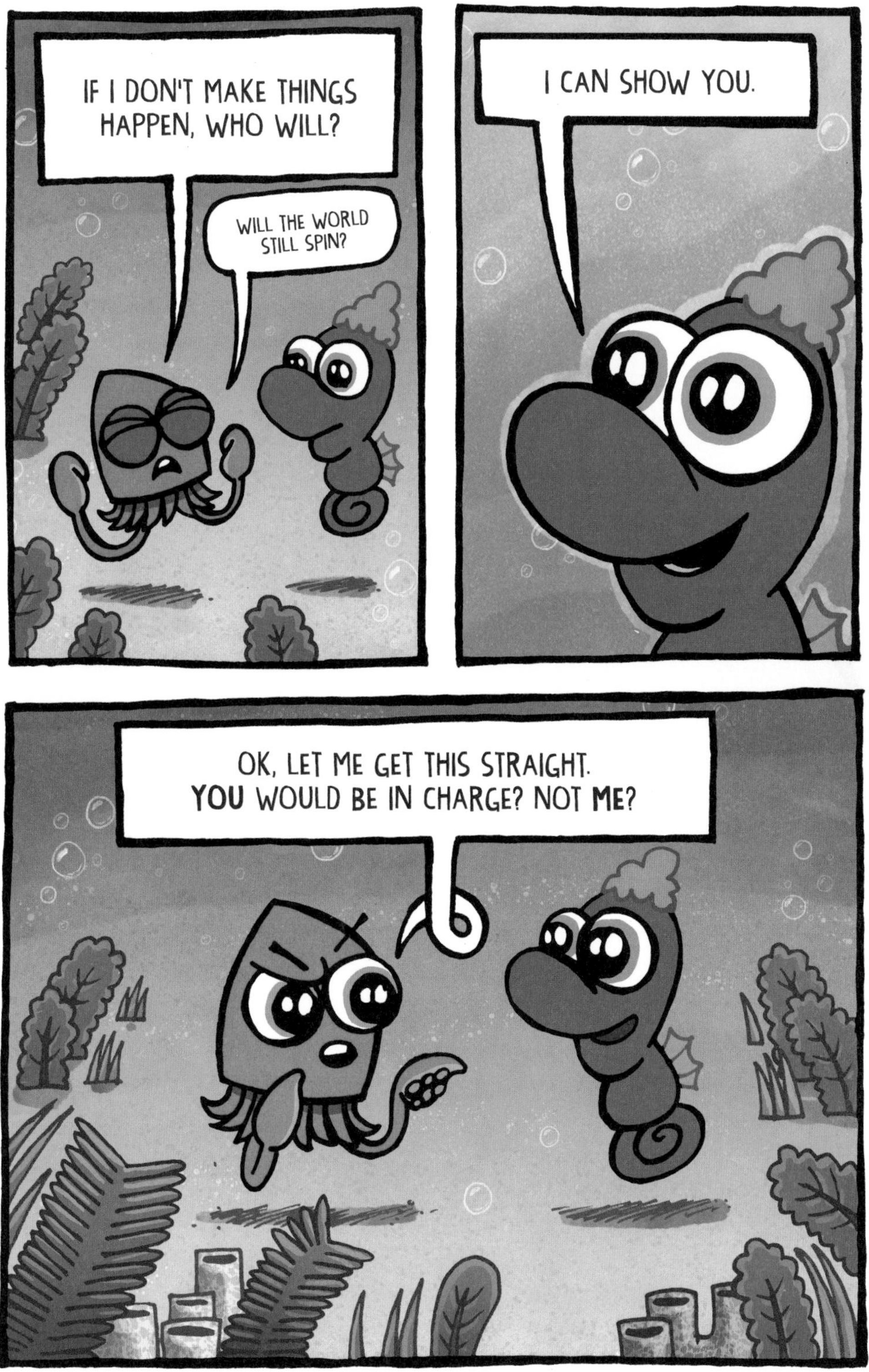
IF I DON'T MAKE THINGS HAPPEN, WHO WILL?
WILL THE WORLD STILL SPIN?
I CAN SHOW YOU.
OK, LET ME GET THIS STRAIGHT. **YOU** WOULD BE IN CHARGE? NOT **ME**?

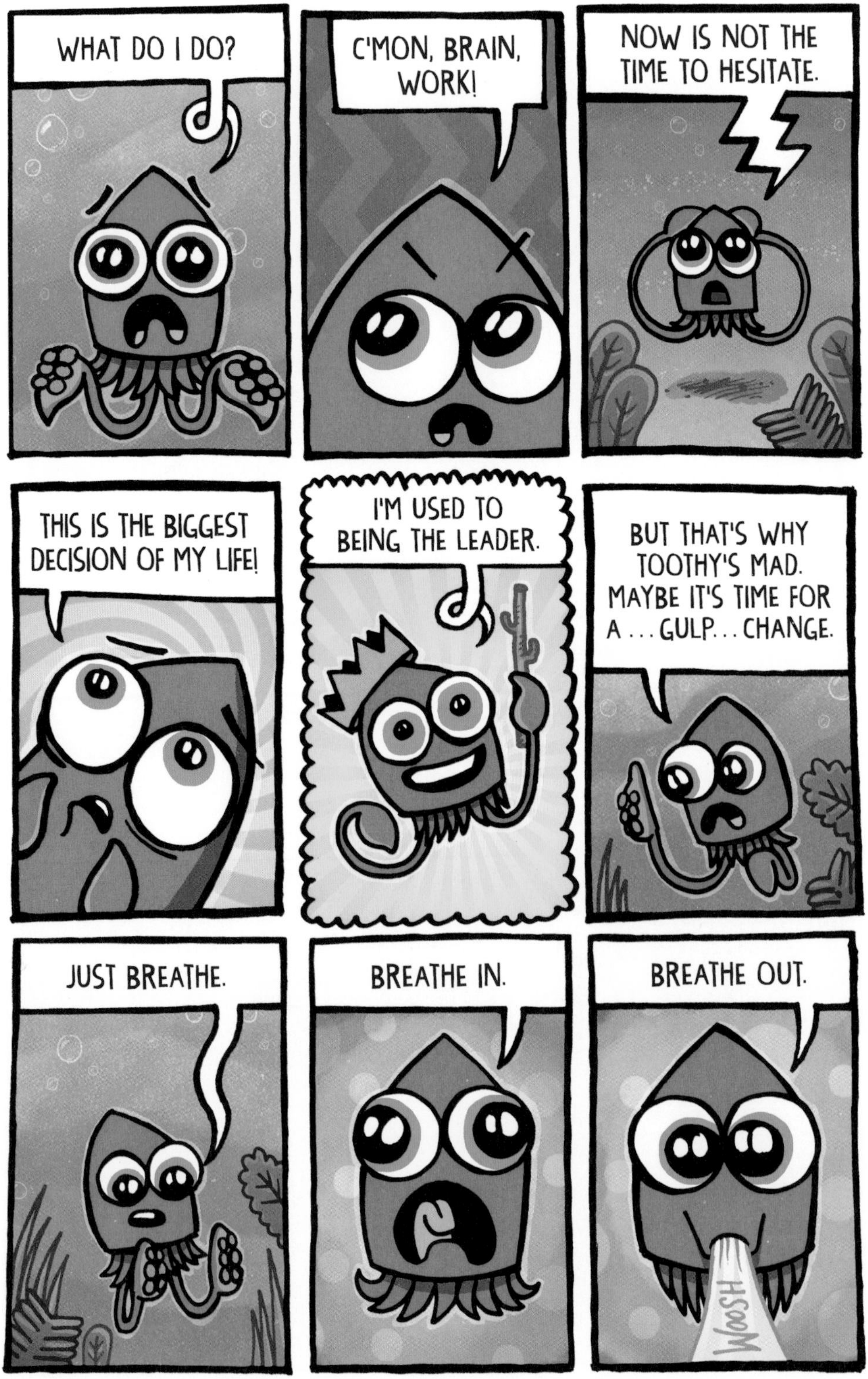
WHAT DO I DO?
C'MON, BRAIN, WORK!
NOW IS NOT THE TIME TO HESITATE.
THIS IS THE BIGGEST DECISION OF MY LIFE!
I'M USED TO BEING THE LEADER.
BUT THAT'S WHY TOOTHY'S MAD. MAYBE IT'S TIME FOR A . . . GULP. . . CHANGE.
JUST BREATHE.
BREATHE IN.
BREATHE OUT.
WOOSH

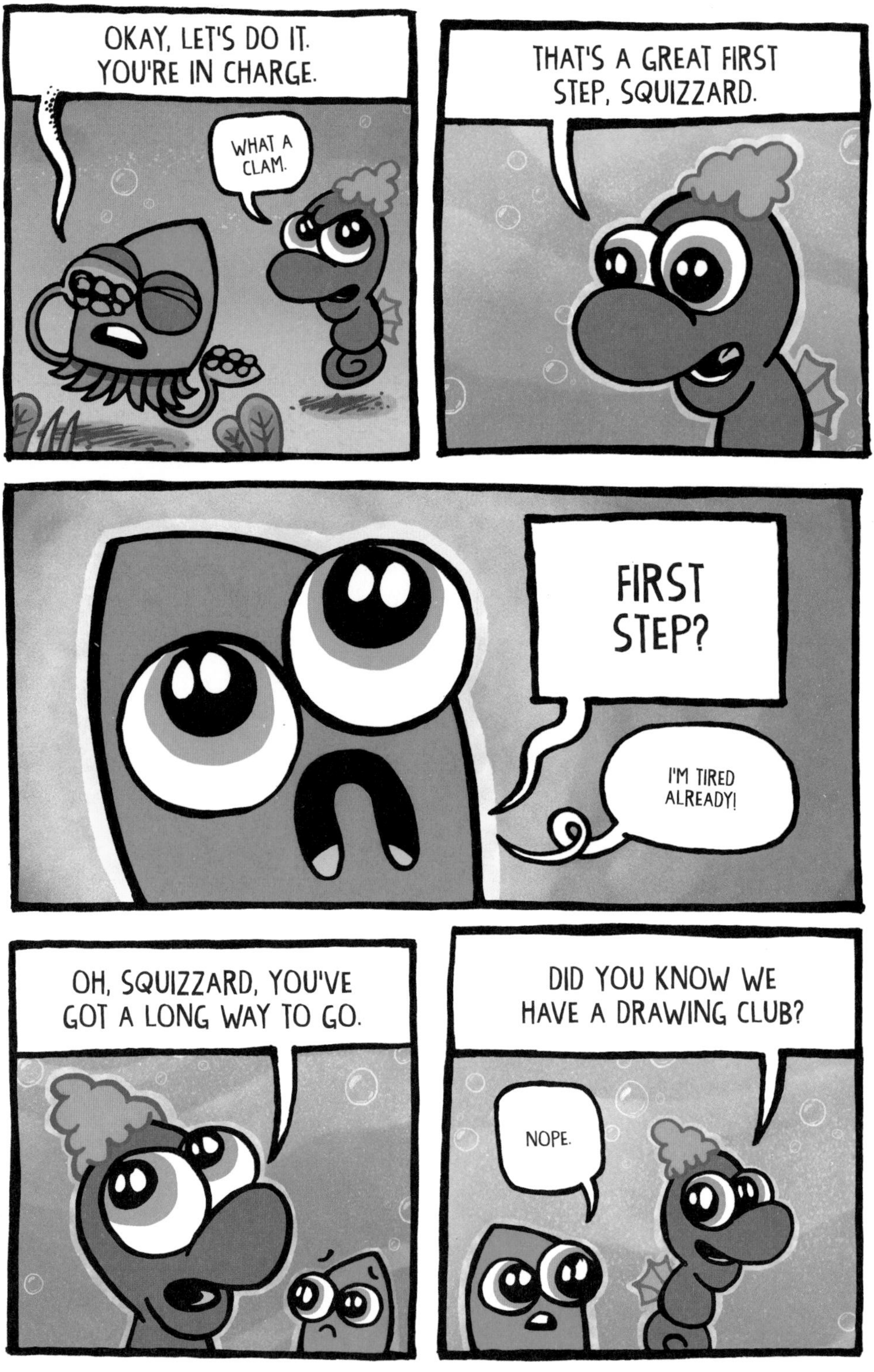
OKAY, LET'S DO IT. YOU'RE IN CHARGE.
WHAT A CLAM.
THAT'S A GREAT FIRST STEP, SQUIZZARD.
FIRST STEP?
I'M TIRED ALREADY!
OH, SQUIZZARD, YOU'VE GOT A LONG WAY TO GO.
DID YOU KNOW WE HAVE A DRAWING CLUB?
NOPE.

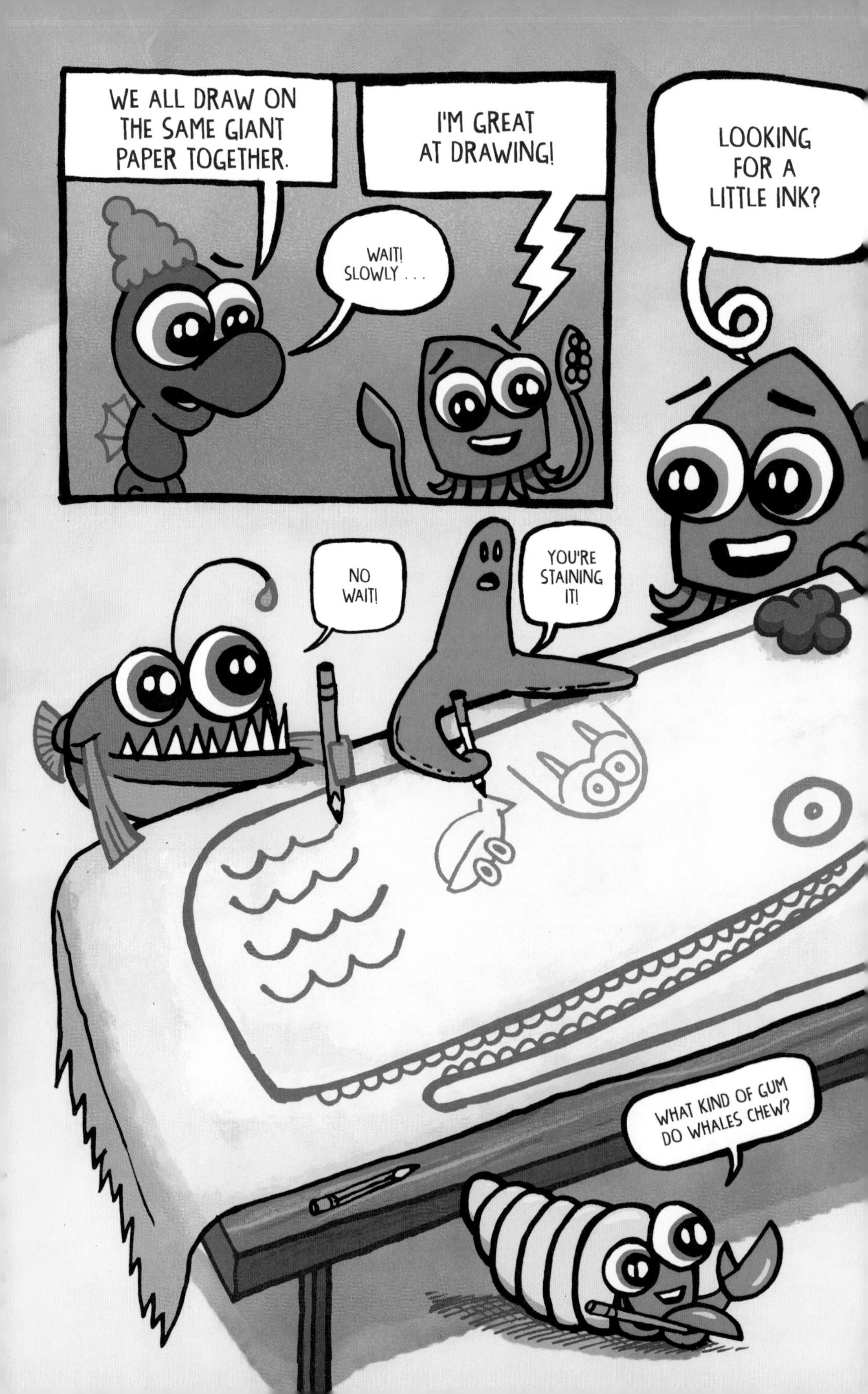
WE ALL DRAW ON THE SAME GIANT PAPER TOGETHER.
I'M GREAT AT DRAWING!
LOOKING FOR A LITTLE INK?
WAIT! SLOWLY . . .
NO WAIT!
YOU'RE STAINING IT!
WHAT KIND OF GUM DO WHALES CHEW?

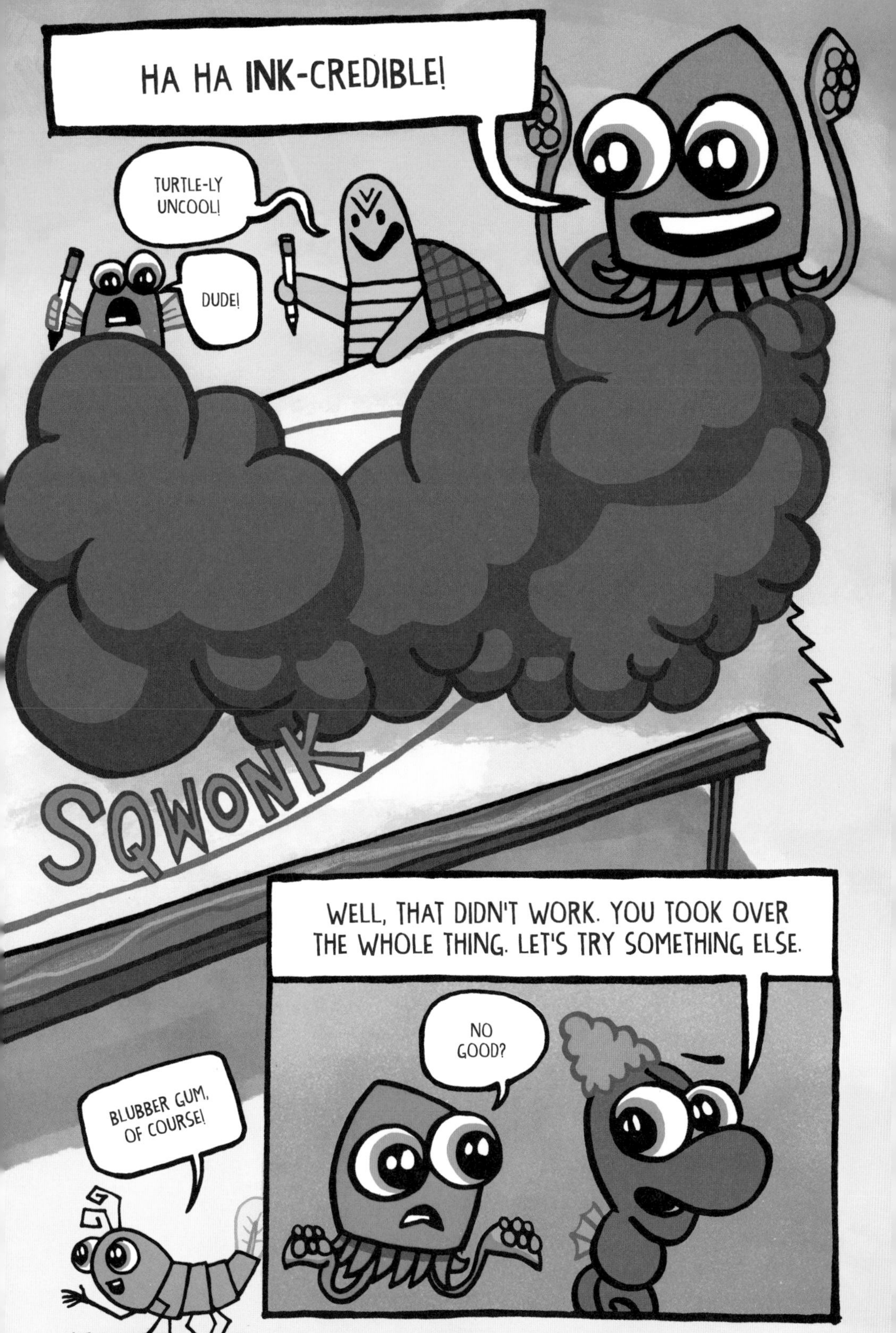
HA HA INK-CREDIBLE!
TURTLE-LY UNCOOL!
DUDE!
SQWONK
WELL, THAT DIDN'T WORK. YOU TOOK OVER THE WHOLE THING. LET'S TRY SOMETHING ELSE.
NO GOOD?
BLUBBER GUM, OF COURSE!

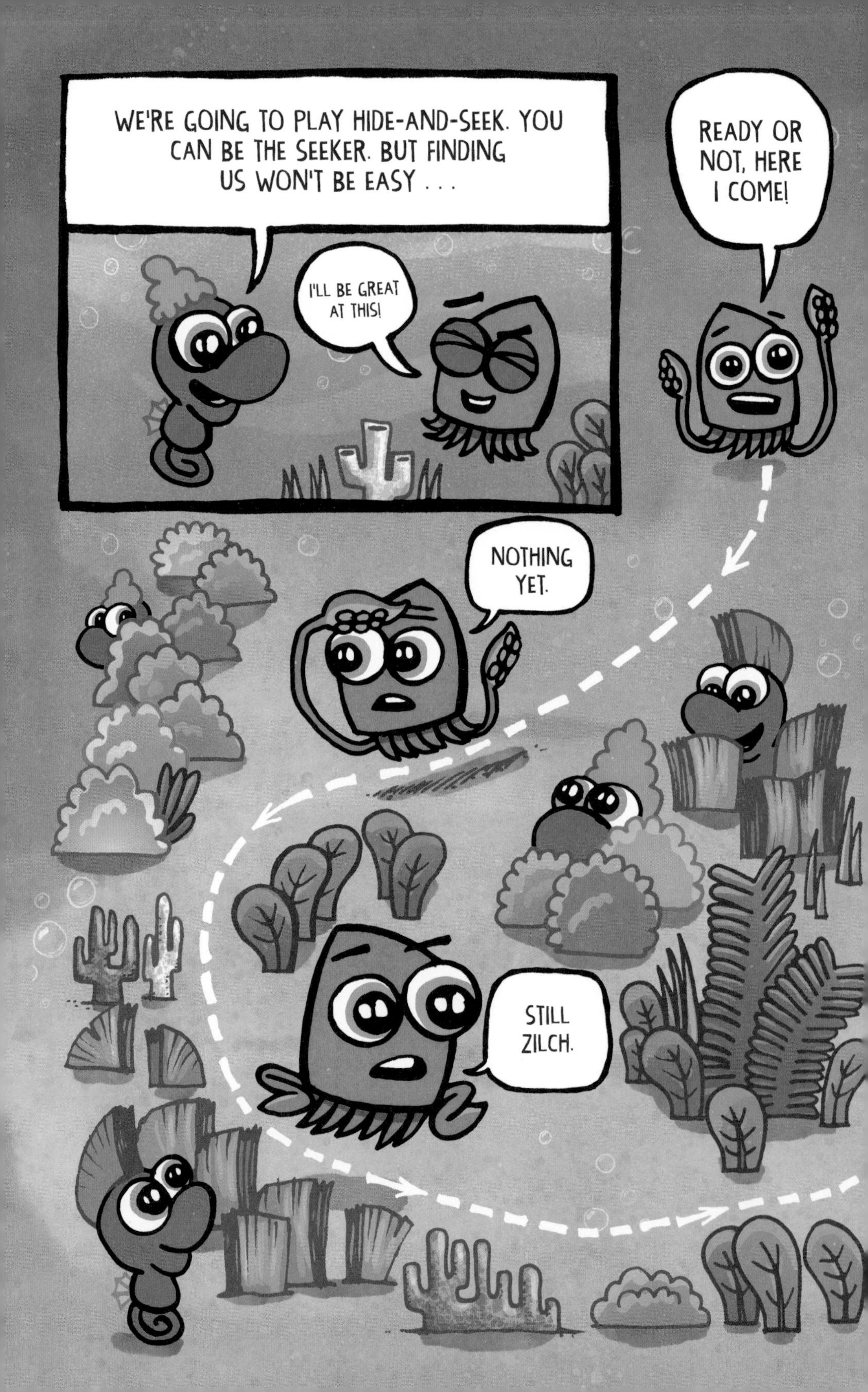
WE'RE GOING TO PLAY HIDE-AND-SEEK. YOU CAN BE THE SEEKER. BUT FINDING US WON'T BE EASY . . .
I'LL BE GREAT AT THIS!
READY OR NOT, HERE I COME!
NOTHING YET.
STILL ZILCH.

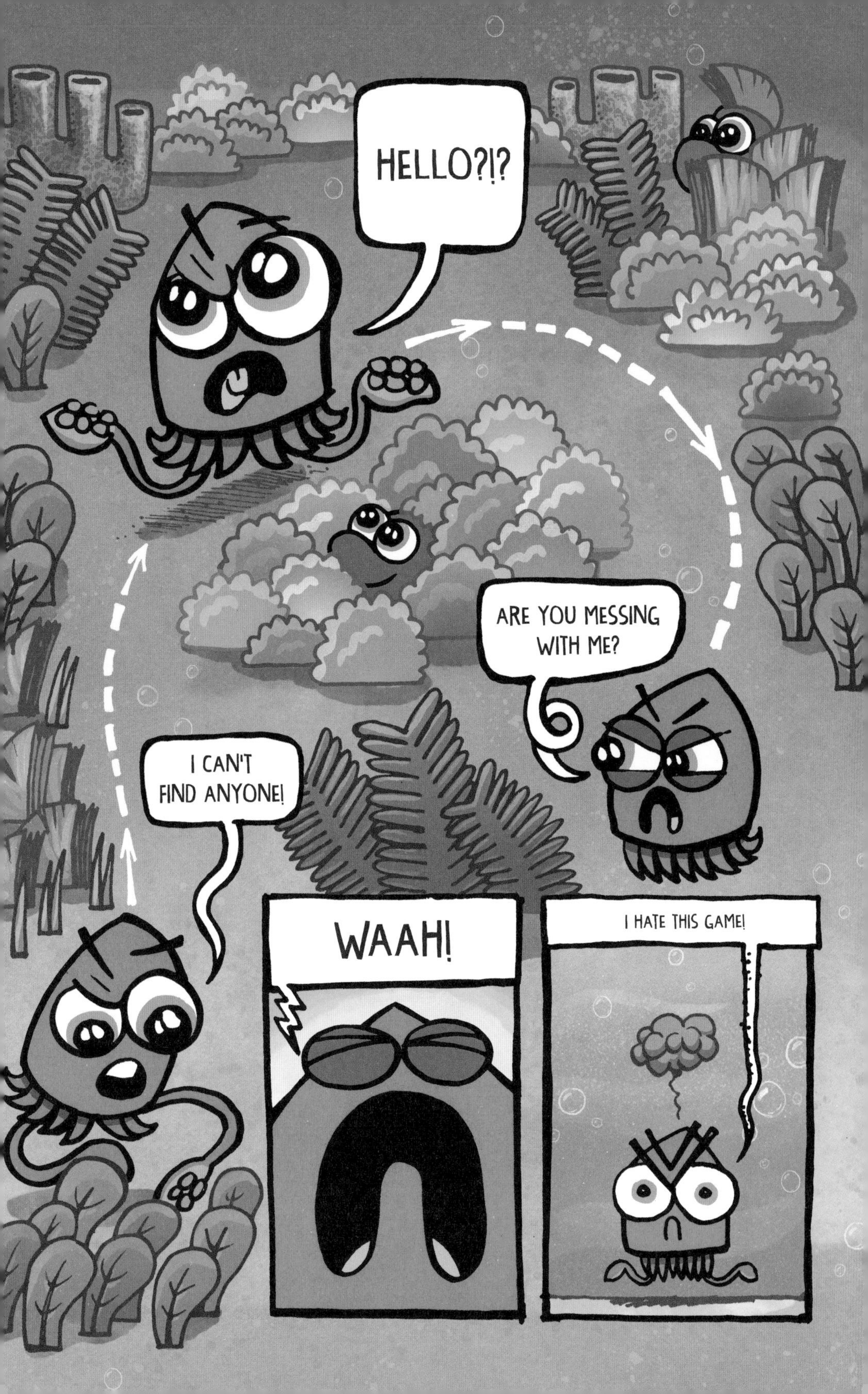
HELLO?!?
I CAN'T FIND ANYONE!
ARE YOU MESSING WITH ME?
WAAH!
I HATE THIS GAME!

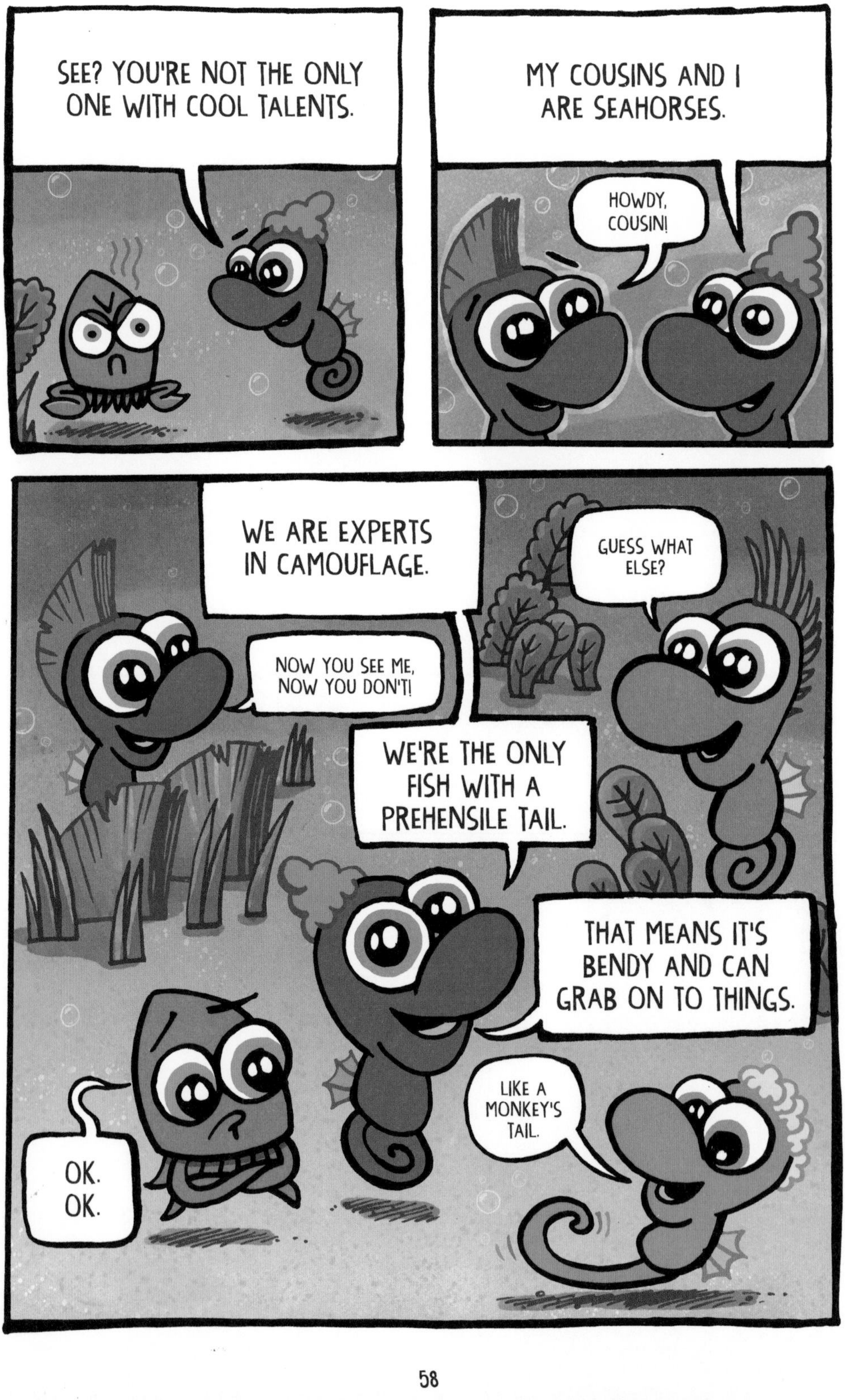
SEE? YOU'RE NOT THE ONLY ONE WITH COOL TALENTS.
MY COUSINS AND I ARE SEAHORSES.
HOWDY, COUSIN!
WE ARE EXPERTS IN CAMOUFLAGE.
NOW YOU SEE ME, NOW YOU DON'T!
GUESS WHAT ELSE?
WE'RE THE ONLY FISH WITH A PREHENSILE TAIL.
THAT MEANS IT'S BENDY AND CAN GRAB ON TO THINGS.
LIKE A MONKEY'S TAIL.
OK. OK.

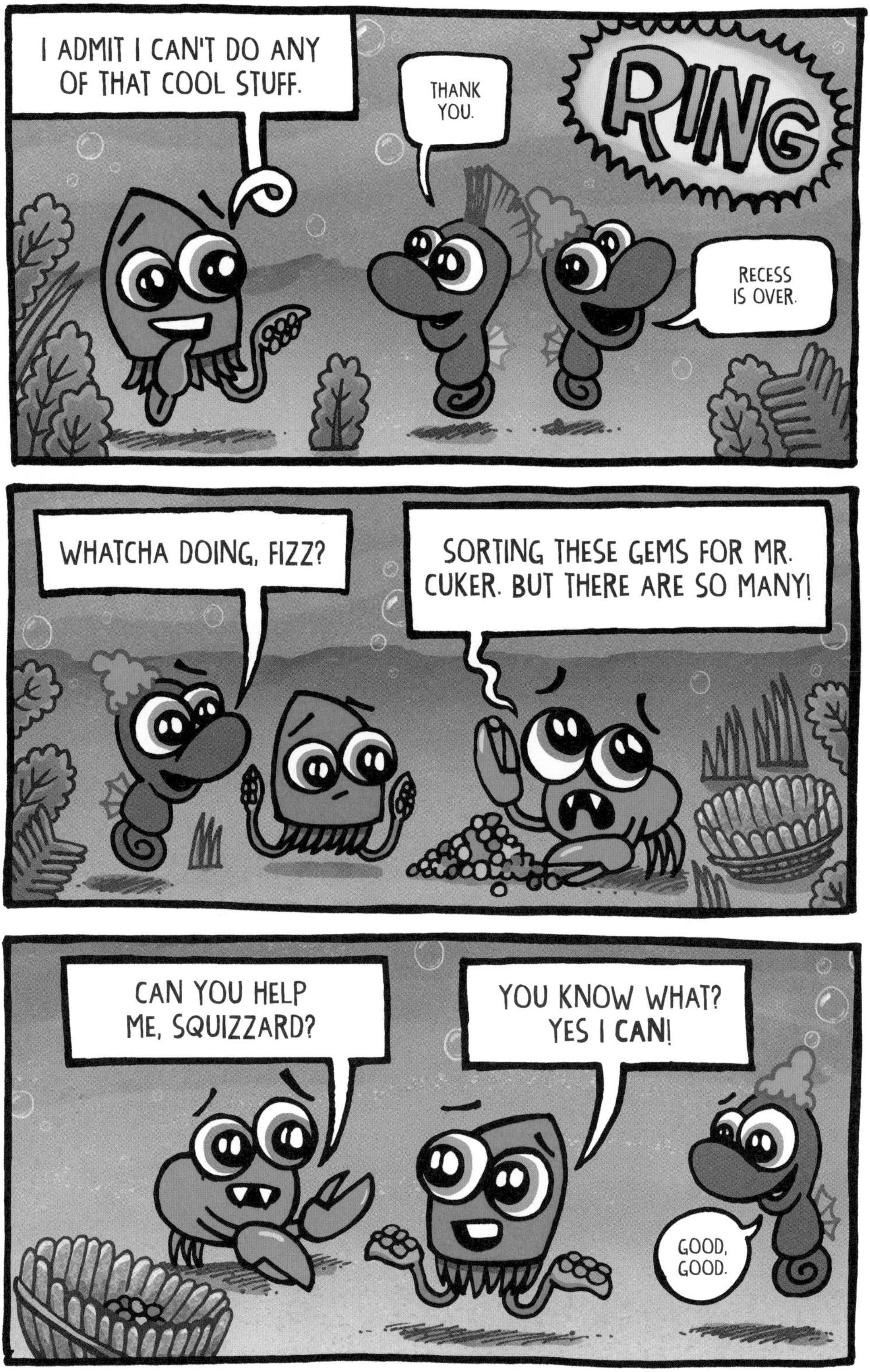
I ADMIT I CAN'T DO ANY OF THAT COOL STUFF.
THANK YOU.
RING
RECESS IS OVER.
WHATCHA DOING, FIZZ?
SORTING THESE GEMS FOR MR. CUKER. BUT THERE ARE SO MANY!
CAN YOU HELP ME, SQUIZZARD?
YOU KNOW WHAT? YES I **CAN**!
GOOD, GOOD.

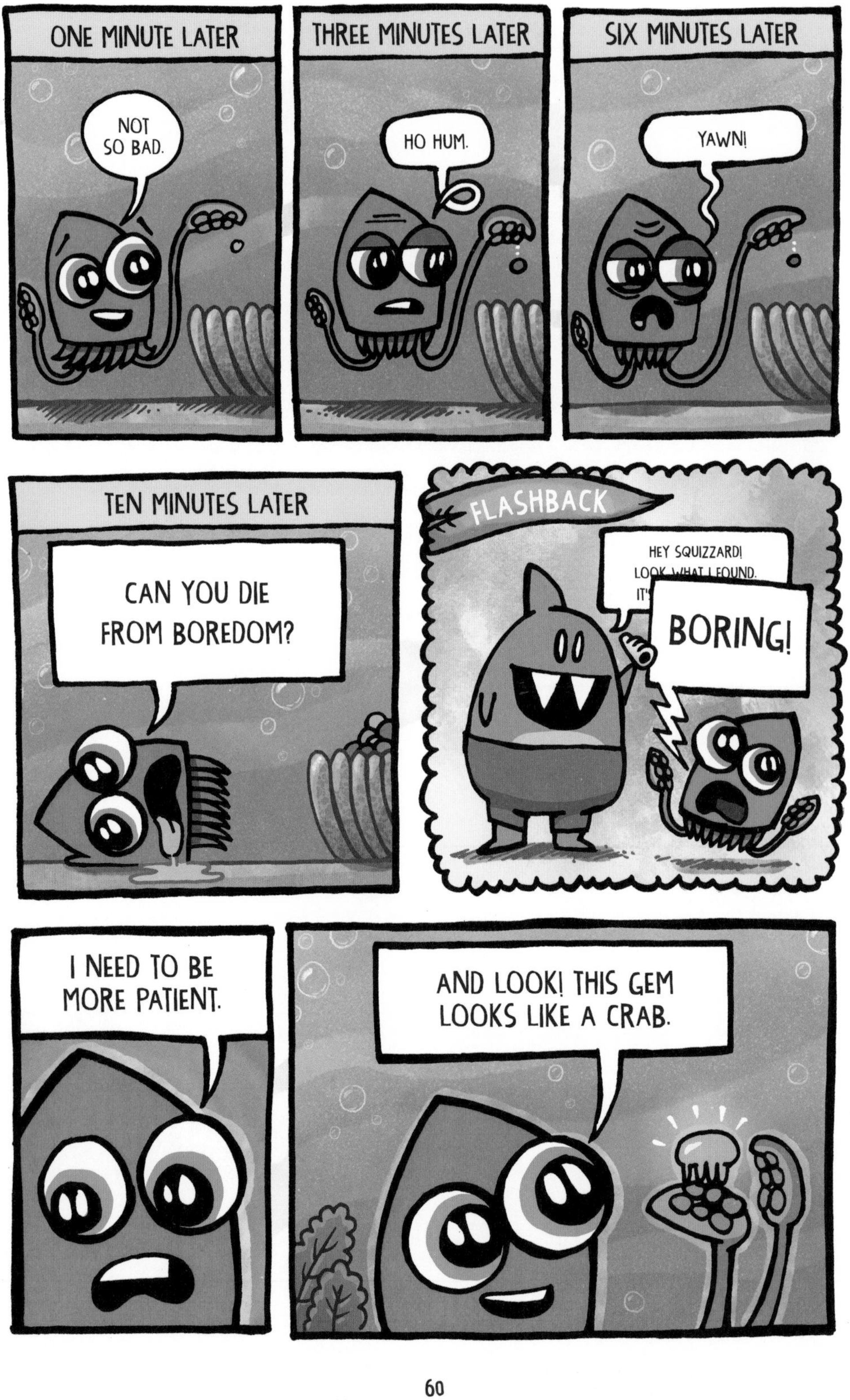

ONE MINUTE LATER
NOT SO BAD.
THREE MINUTES LATER
HO HUM.
SIX MINUTES LATER
YAWN!
TEN MINUTES LATER
CAN YOU DIE FROM BOREDOM?
FLASHBACK
HEY SQUIZZARD!
BORING!
I NEED TO BE MORE PATIENT.
AND LOOK! THIS GEM LOOKS LIKE A CRAB.

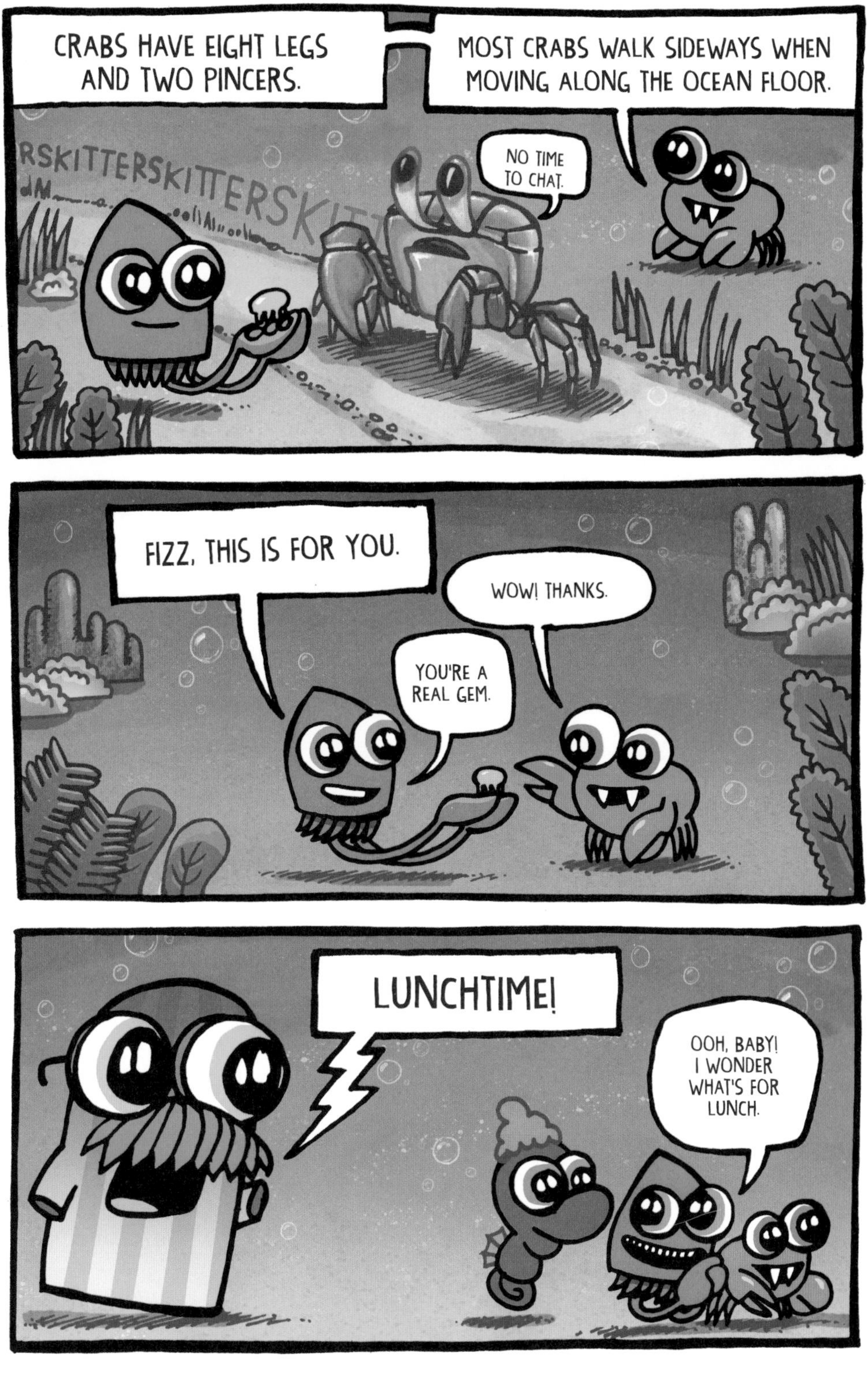
CRABS HAVE EIGHT LEGS AND TWO PINCERS.
MOST CRABS WALK SIDEWAYS WHEN MOVING ALONG THE OCEAN FLOOR.
RSKITTERSKITTERSKITT
NO TIME TO CHAT.
FIZZ, THIS IS FOR YOU.
YOU'RE A REAL GEM.
WOW! THANKS.
LUNCHTIME!
OOH, BABY! I WONDER WHAT'S FOR LUNCH.

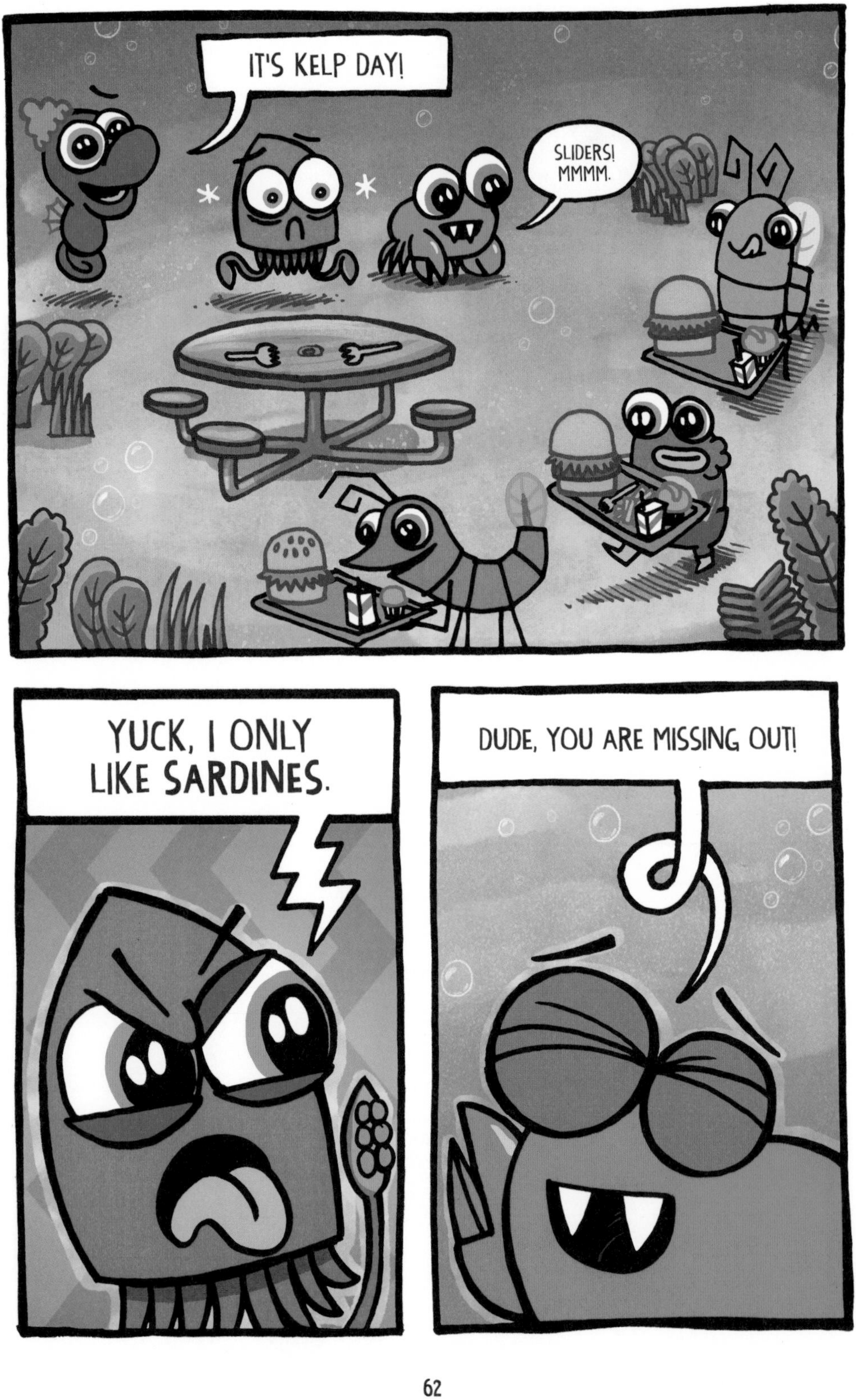
IT'S KELP DAY!
SLIDERS! MMMM.
YUCK, I ONLY LIKE SARDINES.
DUDE, YOU ARE MISSING OUT!

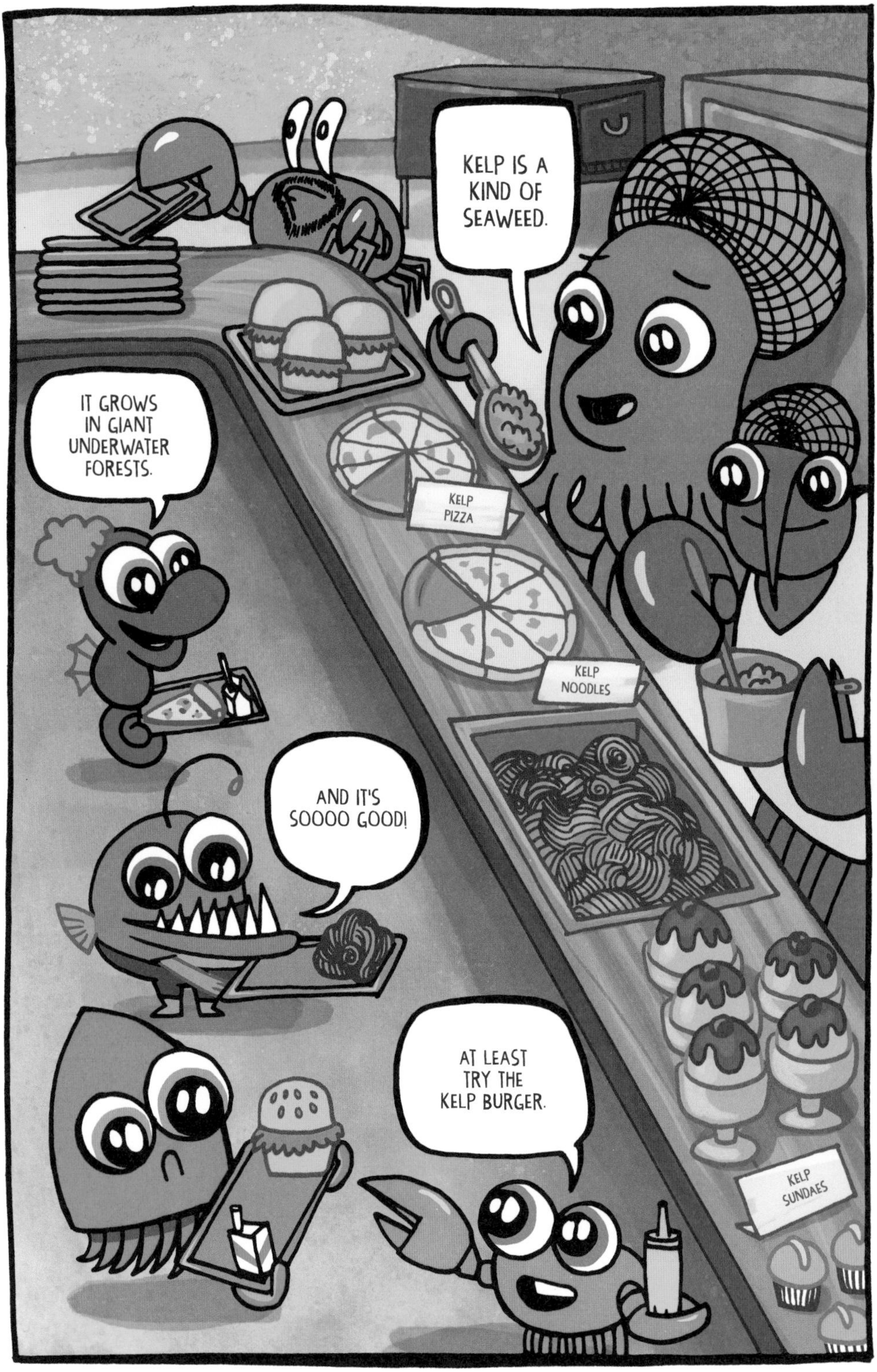
KELP IS A KIND OF SEAWEED.
IT GROWS IN GIANT UNDERWATER FORESTS.
KELP PIZZA
KELP NOODLES
AND IT'S SOOOO GOOD!
AT LEAST TRY THE KELP BURGER.
KELP SUNDAES

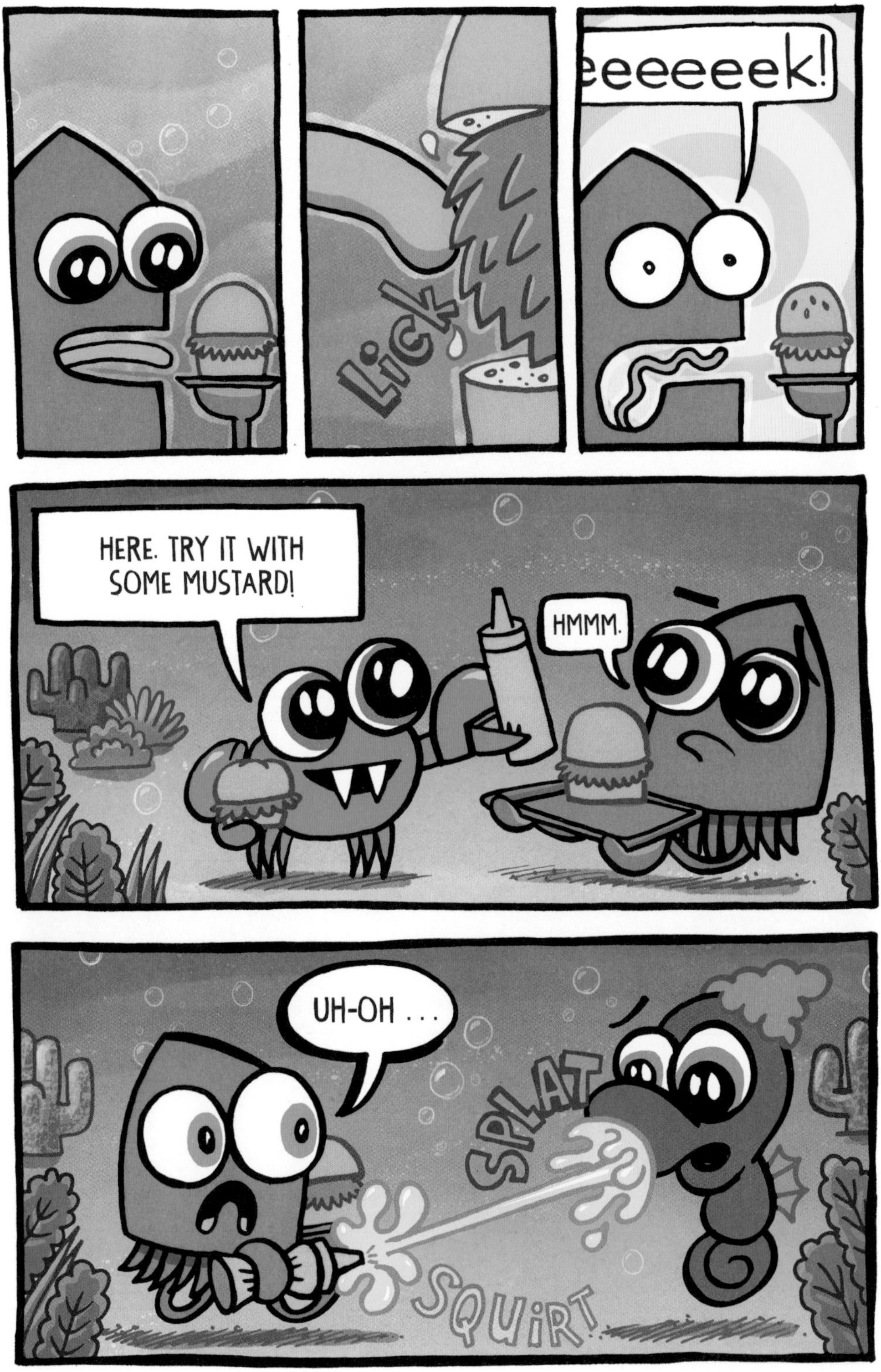
Lick
eeeeeek!
HERE. TRY IT WITH SOME MUSTARD!
HMMM.
UH-OH . . .
SPLAT
SQUIRT

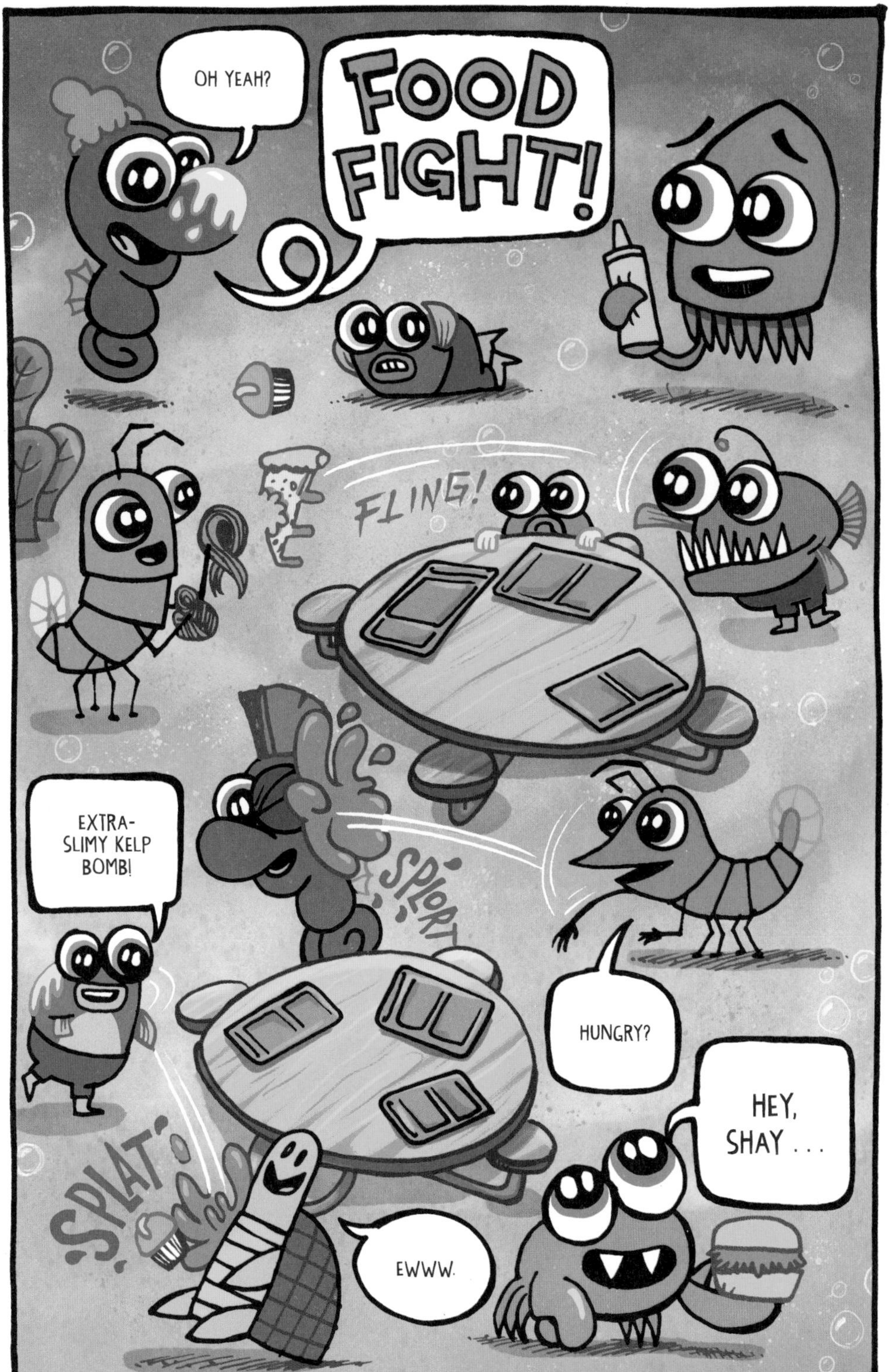
OH YEAH?
FOOD FIGHT!
FLING!
EXTRA-SLIMY KELP BOMB!
SPLORT
HUNGRY?
HEY, SHAY . . .
SPLAT
EWWW.

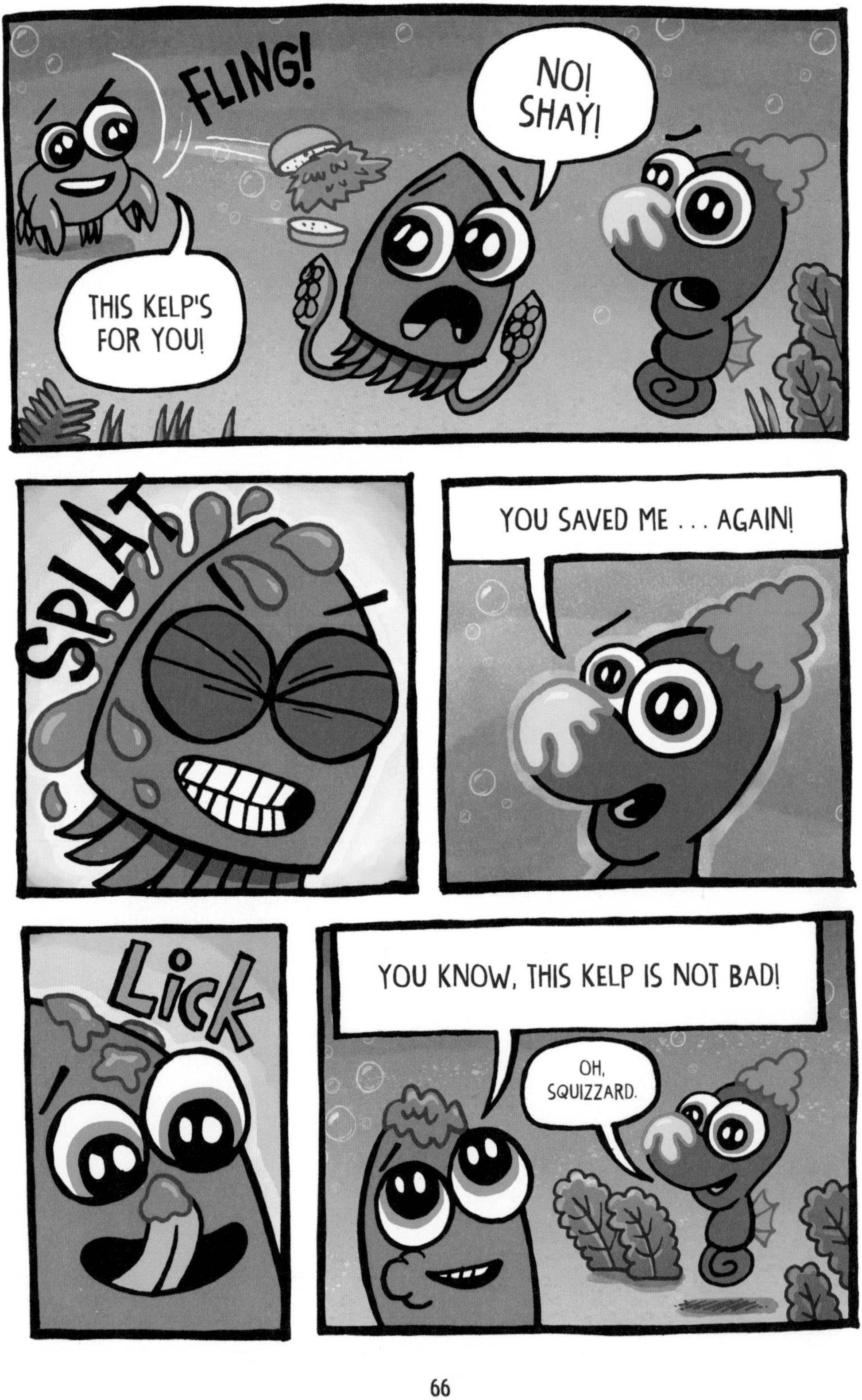
FLING!
THIS KELP'S FOR YOU!
NO! SHAY!
SPLAT
YOU SAVED ME . . . AGAIN!
Lick
YOU KNOW, THIS KELP IS NOT BAD!
OH, SQUIZZARD.

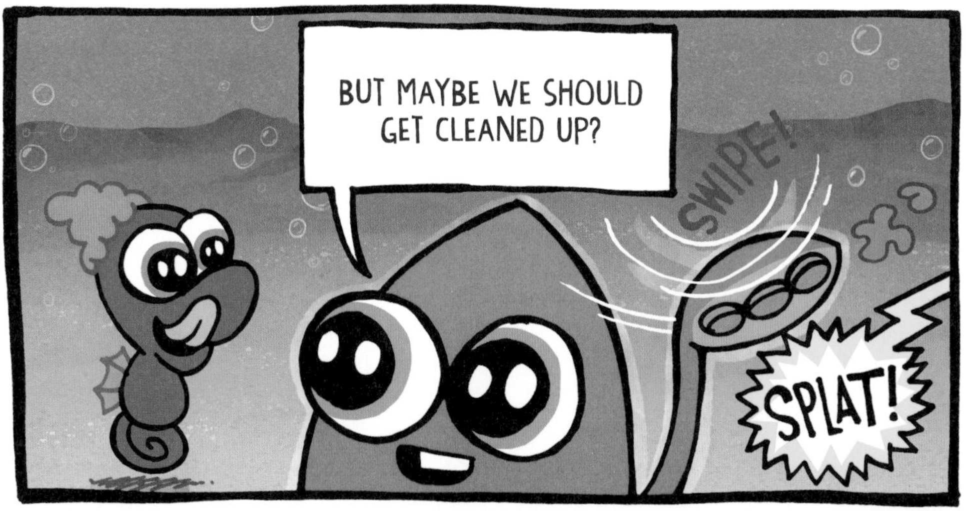
BUT MAYBE WE SHOULD GET CLEANED UP?
SWIPE!
SPLAT!

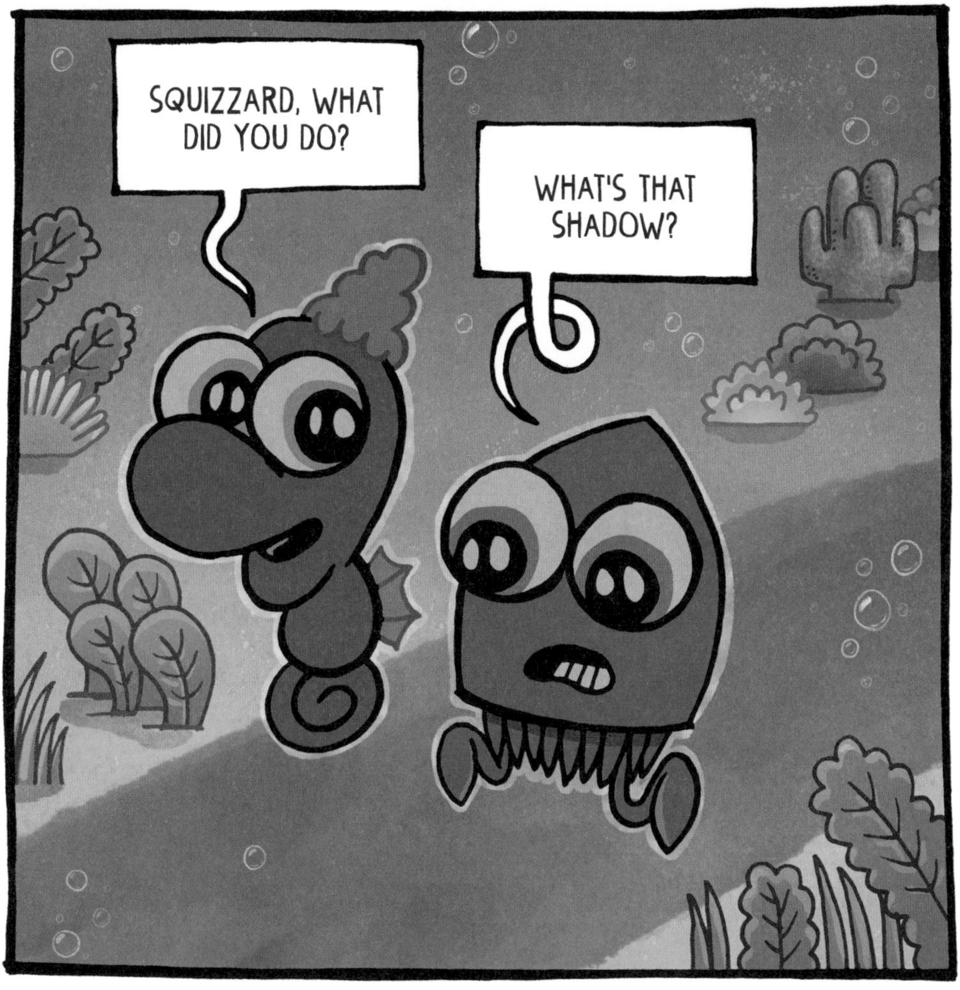
SQUIZZARD, WHAT DID YOU DO?
WHAT'S THAT SHADOW?

CHAPTER 5

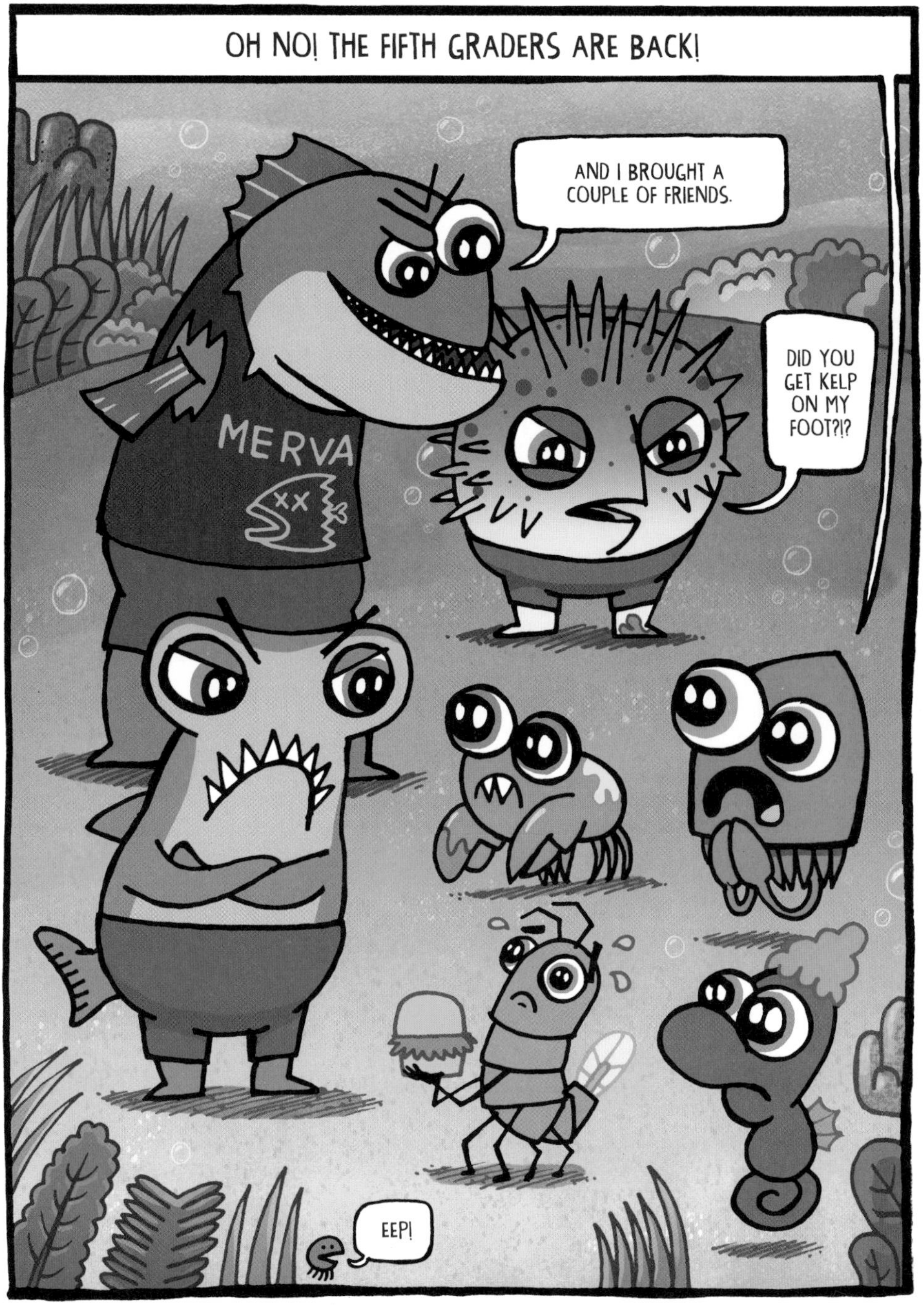
OH NO! THE FIFTH GRADERS ARE BACK!
AND I BROUGHT A COUPLE OF FRIENDS.
MERVA
DID YOU GET KELP ON MY FOOT?!?
EEP!

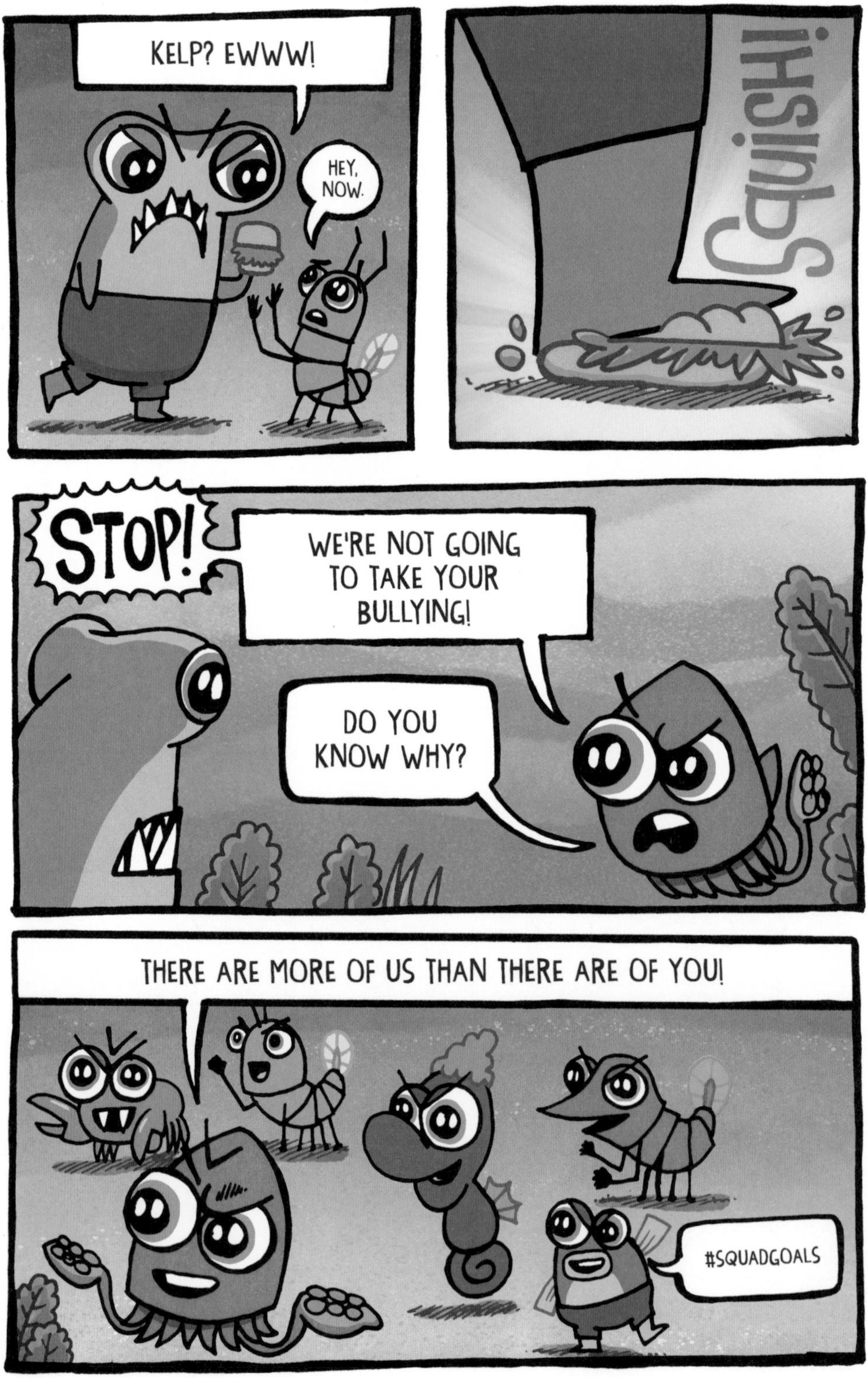
KELP? EWWW!
HEY, NOW.
SQUISH!
STOP!
WE'RE NOT GOING TO TAKE YOUR BULLYING!
DO YOU KNOW WHY?
THERE ARE MORE OF US THAN THERE ARE OF YOU!
#SQUADGOALS

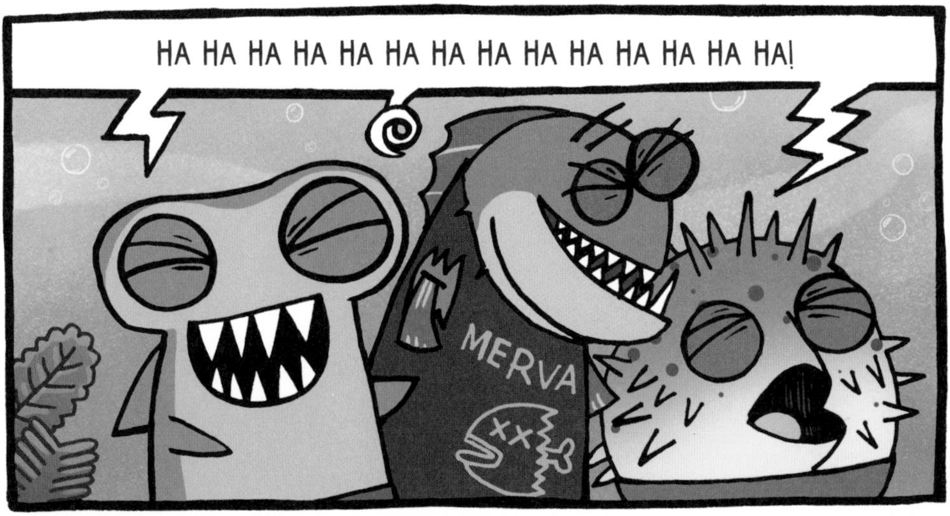
HA HA HA HA HA HA HA HA HA HA HA HA HA HA!
MERVA

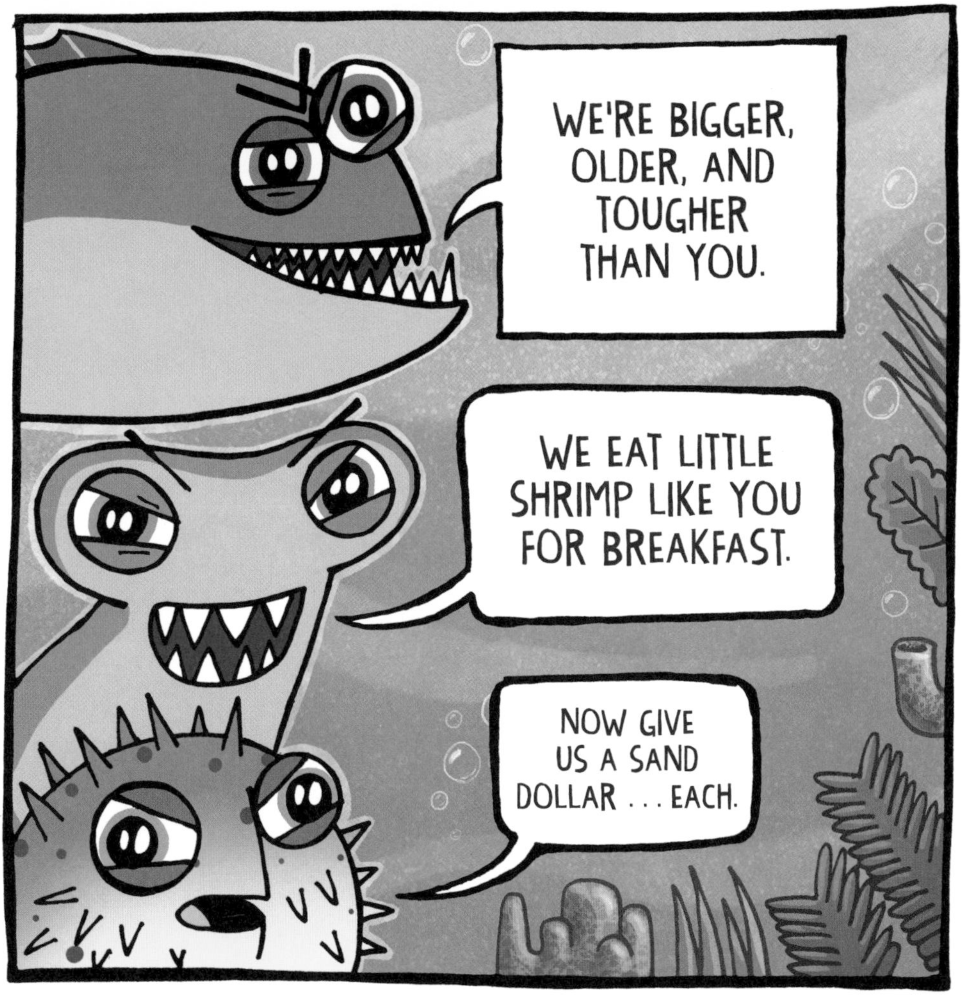
WE'RE BIGGER, OLDER, AND TOUGHER THAN YOU.
WE EAT LITTLE SHRIMP LIKE YOU FOR BREAKFAST.
NOW GIVE US A SAND DOLLAR . . . EACH.

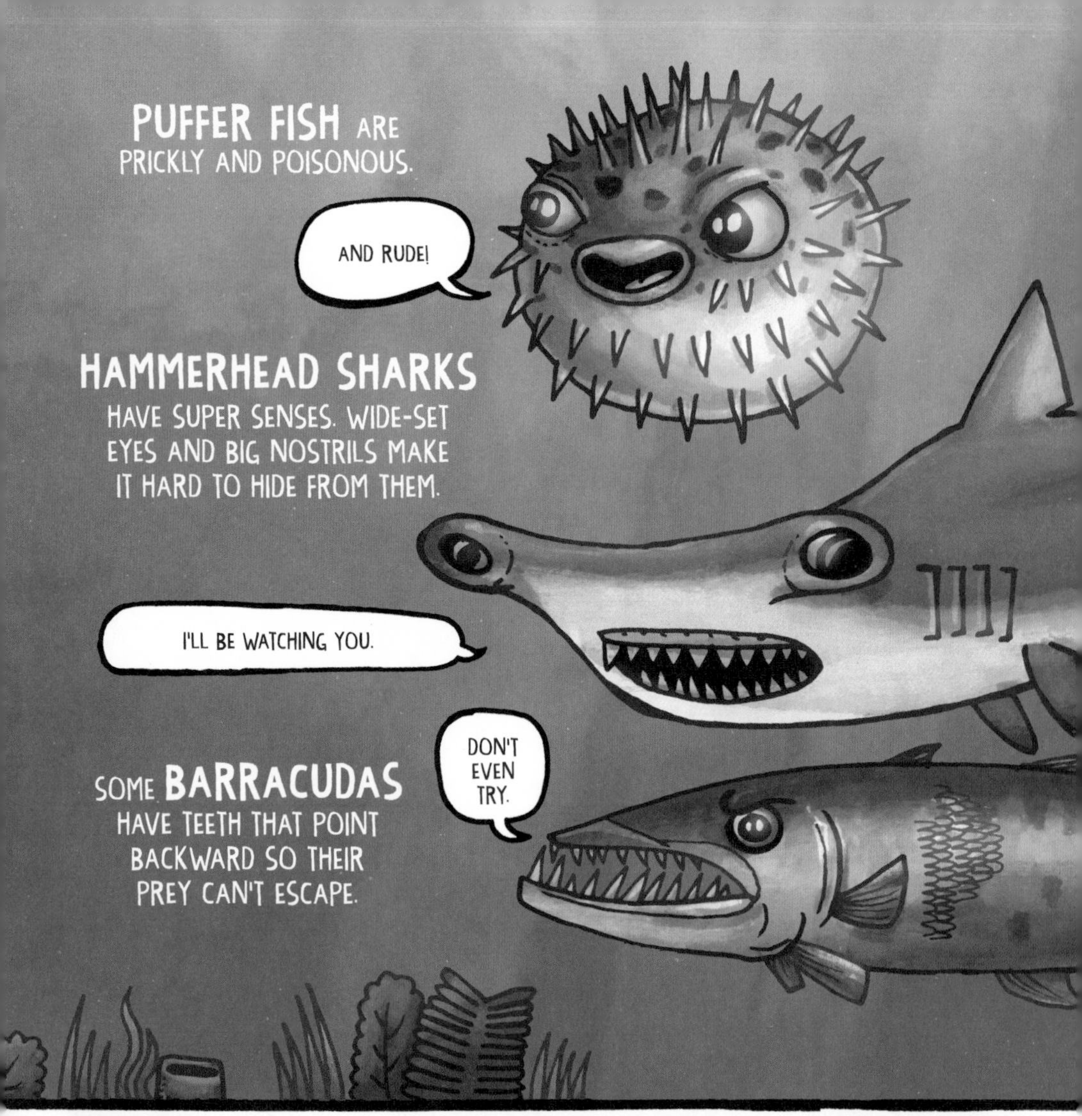
PUFFER FISH ARE PRICKLY AND POISONOUS.
AND RUDE!
HAMMERHEAD SHARKS HAVE SUPER SENSES. WIDE-SET EYES AND BIG NOSTRILS MAKE IT HARD TO HIDE FROM THEM.
I'LL BE WATCHING YOU.
SOME BARRACUDAS HAVE TEETH THAT POINT BACKWARD SO THEIR PREY CAN'T ESCAPE.
DON'T EVEN TRY.

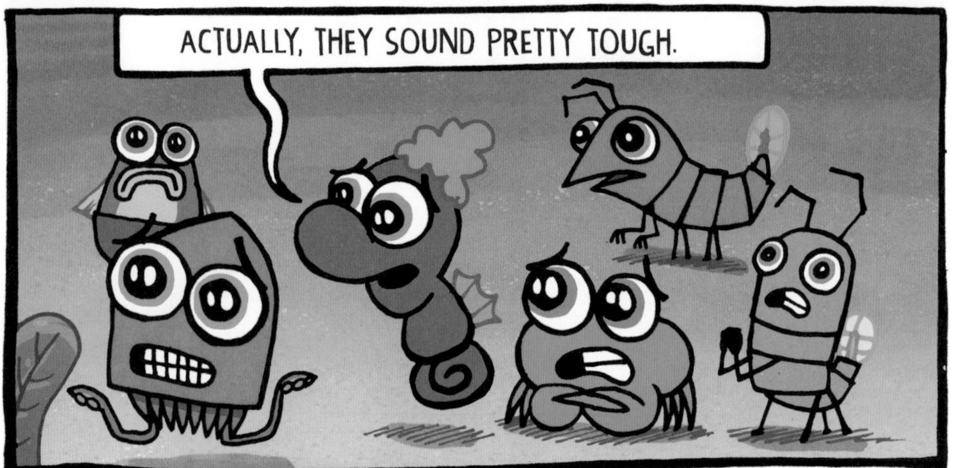
ACTUALLY, THEY SOUND PRETTY TOUGH.

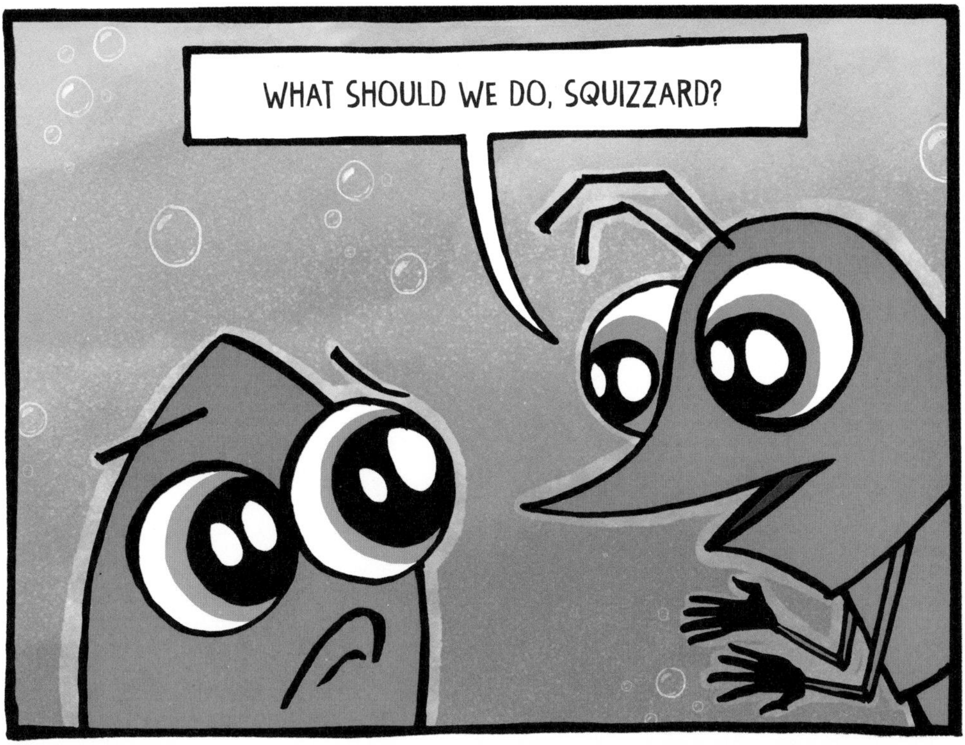
WHAT SHOULD WE DO, SQUIZZARD?

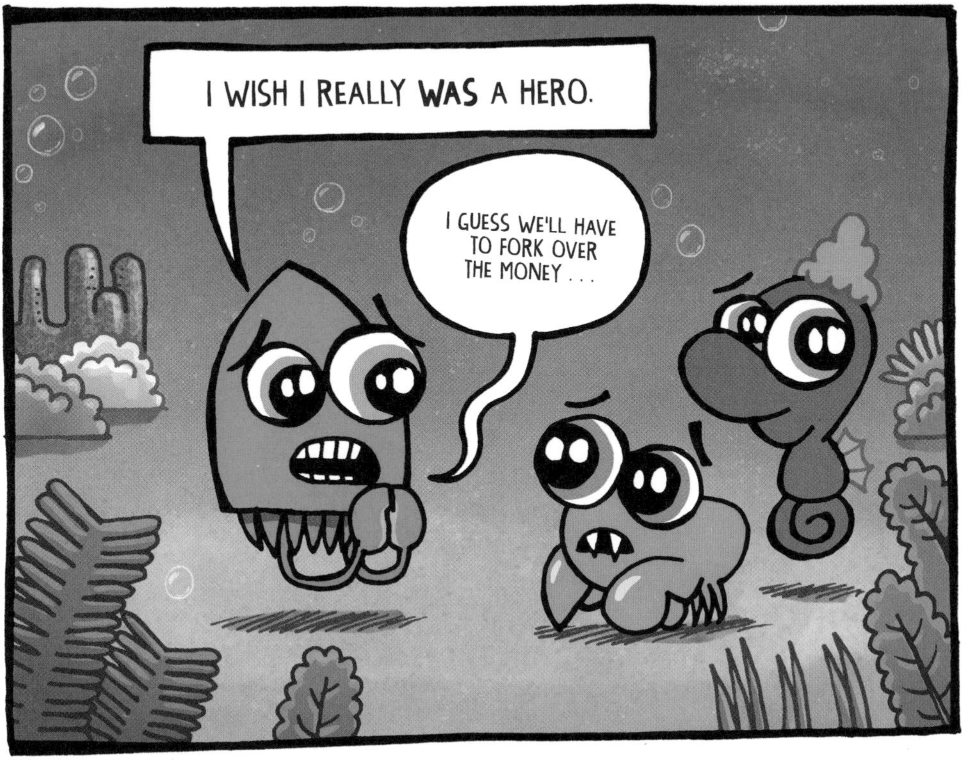
I WISH I REALLY **WAS** A HERO.
I GUESS WE'LL HAVE TO FORK OVER THE MONEY . . .

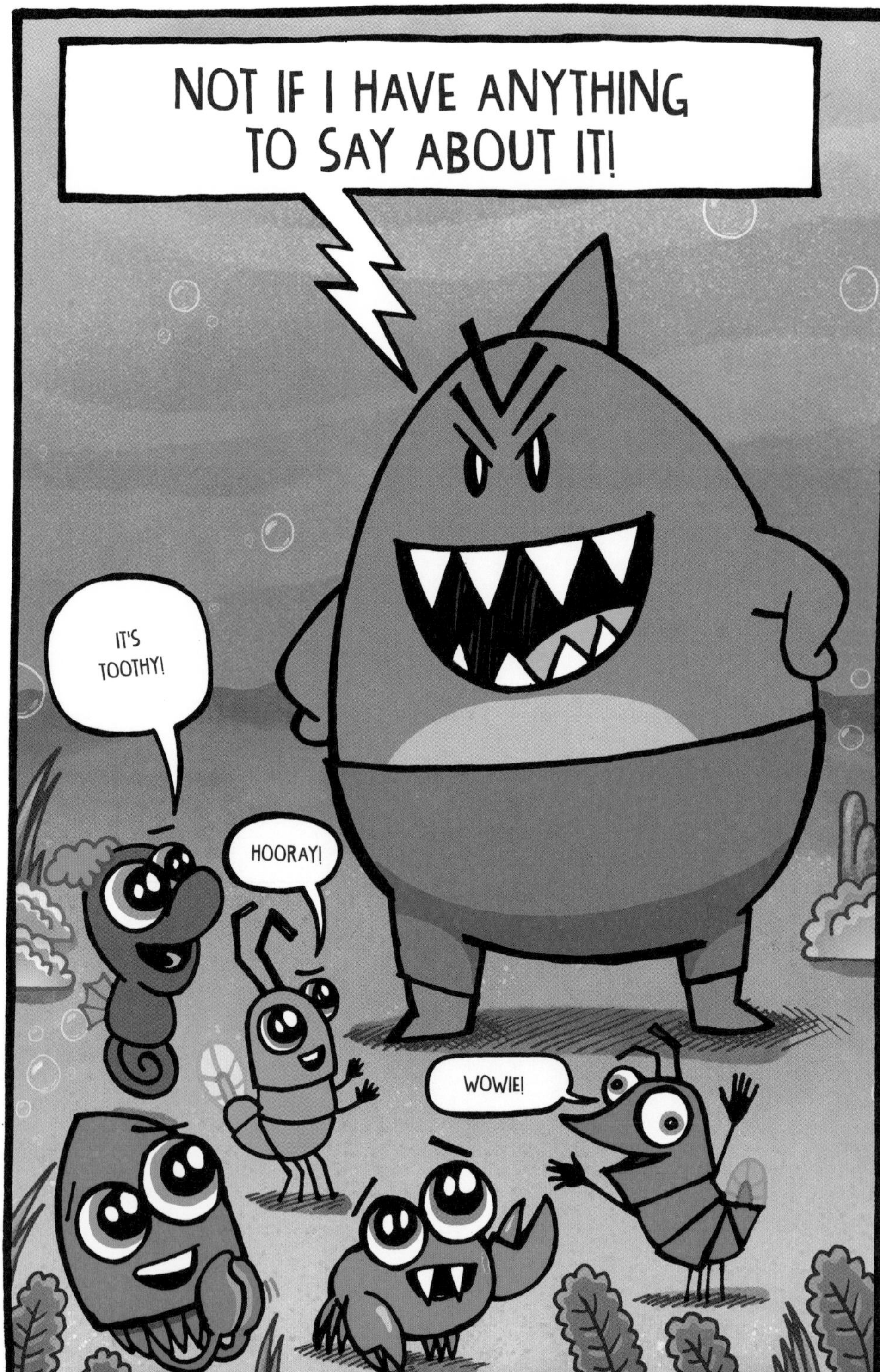
NOT IF I HAVE ANYTHING TO SAY ABOUT IT!
IT'S TOOTHY!
HOORAY!
WOWIE!

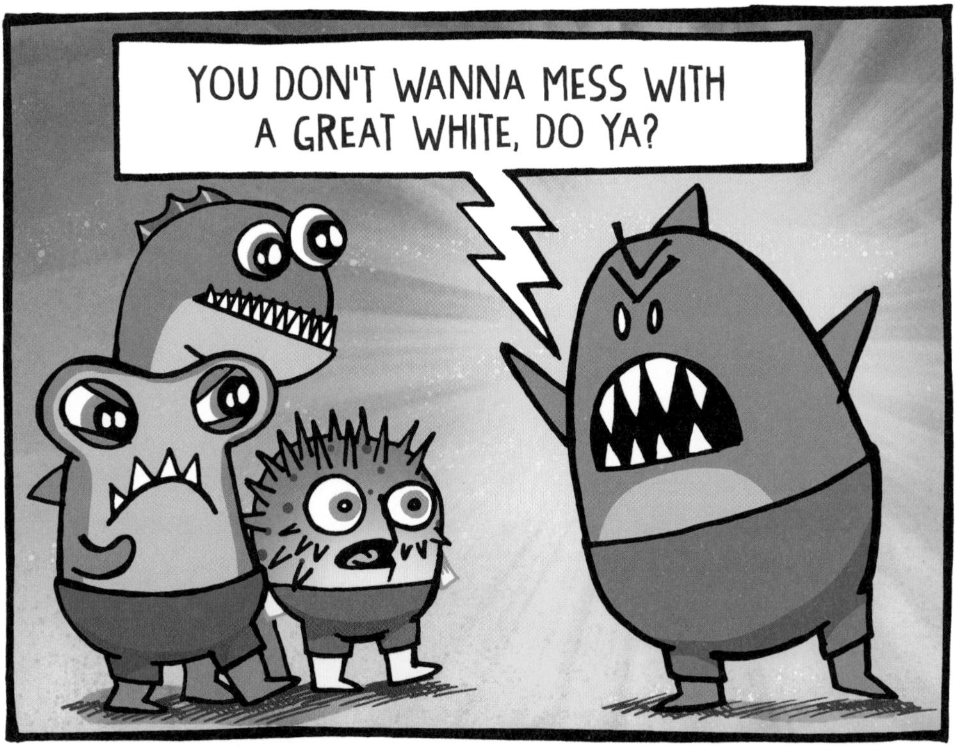
YOU DON'T WANNA MESS WITH A GREAT WHITE, DO YA?

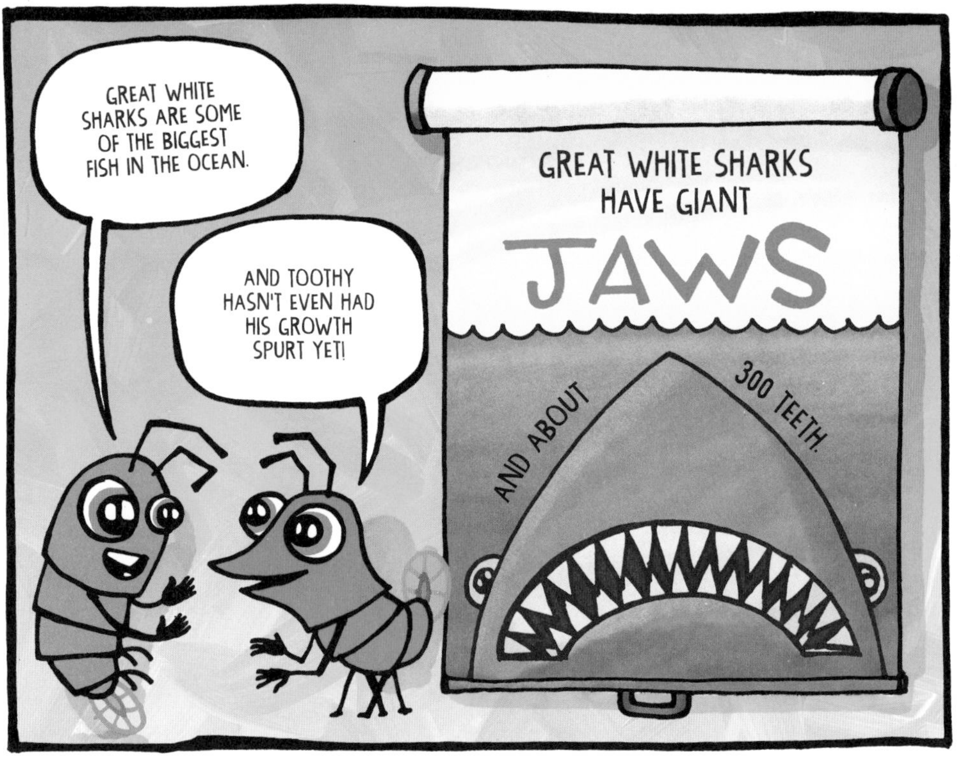
GREAT WHITE SHARKS ARE SOME OF THE BIGGEST FISH IN THE OCEAN.
AND TOOTHY HASN'T EVEN HAD HIS GROWTH SPURT YET!
GREAT WHITE SHARKS HAVE GIANT
JAWS
AND ABOUT
300 TEETH.

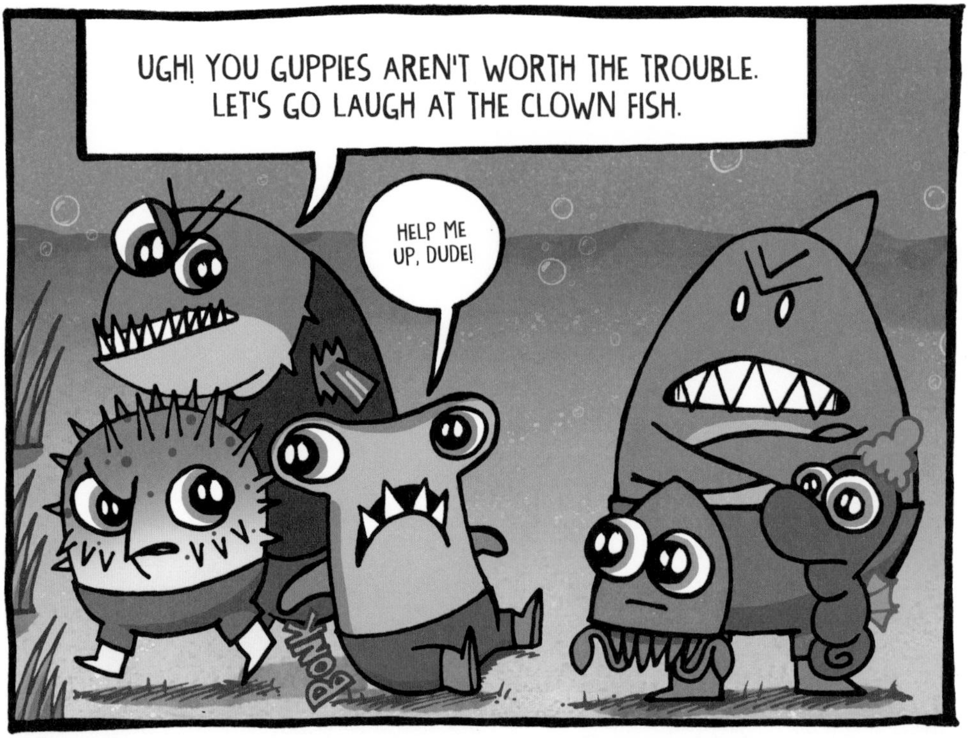
UGH! YOU GUPPIES AREN'T WORTH THE TROUBLE. LET'S GO LAUGH AT THE CLOWN FISH.
HELP ME UP, DUDE!
BONK

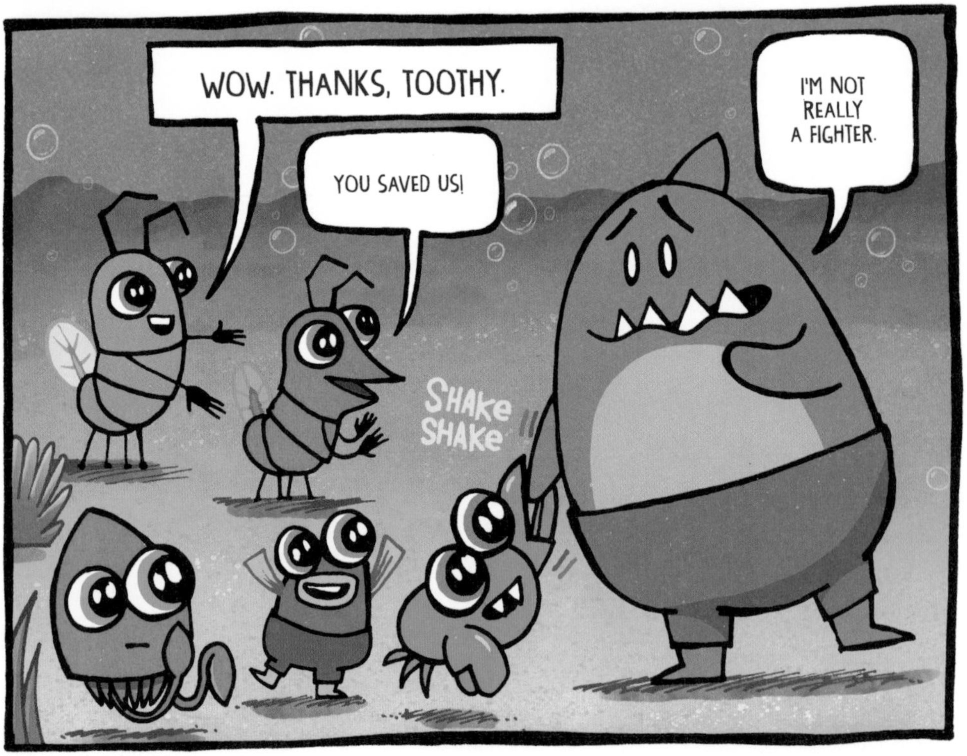
WOW. THANKS, TOOTHY.
YOU SAVED US!
I'M NOT REALLY A FIGHTER.
SHAKE SHAKE

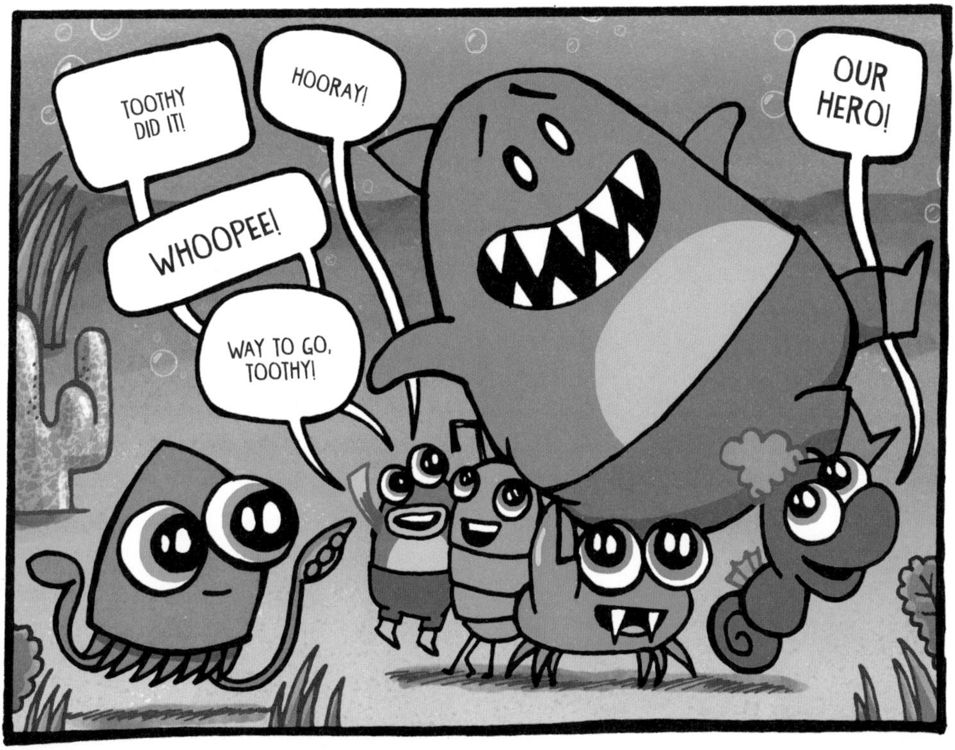
TOOTHY DID IT!
HOORAY!
WHOOPEE!
WAY TO GO, TOOTHY!
OUR HERO!

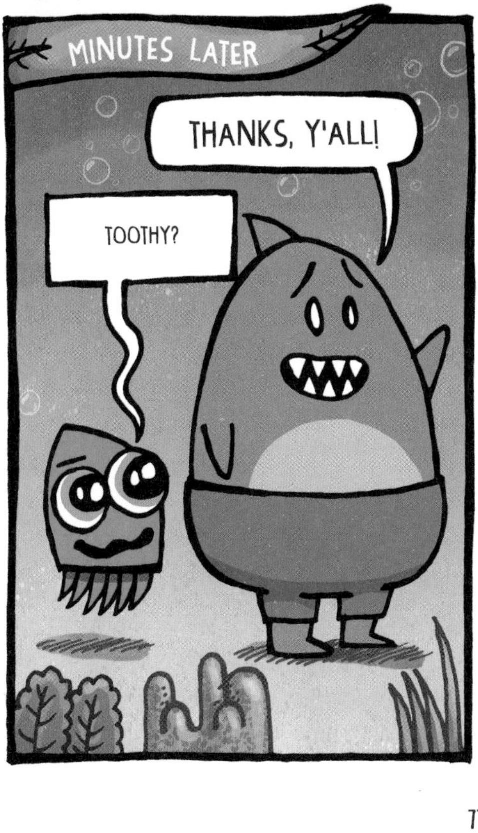
MINUTES LATER
THANKS, Y'ALL!
TOOTHY?

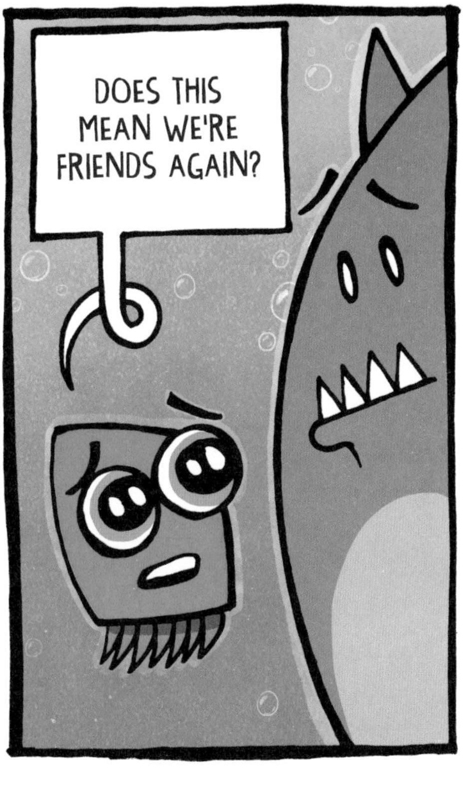
DOES THIS MEAN WE'RE FRIENDS AGAIN?

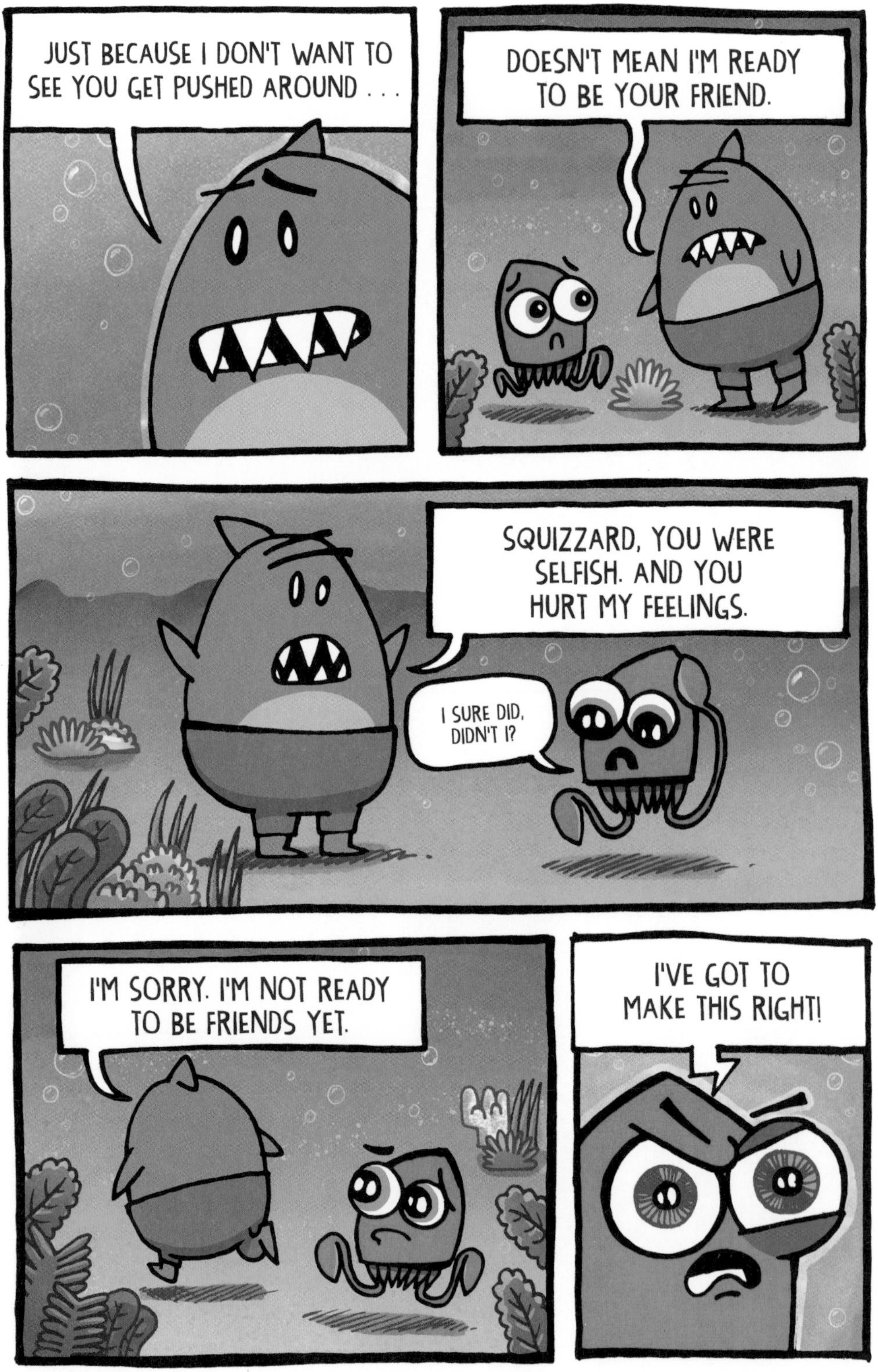
JUST BECAUSE I DON'T WANT TO SEE YOU GET PUSHED AROUND . . .
DOESN'T MEAN I'M READY TO BE YOUR FRIEND.
SQUIZZARD, YOU WERE SELFISH. AND YOU HURT MY FEELINGS.
I SURE DID, DIDN'T I?
I'M SORRY. I'M NOT READY TO BE FRIENDS YET.
I'VE GOT TO MAKE THIS RIGHT!

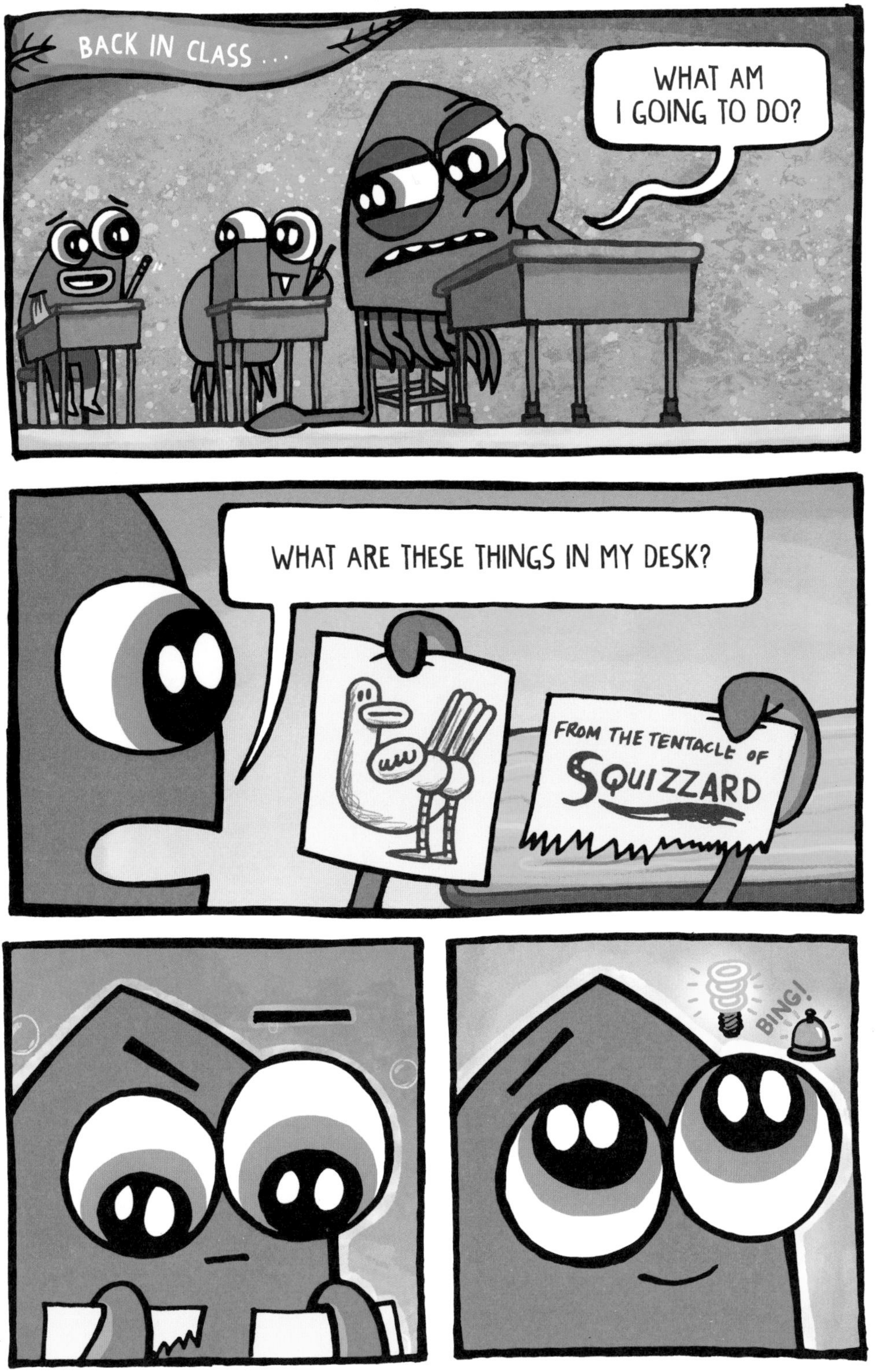
BACK IN CLASS . . .
WHAT AM I GOING TO DO?
WHAT ARE THESE THINGS IN MY DESK?
FROM THE TENTACLE OF SQUIZZARD
BING!

CHAPTER 6

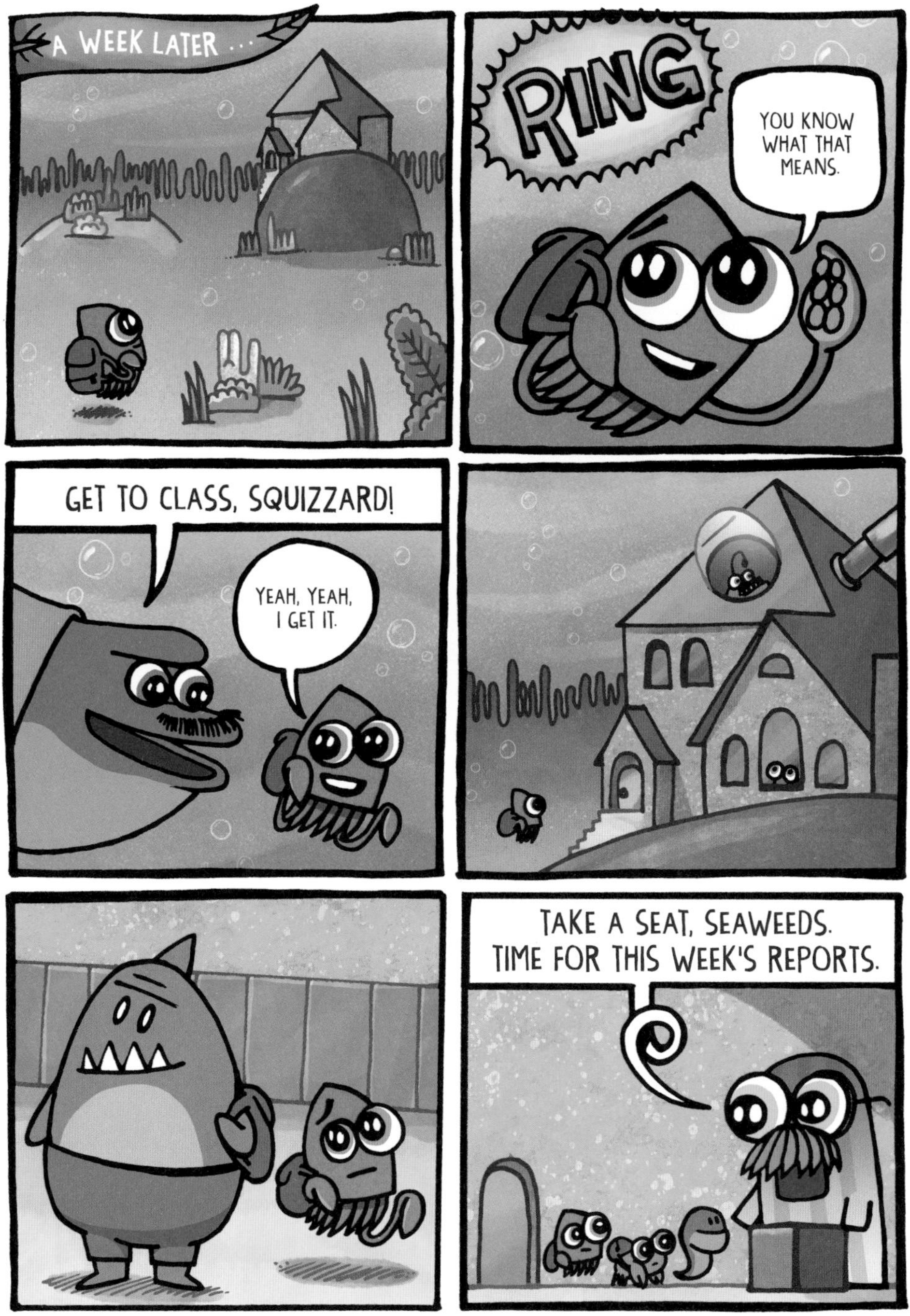
A WEEK LATER . . .
RING
YOU KNOW WHAT THAT MEANS.
GET TO CLASS, SQUIZZARD!
YEAH, YEAH, I GET IT.
TAKE A SEAT, SEAWEEDS. TIME FOR THIS WEEK'S REPORTS.

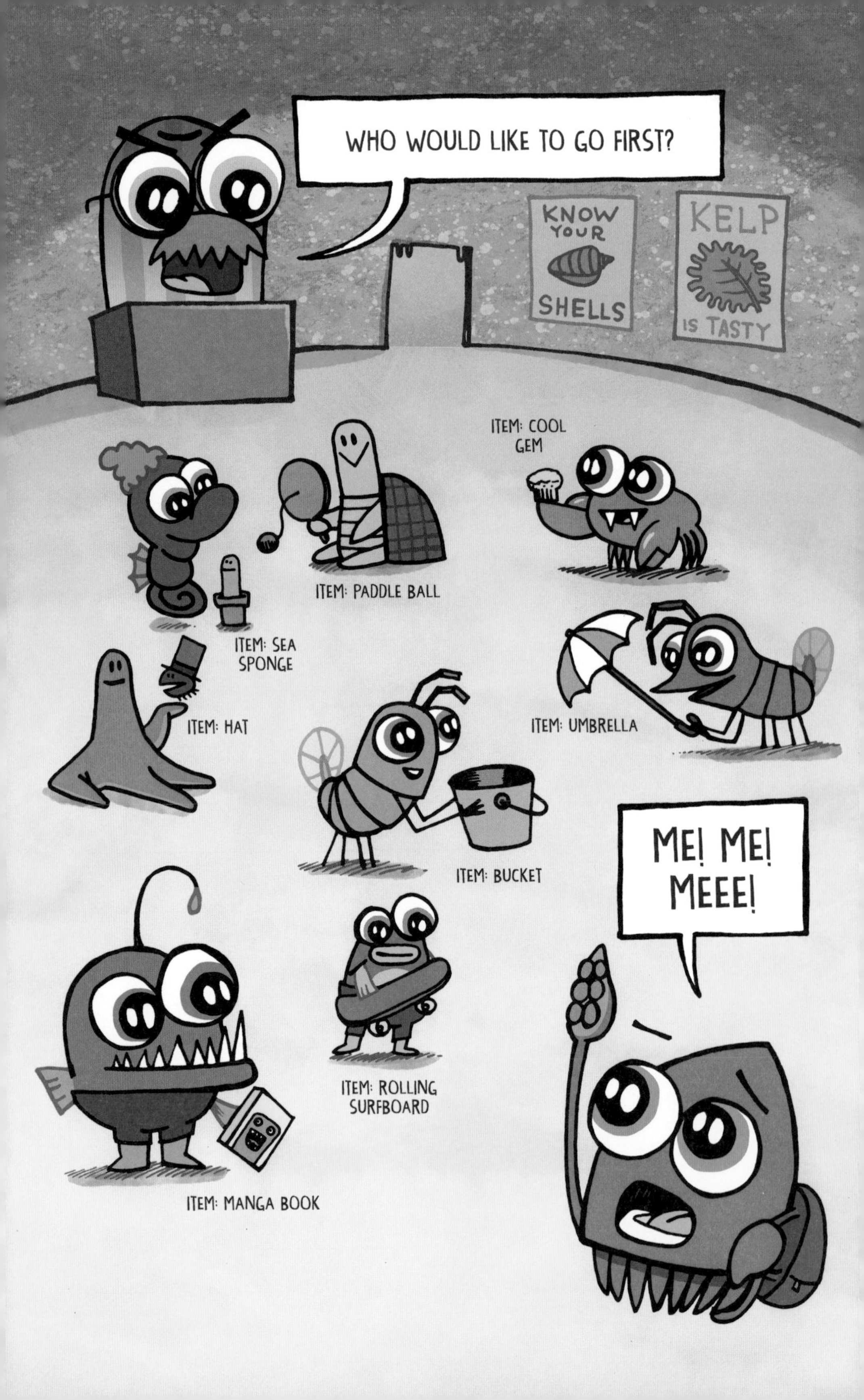
WHO WOULD LIKE TO GO FIRST?
KNOW YOUR SHELLS
KELP IS TASTY
ITEM: COOL GEM
ITEM: PADDLE BALL
ITEM: SEA SPONGE
ITEM: HAT
ITEM: UMBRELLA
ITEM: BUCKET
ME! ME! MEEE!
ITEM: ROLLING SURFBOARD
ITEM: MANGA BOOK

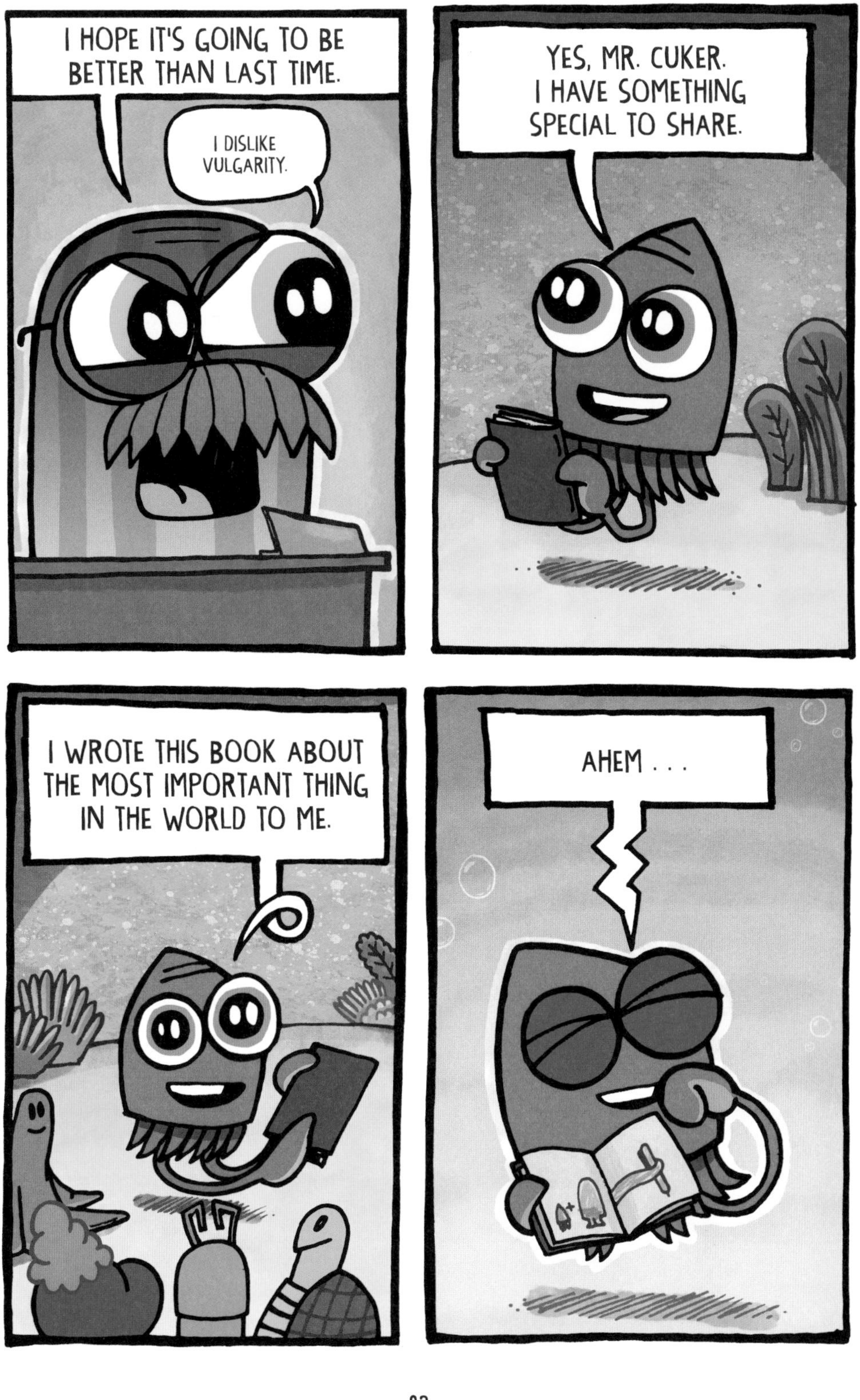
I HOPE IT'S GOING TO BE BETTER THAN LAST TIME.
I DISLIKE VULGARITY.
YES, MR. CUKER. I HAVE SOMETHING SPECIAL TO SHARE.
I WROTE THIS BOOK ABOUT THE MOST IMPORTANT THING IN THE WORLD TO ME.
AHEM . . .

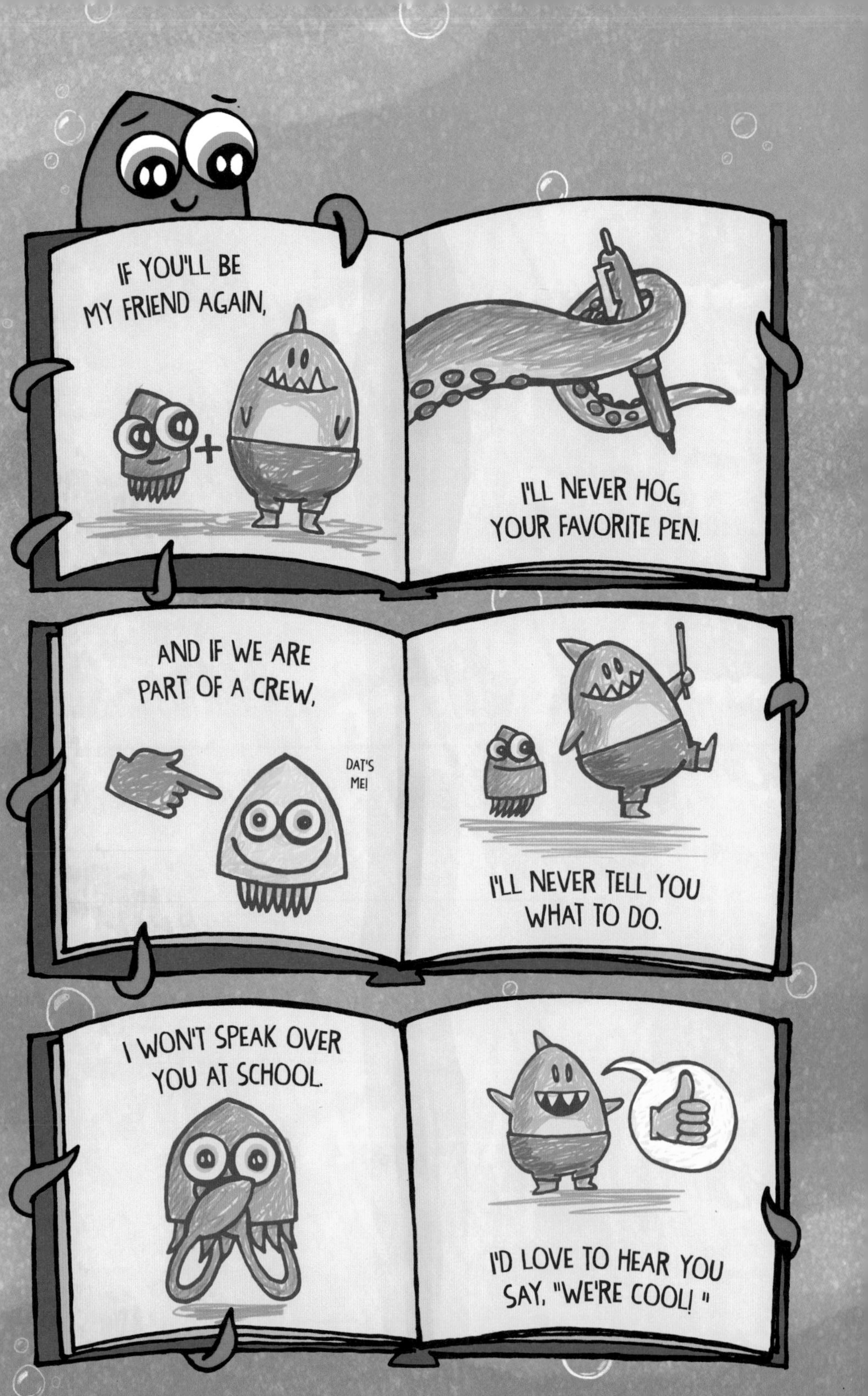
IF YOU'LL BE
MY FRIEND AGAIN,
I'LL NEVER HOG
YOUR FAVORITE PEN.
AND IF WE ARE
PART OF A CREW,
DAT'S
ME!
I'LL NEVER TELL YOU
WHAT TO DO.
I WON'T SPEAK OVER
YOU AT SCHOOL.
I'D LOVE TO HEAR YOU
SAY, "WE'RE COOL!"

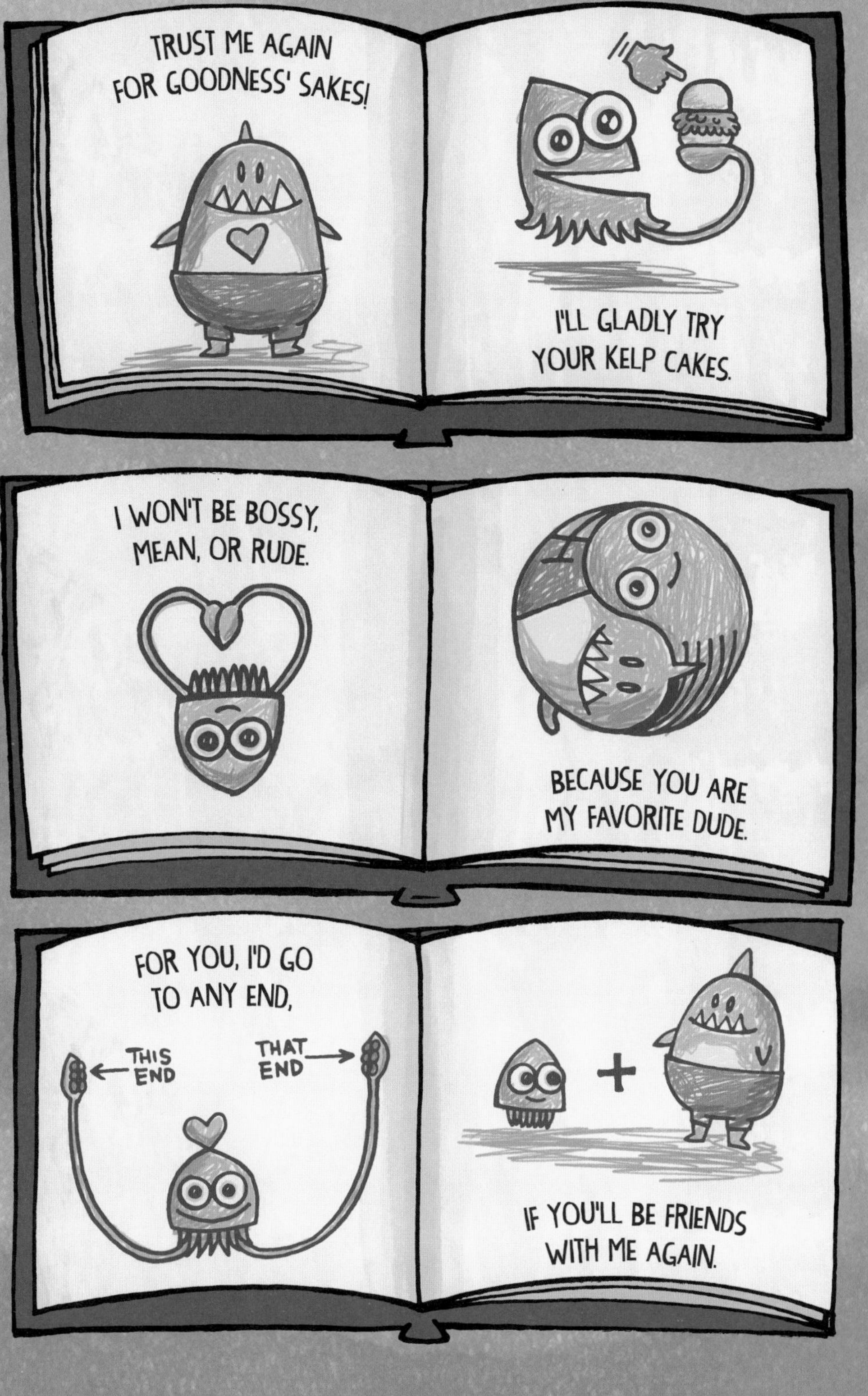
TRUST ME AGAIN
FOR GOODNESS' SAKES!
I'LL GLADLY TRY
YOUR KELP CAKES.
I WON'T BE BOSSY,
MEAN, OR RUDE.
BECAUSE YOU ARE
MY FAVORITE DUDE.
FOR YOU, I'D GO
TO ANY END,
THIS END
THAT END
IF YOU'LL BE FRIENDS
WITH ME AGAIN.

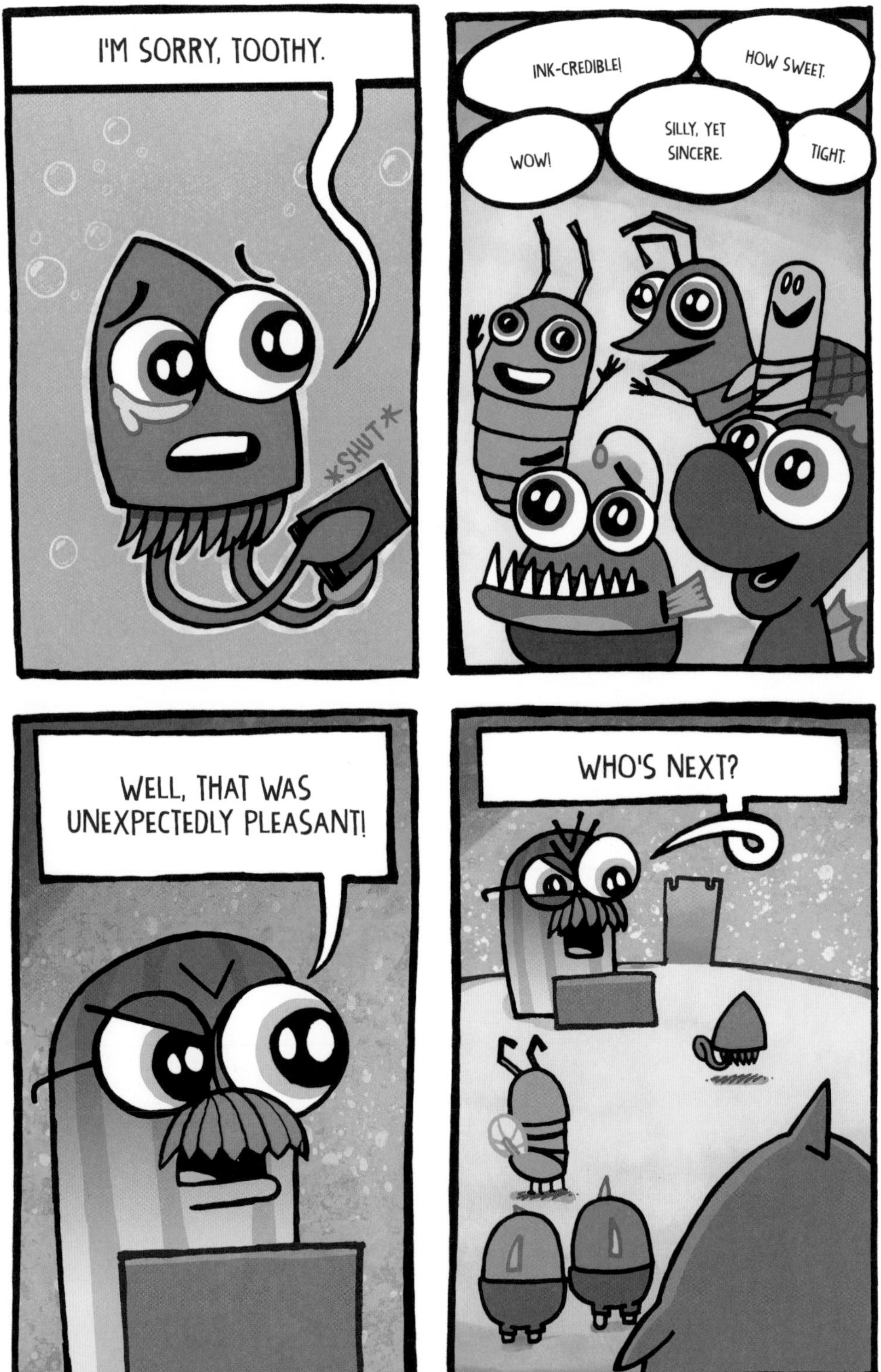
I'M SORRY, TOOTHY.
SHUT
INK-CREDIBLE!
HOW SWEET.
WOW!
SILLY, YET SINCERE.
TIGHT.
WELL, THAT WAS UNEXPECTEDLY PLEASANT!
WHO'S NEXT?

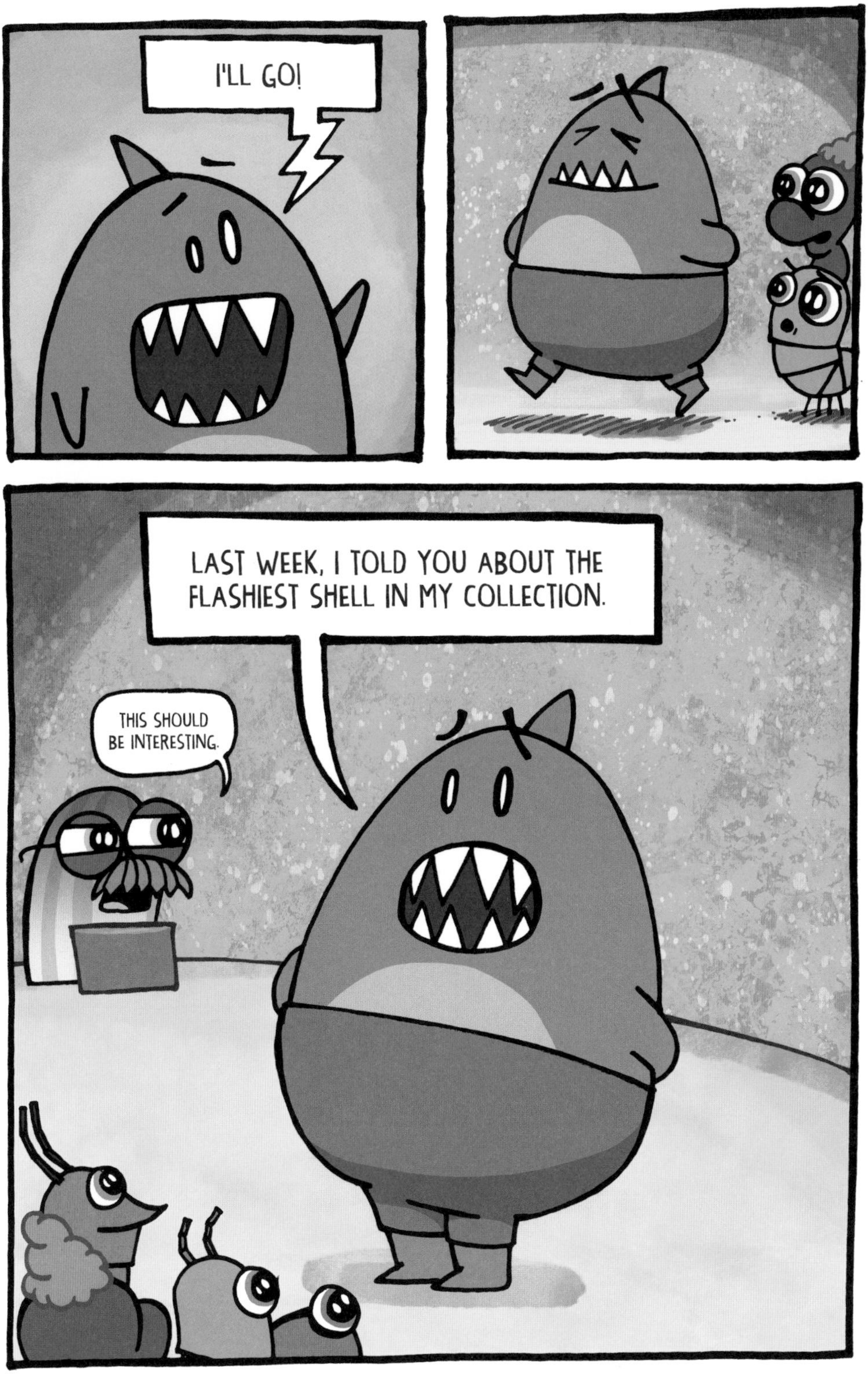
I'LL GO!
LAST WEEK, I TOLD YOU ABOUT THE FLASHIEST SHELL IN MY COLLECTION.
THIS SHOULD BE INTERESTING.

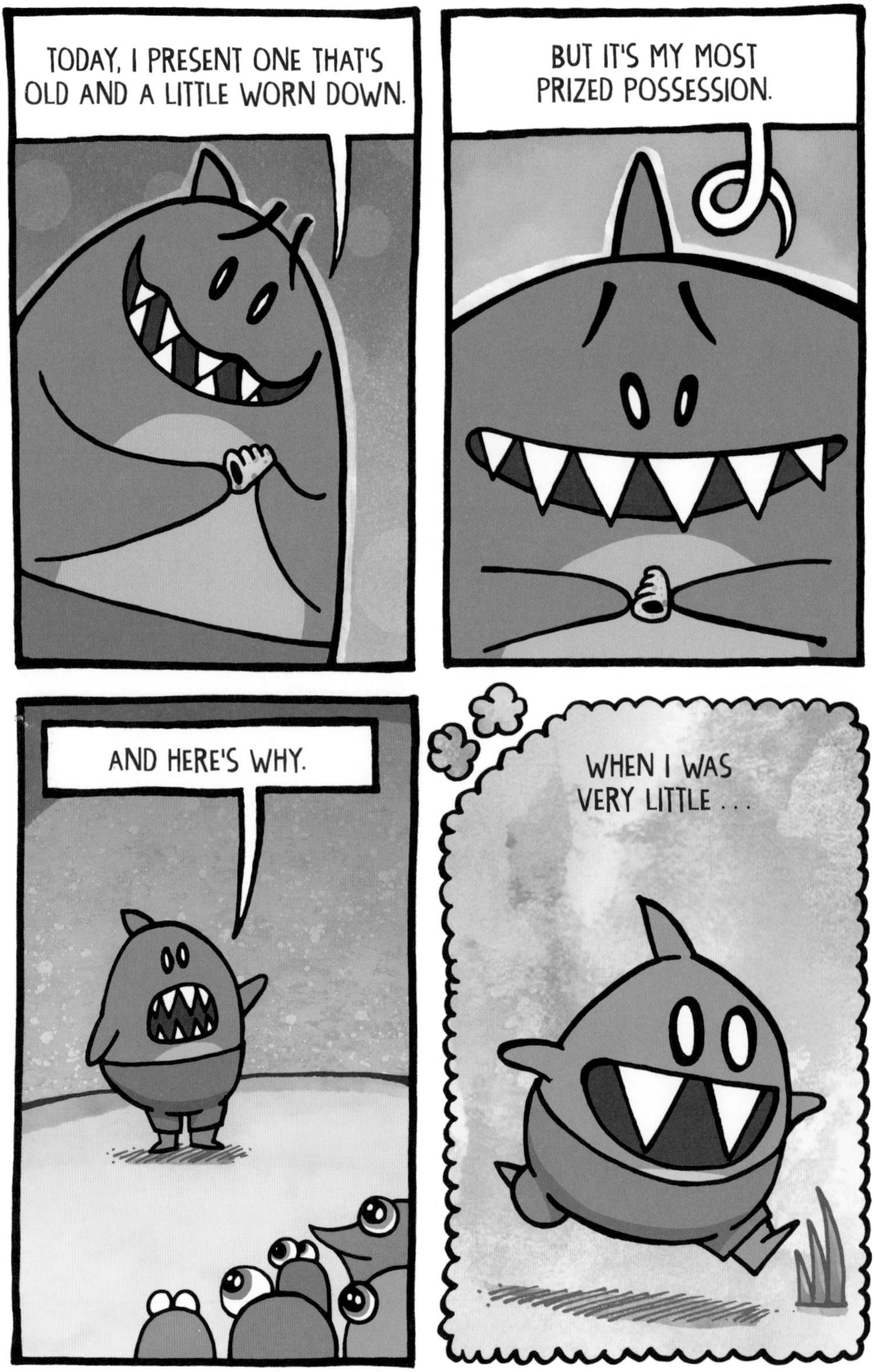
TODAY, I PRESENT ONE THAT'S OLD AND A LITTLE WORN DOWN.
BUT IT'S MY MOST PRIZED POSSESSION.
AND HERE'S WHY.
WHEN I WAS VERY LITTLE . . .

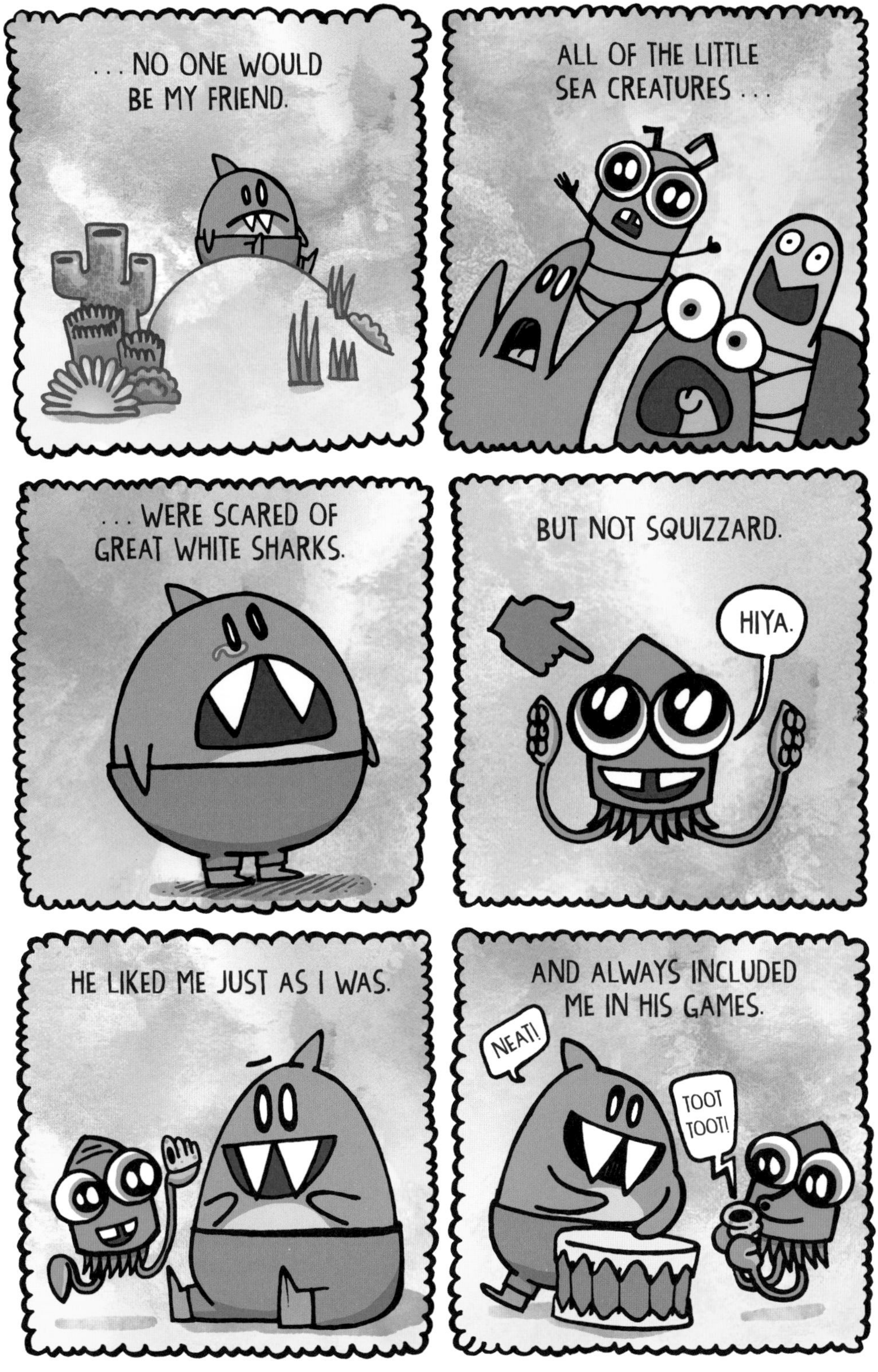

. . . NO ONE WOULD BE MY FRIEND.
ALL OF THE LITTLE SEA CREATURES . . .
. . . WERE SCARED OF GREAT WHITE SHARKS.
BUT NOT SQUIZZARD.
HIYA.
HE LIKED ME JUST AS I WAS.
AND ALWAYS INCLUDED ME IN HIS GAMES.
NEAT!
TOOT TOOT!

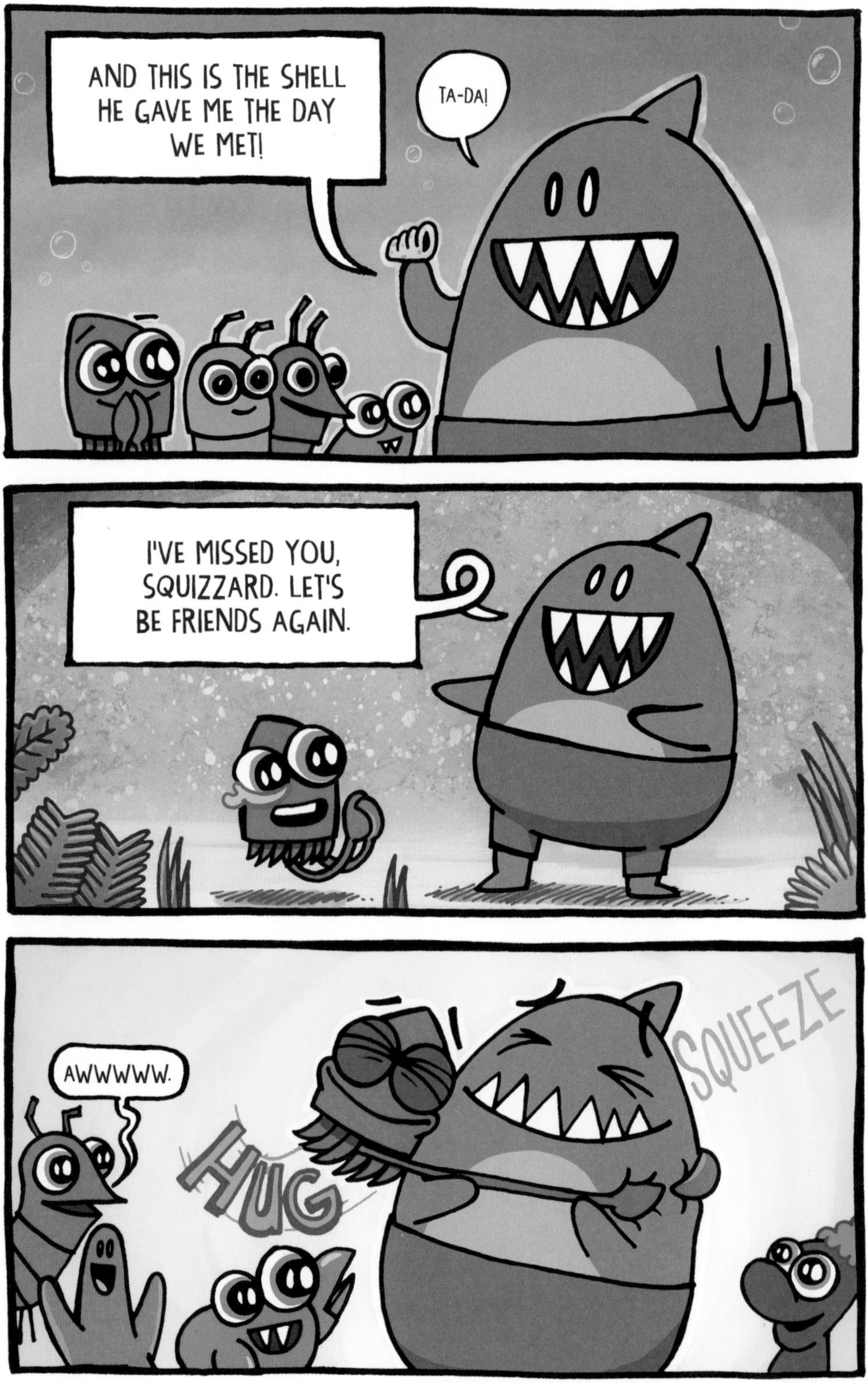
AND THIS IS THE SHELL HE GAVE ME THE DAY WE MET!
TA-DA!
I'VE MISSED YOU, SQUIZZARD. LET'S BE FRIENDS AGAIN.
AWWWWW.
HUG
SQUEEZE

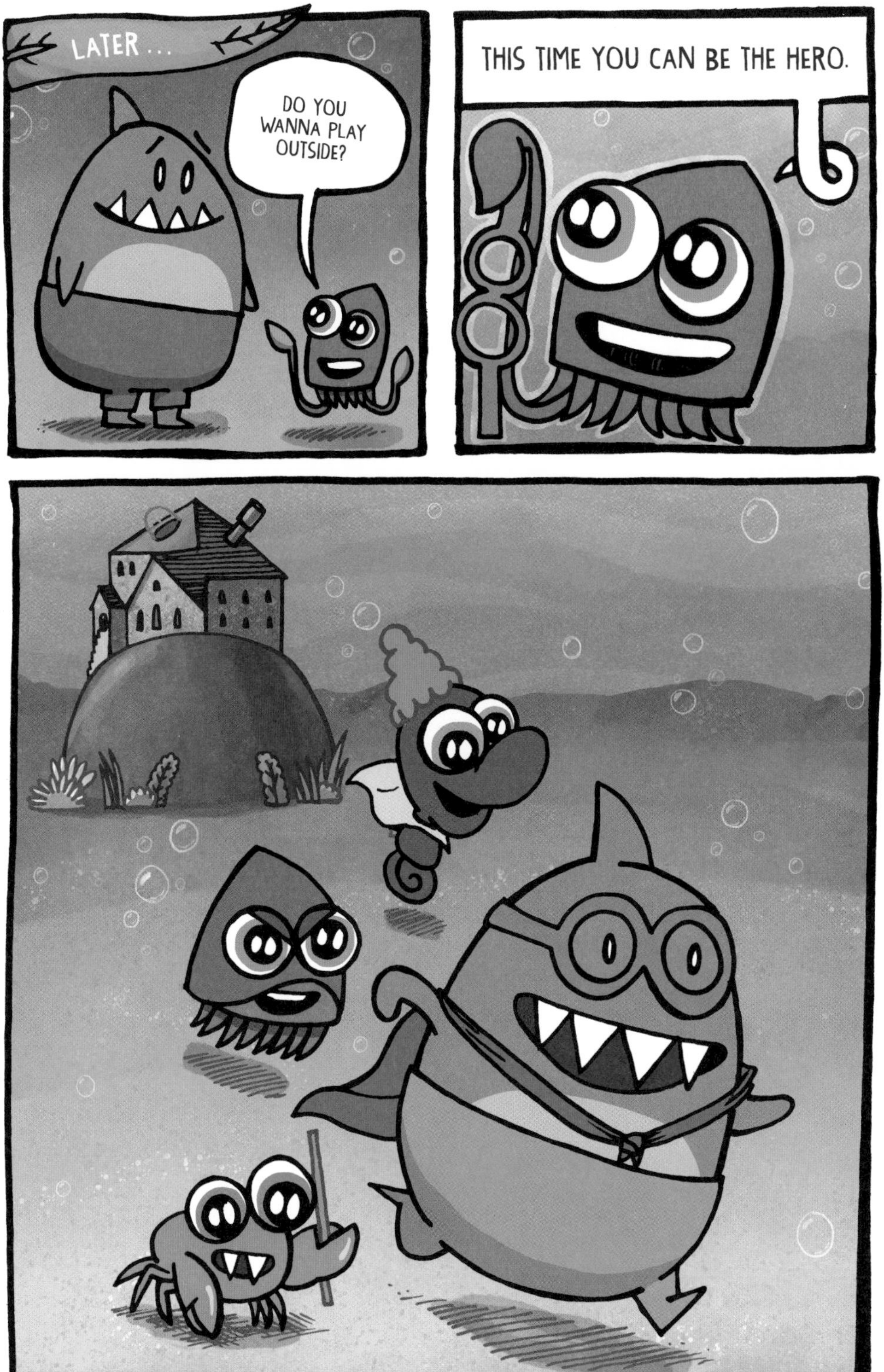
LATER . . .
DO YOU WANNA PLAY OUTSIDE?
THIS TIME YOU CAN BE THE HERO.

FRIENDSHIP UNDER THE SEA

There are around one million different kinds of animals living in the ocean. Some of those animals hunt each other, but others live together in peace.

When two creatures live closely together for a long period of time, they share a bond that's called symbiosis (sim-be-OH-sis). Sometimes this bond can be helpful for both creatures.

For example, clown fish like to hide inside a sea anemone because the anemone protects it from predators. In return, the clown fish cleans the anemone and gets rid of harmful parasites.

And when a blind pistol shrimp burrows down into the mud to forage for food, a little goby comes along to act as a bodyguard, but also to find a safe place to store its eggs.

We can't know how animals really feel, but I'm pretty sure anyone would call Squizzard and Toothy's friendship totally symbiotic!

KEVIN SHERRY is the author and illustrator of many children's picture books, most notably The Yeti Files and Remy Sneakers series, and the picture book I'M THE BIGGEST THING IN THE OCEAN, which received starred reviews and won an original artwork award from the Society of Illustrators. He's a man of many interests: a chef, an avid cyclist and screen printer, and a performer of hilarious puppet shows for kids and adults. Kevin lives in Baltimore, Maryland.

ACKNOWLEDGMENTS

With thanks to Mom, Dad, Brian, Margie, Erin, Dale, Rachel, Ryan, Dan, Justin, Mary, Hunky Mr. Dev, Ed, Akiko Day, Jaclyn Wander Paris, and the Black Cherry Puppet Theater.

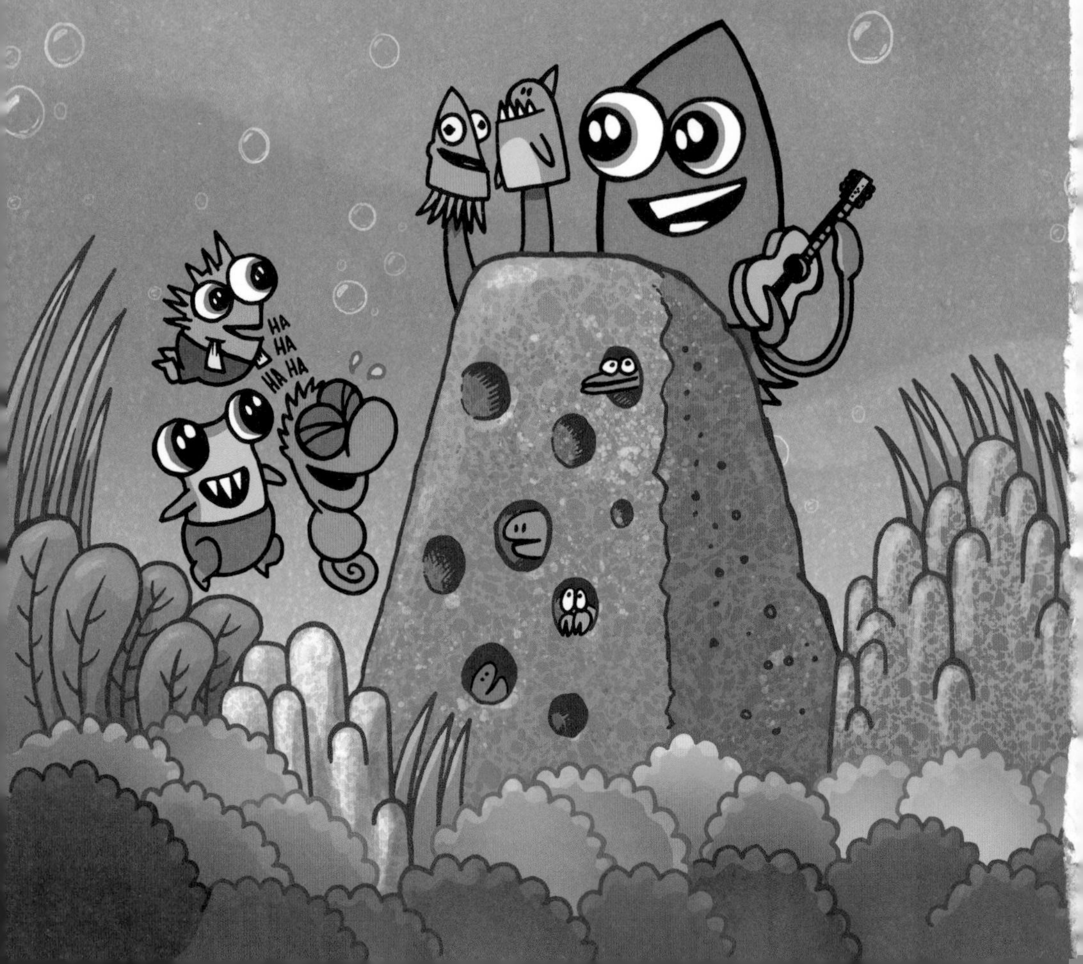

HA
HA
HA
HA